W9-APO-481

07/2019

THE
LAST
LIE

Alex Lake is a British novelist who was born in the North West of England. *After Anna*, the author's first novel written under this pseudonym, was a No.1 bestselling ebook sensation and a top-ten *Sunday Times* bestseller. The author now lives in the North East of the US.

🐦 @AlexLakeAuthor

PALM BEACH COUNTY
LIBRARY SYSTEM
3650 Summit Boulevard
West Palm Beach, FL 33406-4198

Also by Alex Lake

After Anna
Killing Kate
Copycat

THE LAST LIE

ALEX LAKE

HarperCollins*Publishers*

HarperCollins*Publishers* Ltd
1 London Bridge Street,
London SE1 9GF

www.harpercollins.co.uk

First published by HarperCollins*Publishers* 2018
19 20 21 22 LSCC 10 9 8 7 6 5 4 3

Copyright © Alex Lake 2018

Alex Lake asserts the moral right to
be identified as the author of this work

A catalogue record for this book is available from the British Library

ISBN: 978-0-00-829512-7 (PB b-format)

This novel is entirely a work of fiction.
The names, characters and incidents portrayed in it are
the work of the author's imagination. Any resemblance to
actual persons, living or dead, events or localities is
entirely coincidental.

Typeset in Sabon LT Std by Palimpsest Book Production Ltd,
Falkirk, Stirlingshire
Printed and bound in the United States of America
by LSC Communications

All rights reserved. No part of this publication may be
reproduced, stored in a retrieval system, or transmitted,
in any form or by any means, electronic, mechanical,
photocopying, recording or otherwise, without the prior
permission of the publishers.

For more information visit: www.harpercollins.co.uk/green

To Paul Ponder

Prologue

The woman driving the car knew better than to stop for hitchhikers. Maybe, decades ago, she would have considered it. Things were different then. People had good intentions. Kids were polite, and respectful to adults. They didn't hang around the streets wearing hoodies and intimidating passers-by. A hitchhiker would, more than likely, be in search of nothing other than a lift to their destination. So yes, she might have picked one up years ago.

But only in the right circumstances. If she was with someone. And it was daylight. And the hitchhiker looked respectable.

Even back then she would never have picked someone up alone, at night, on a quiet road through deserted countryside, a road lined by half-bent trees and high hedges.

And she wasn't about to start now.

It was still awkward, though. You didn't want to acknowledge the person as you passed them because that meant acknowledging you were not generous enough to help them out. It was like passing a beggar on the street; you didn't want to look at them, didn't want to have the embarrassment of saying 'no' when they asked for money. So you marched on, eyes forward, as though they weren't even there.

It was easy on a busy street with other people around, other things to look at, but on a country road at night? It was much harder. There was nothing to pretend you'd been distracted by. It was obvious you would have noticed the hitchhiker. You couldn't not.

Who was, she saw as she approached, a young woman. At least she thought so, from a distance. Long hair, slight build. For a moment her resolve wavered – maybe she would pick her up, she shouldn't be out here alone – but then she stiffened. She'd heard of this kind of trick: put an innocent, unthreatening woman out there and then, when the driver stopped, a thug – or gang of thugs – would jump out, steal the car and leave her there, alone.

Or worse. Raped. *Dead*.

She got ready to swerve in case the young woman jumped or stumbled into the road. That was another trick she'd heard about. Or maybe she was drunk. It wouldn't be a surprise. Nowadays young women got drunk all the time, out in town centres that were no-go areas at night, vomit-streaked war zones populated by feral youths intent on fighting and drinking and having sex with each other.

The hitchhiker's head turned towards the sound of the car. She raised her hand. It was a curiously weak movement. Hesitant. Tentative. Fearful, almost. The woman driving the car shook her head. She was definitely not stopping. The girl was probably on drugs, as well as drunk.

And then the beam of the headlights lit her up and the woman driving the car let out a sharp gasp.

The hitchhiker *was* a young woman, in her late twenties, or maybe early thirties.

She was also completely naked.

But that wasn't the most shocking thing about her.

The most shocking thing was that the woman driving the car recognized her.

2

It took her a few moments to realize where from, and then she gasped again.

She wasn't a hitchhiker – although there was no doubt she needed a lift – she was something completely different.

She braked, coming to a halt a few metres past the young woman, then opened her door.

The young woman stared at her, her eyes wide and unseeing. Her hair was matted, and she was streaked with dirt. She took a step towards the car, and the driver flinched, glancing around to see if there was anyone hiding in the shadows.

There was nothing. Just the hedges and the moon and the silence of the night.

She looked back at the young woman.

'Are you—' she said, then paused. 'Are you *her*?'

PART ONE

Alfie and Claire

Claire

Claire Daniels stood on the tiled floor of the bathroom and stared into the mirror. She studied the face that looked back at her. She recognized every feature and freckle and contour. She had seen them a thousand times. More. Many thousands. The face belonged to her. It was utterly familiar.

And yet, in a few minutes, she might be a totally new person.

From time to time a person could change in an instant into someone new. It had happened to her twice: the day her mum died and the day she met Alfie. Once for bad, once for good. And today – this morning – it might be about to happen a third time.

That first time was awful. *Beyond* awful. She was fourteen and had just walked in from Lacrosse practice after school. Her best friend Jodie's mum had brought her home and on the way back she had asked if they wanted to go to a Coldplay concert, on their own. Jodie's mum said she would drop them off and pick them up but they could watch the concert without any adults present.

Thank you, Mrs Pierce, Claire said. *That would be amazing.*

Call me Angie, Jodie's mum said. *But you need to clear it with your parents.*

Which was what Claire had been planning to do when she ran into the house. Her dad would be at work, but she could hear the television in the living room, which was where her mum would be.

She was there, all right, slumped on the cream leather sofa in the living room. At first Claire had thought she was sleeping, but then she noticed the trickle of blood coming from her nostril and the vomit on her jeans and the glassy-eyed stare into nowhere.

She was dead. Claire knew it as soon as she saw her, but that didn't stop her slapping then hugging then slapping her to wake her up. What followed was a whirl she had never been able to put in order however many times she had thought about it. She'd called her dad and then it was sirens, medics, police officers. A doctor had given her something and she'd gone to bed, only to wake up the next day to the same horror.

Her mother never gave permission for Claire to go to the Coldplay concert. She never gave permission for anything else ever again.

Heroin, her dad told her a few days later. Her mum had overdosed, an addiction from her twenties that she'd managed to beat down had come roaring back in her forties and burned her out.

It snuffed out Claire, too. Left her hollow. When she looked at herself in the mirror she saw someone else. Someone lost, unsmiling, changed. There was a gap at the centre of her, a gap that was only filled when she met Alfie. She remembered getting home after their first date, a date that had begun as an afternoon coffee and grown into dinner and drinks and a night-time walk through central London. She'd glimpsed herself in the mirror. Something about her reflection had caught her eye and she'd paused, and looked again, and seen a new woman. Seen herself again.

And she knew she had changed in the space of that night, had started to emerge from the hole her mum's death had left her in.

Started. Even after three years of marriage – three happy years – there was still something missing. And hopefully that final piece of the puzzle would be in place any minute. If it went as she hoped, she'd look in the mirror and see, once again, a new person.

A mother.

At least, a mother-to-be.

A mother who would not overdose on heroin and leave her daughter alone. A mother who would love and cherish her child, her *children*. A mother who would heal her own wounds by making sure she didn't inflict them on her children.

And then she'd go and wake up her husband, the man who had made her feel warm and safe and whole from the moment they'd met and every moment since, and tell him that she was pregnant. After all these months trying, finally, they were going to be parents, going to have new titles, new roles.

Claire and Alfie, daughter and son, wife and husband.

Mum and dad.

She blinked, and opened the bathroom cabinet. She took out a pregnancy test. It was the first of a packet of two. She'd bought them nine months earlier in anticipation of needing them sooner, but her period had come, on time, month after month. She and Alfie did everything right: they had sex constantly when she was ovulating, and plenty besides, but it didn't matter. Inevitably at the appointed time she started to feel bloated and lethargic and then her period arrived.

But not this month. This month she was two days late. Two whole days. She knew there could be many reasons why, but she didn't care.

She was pregnant. She *felt* it.

And it was her birthday this weekend. She had drinks planned after work – it was a Friday – and then a party at her dad's house on Saturday. It was the perfect present. It all hung together. It was too right *not* to be true.

She took the test from the cardboard and sat on the toilet. She positioned it between her legs and a few seconds later a stream of warm urine ran over the white plastic. She left it there until the stream stopped and then placed it by the sink. She didn't look at it; the line she craved could take a minute or so to show up and she wanted to give it every opportunity.

She washed her hands, her heart racing and her stomach tight. She pictured herself walking into their bedroom and shaking Alfie awake. Telling him the news. Watching him smile. No – she stopped herself. She shouldn't get carried away. Her dad called it the commentators' curse: just when a commentator was saying how some football team was about to score or some player was playing well, something bad would happen.

But this was it; she was sure of it. There'd be a line and she'd be pregnant and even if it didn't work out, if there was a problem of some sort, she'd know she *could* get pregnant, and even that would be enough, would be better than the doubt and worry and anguish of wondering if it would ever happen.

She picked up the pregnancy test. Turned it around. Let her eyes travel to the end where the little window contained—

Nothing.

No line. Not the faintest imprint of a line.

She shook it. She put it down next to the sink and waited a minute or two. Then she picked it up again.

No line.

She pressed the pedal at the base of the bin and flipped

the lid open. She looked one last time – to be sure – and then threw the test, the negative test, into the trash. She'd ask Alfie to take it out later. She didn't want to. She didn't want any reminder of her failure.

Alfie

Alfie Daniels lay in bed listening to his wife move around in the bathroom. He knew what she was doing, despite the fact she'd said nothing. He knew when her period was due and he knew it hadn't come because Claire had not walked into the living room with tears in her eyes or sent him a text message with sad emojis saying she had her period.

For nine months he had hugged her each time and promised her it would happen eventually, only to watch her hope build through the month and be dashed again.

And now she was late and he could tell she was convinced that this was it. For the last two days he had watched her move from a state of quiet introspection to nervous excitement. She thought she was pregnant.

If she'd told him, he would have suggested not getting her hopes up, but it was too late for that now. Her hopes were flying high and turning into dreams of the future and there was only one thing that would bring them down.

Which, from the sound of things, had just happened. There was no cry of excitement or rush of steps to come and tell him the good news. Only the thud of the bathroom door closing and a slow, heavy tread towards the bedroom.

The door opened and she came in. She stood by their bed, her face set and unsmiling.

'Hey,' he said. 'What's the matter?'

'My period was late. I took a test.'

Alfie sat up on his elbows. 'And?'

Tears formed in her eyes and rolled down her cheeks. She shook her head.

'I'm sorry,' he said, and held out his arms. 'Come here.'

'No,' she said. 'I want to be alone. I'm going to have a shower.'

'I don't think so. Not before a hug.'

'I'm OK.'

'It's not for you. It's for me. I'm disappointed too.'

It was clearly the wrong thing to say. Her lips quivered and tears welled in her eyes. She let out a loud, wracking sob then slumped on the edge of the bed and buried her face in his neck.

'I tried not to hope,' she said. 'I told myself not to get my hopes up, but it's impossible. I want this so much.'

'Me too,' he said. 'And it'll happen. It takes time for lots of people.'

'I know,' she replied. 'But what if we're the ones who it never happens for? What then?'

'We're a long way from that,' Alfie said. 'A long way.'

'But what if?' Claire said. 'What if we can't have kids?'

'Don't think like that.'

She nodded. 'I won't. I'm going to have a shower.'

When she came back her eyes were red.

'You not feeling too good?' Alfie said.

'I was sure I was pregnant this time,' she said. 'I felt different, somehow. And I've been so regular. I don't know why my period would suddenly be late.'

'Stress can do that,' Alfie said. 'This is a difficult time for you. For us.'

She wiped a tear from her eyes. 'I can't stop crying. It's the sense of loss. Even though I wasn't pregnant – so there was nothing to lose – I'd let myself think I was, and I was already imagining a future with us as parents. And now it's gone.'

'Only for now,' Alfie said. 'We'll get there in the end, I know it.'

He held her tight, then sat up.

'I have to get ready for work,' he said. 'I've got an early meeting.'

In the bathroom, Alfie stripped off. He looked in the full-length mirror. He flexed his pectoral muscles, then turned sideways and admired his flat abdominals. His chest and back were waxed and smooth, unlike the thick, brown hair on his scalp. He kept himself in shape; the only thing he couldn't do anything about were the pock-marks on his face, the scars left by the acne he'd suffered from as a teenager.

He turned on the shower and stepped in. He let the hot water run over him. He washed his hair, massaging the shampoo into his scalp. The shampoo he used cost over thirty pounds a bottle, but it was worth it. According to his hair stylist, he had the kind of hair that movie stars had. He could be a hair model, she said, and it was worth paying the extra for good shampoo. So he treated himself.

And besides, they could afford it. Claire's dad was both rich and generous.

When he was finished, he wrapped a towel around his waist and grabbed his razor. As he started to shave the bathroom door opened.

'Would you take out the bin?' Claire said. 'The test is in there. I don't want to go near it.'

Alfie nodded. 'OK.'

14

'And thanks,' she said. 'For being so supportive. I'm lucky to have you. And we'll be pregnant, one day.'

He smiled. 'We will. I know we will.'

She closed the door and the smile fell from his face. He looked at himself in the mirror and shook his head.

Stupid bitch.

She wanted him to take out the bin. Of course she did. She was too infantile to deal with a negative pregnancy test so she needed him to deal with it for her, like it was a fucking python or something. It was pathetic.

It was typical of her.

As was the way she used 'we' instead of 'I'. 'We'll be pregnant, one day.' He hated that 'we'. Hated the cloying, saccharine refusal to accept the biological truth of the situation: it was her who would be pregnant, not him.

The irony – and he took great pleasure in it – was that, whatever words she used, she was wrong. They – she – wouldn't be pregnant any time soon. Ever, in fact.

Because what she didn't know was that her husband had no intention of having children. They were the *last* thing he wanted. There were many reasons why, but the main one was because the arrival of kids would render all his careful plans redundant.

They would tie him to the simpering bitch forever, and there was no way he was letting that happen.

But she couldn't find out he didn't want them. Not yet, at any rate. He still needed her for a while, which was why he had never mentioned – and did not plan to – the reason *why* she would not be getting pregnant any time soon.

Her husband had had a vasectomy.

He'd had it done a year after they married – almost exactly two years earlier, now – when she had started talking about having kids in earnest. He'd gone to see the doctor, told him what he wanted – the doctor was surprised given how young he was and had tried to talk him out of it, but he had referred him nonetheless – and then, one morning, Alfie had gone to the hospital and had the operation.

He'd been back at his desk the same afternoon. He was a bit sore, but it was OK.

And it would remain his little secret.

He glanced at the bin. The negative pregnancy test lay there, pointing at him, accusing him.

'Fuck you,' he said, then wiped the shaving cream from his face.

Claire

Claire picked up her phone from the bedside table and glanced at the time:

Ten a.m.

She lay back on her pillow, her head thick with a nasty hangover. Friday had been awful, but at least it was Friday. She'd gone out with her colleagues to a bar in the West End and drunk away the disappointment of the pregnancy test. She didn't even mind the headache. It took her mind off it all.

She *did* mind the cramps. Her period had arrived and the cramps were worse than they had been for a while, each one reminding her of what had happened.

She turned on her front and buried her head underneath her pillow. She heard the muffled sound of the door opening. She smelled coffee. It made her feel sick.

'Hey,' Alfie said. 'Did I hear you moving around? I brought you breakfast in bed.'

She peeked out at him. He was holding a tray with a bowl of something and a mug of coffee on it.'

'You didn't have to do that,' she said.

'Of course I did!' Alfie said. 'It's your special day! Happy birthday, darling.'

Claire groaned. She'd forgotten it was her birthday.

She'd forgotten they had to go to the party at her dad's house later.

Claire sat on the bed in her childhood bedroom. It was a single bed with a pink-and-purple duvet cover. On the wall next to it were faint stains of Blu-tack from the posters she'd had up there – David Beckham, Robbie Williams, the usual teenage girl crushes. It was an hour until the party. Her hangover was gone – two ibuprofen and a mid-afternoon nap had seen it off – and Alfie had texted to say he was on his way. He'd been playing golf that afternoon. It was his new hobby, and he'd been spending a lot of his weekend afternoons on the golf course. He'd tried to persuade her to join him, but she couldn't think of any way she'd less like to spend an afternoon than hitting balls around an over-sized garden.

She'd been hoping the party would be a celebration of a little more than her birthday. Not that she would have announced the pregnancy to everyone this early, but she'd wanted her and Alfie and her dad to know a baby was on the way and to spend the day giving each other secret smiles, the knowledge too momentous to ignore. She'd pictured herself holding a glass of wine (but not drinking it), so nobody would suspect she was pregnant but the baby would come to no harm.

It was not to be. It was a birthday party and no more.

She'd learned her lesson, though. Don't get carried away with the hope. It only led to disappointment, which was a new and unwelcome shock to her. She had never really had to face not having something she wanted. Her parents had come from humble backgrounds in the North East, but had managed to build up a chain of estate agents together. They had both worked long hours to do it and, in her mum's case, developed unhealthy ways of coping with the stress. After her mum died, her dad threw himself into the business even more, assuaging his guilt at his absence from the home with extravagant gifts.

And as the years had gone by the gifts had grown more and more extravagant, from the house in Fulham where she and Alfie lived, to the holiday they'd recently had in Cannes, to the Range Rover they drove. In truth, she found his generosity a bit uncomfortable. A few times she and Alfie had discussed telling him they didn't need any help, but Alfie had persuaded her there was no harm in it. He also pointed out how happy it made her dad, so they kept accepting his gifts.

Apart from in her career. That was the one area Claire refused to let him help her. She was a partner in a design firm, a world her dad knew nothing about, and she had worked her way up from the ground floor.

But now, all pride aside, she would have accepted any help her dad could have given her, but there was nothing he could do. She had everything going for her: a loving dad, a wonderful husband, her career. She was smart, athletic, healthy.

And she would have given it all to be a mother.

But she couldn't shake the feeling that being a mother was the one thing the universe was going to deny her. She felt almost as though she was in a fairy story, the lucky princess given everything, except the thing she wanted most.

She knew she was getting sick with worry – she'd been losing weight – and it made her want to hide away from the world, but she'd have to put on a brave face for the party, would have to smile and say *Oh, no, we're so busy we haven't even thought about it yet* when people asked her whether she and Alfie were planning to start a family.

She took off her jeans and sweater and opened a large cardboard box. It came from an internet company that sent new clothes; depending on what you kept and what you returned someone – although, according to Jodie, it was most likely not a person at all but an algorithm of some type, whatever the hell an algorithm was – figured out what you liked. Whoever or whatever was doing it, was uncannily accurate.

She pulled out a sleeveless navy-blue dress. It had a one-shoulder neckline, and an asymmetric hem. She pulled it on and looked over her shoulder at the back.

There was a knock on the bedroom door.

'Hello,' Alfie said, the door opening a crack. 'Are you decent?'

'Come in,' Claire replied. 'I'm trying on a dress.'

Alfie whistled softly. 'Wow. You look amazing.'

'You like it?'

He nodded, and moved behind her, running his hands from her hips to her buttocks, then around to her stomach. He pressed his lips to her neck.

'Very much,' he said. He reached down and pulled the dress up, stroking the backs of her thighs as he did so.

'Alfie,' she said, her voice low and breathless. 'We can't. I have my period.'

He turned her round and kissed her.

'I don't care,' he said. 'I want you too much.'

'No,' she said. 'I want to, but no. It'll only be a few days.'

'Ok,' he said. 'I can wait. Let's get ready for the party. I have a surprise for you.'

'Really?' She was not in the mood for surprises. 'What kind of surprise?'

'You'll see,' he said. 'You'll see.'

Alfie

Standing in front of the fireplace, Alfie tapped his glass – crystal, full of vintage champagne, he loved this stuff, he really did – with the handle of his fork – silver, antique – and watched as conversations died down and heads turned to face him. When the room was silent, he smiled and started to speak.

'Thank you all,' he said, 'for coming to celebrate this very special day. My wife' – he turned to Claire and smiled – 'it's still a thrill to call her that, even after three years, is celebrating her thirtieth birthday. I told her before the party that I had something special for her, and I do.'

He gestured to Jodie, who moved to the front of the guests and handed him a guitar. It was a Martin D50 which Claire had bought him, after some not-too-subtle hints, for his last birthday. It was an instrument he had dreamed of owning all through his childhood, but which, until he met Claire, had been woefully out of his reach. Woefully out of most people's reach.

'Alfie,' Claire said, 'what are you doing?' She looked at Jodie, eyebrows raised.

Jodie held up her hands, palms facing Claire. 'Merely doing what I was told,' she said.

'Thank you, Jodie,' Alfie said, and then turned to Claire. 'I wrote you a song,' he said. He slipped the strap over his neck and held up his right hand. 'I know, it's soppy and over the top but I don't care. I'm the luckiest man alive, and I want everyone to know it. So, here we go. It's called "Since the Start".'

He strummed an E chord and started to sing.

'*Since the start*
Since the day I met you
Since the start
I have known I loved you.'

He sang the rest of the song. It was pretty good, in a way. Highly derivative, basic chords, minimal musicianship required, but writing and playing and singing it would be far beyond most people, which was what mattered. When he finished, he could tell that the guests' reactions were mixed: the women were touched at his display of naked emotion, the men looked faintly embarrassed for him.

Which was good. That was exactly what he wanted them to feel. He wanted everyone to see how much in love with his wife and how different to all the other guys he was.

Claire, predictably, had tears in her eyes. As the applause died down she hugged him, kissing his cheek and ear and mouth.

'Thank you,' she whispered. 'That was beautiful. I love you.'

'I love you too,' he said. 'Happy birthday.'

After the song, Mick, Claire's dad spoke. He gave a tearful tribute to her and talked about how proud Penny, his wife and Claire's mum, would have been of her daughter. He didn't mention Alfie – or his song – which was par for the course. When he had finished and the guests had returned to their increasingly drunk and loud conversation about politics or sport or something else they knew nothing about, Alfie slipped out to the kitchen.

He put on his jacket. He had a packet of Chesterfields and a book of matches and he was planning to sneak off and find a secluded spot – there was a bench in a corner of Mick's vast back garden that would do – where he could light up and have a quiet smoke. He had a packet of mints, too; on one occasion before they got married he'd said he'd do anything for her and Claire had asked him to give up – for his sake, she said, because she loved him so much and couldn't bear the thought of him poisoning himself, the soppy bitch – and he didn't want her finding out he'd lied.

He walked through the kitchen and opened the back door to the terrace. There was a footstep behind him.

He turned around. It was Mick. He was holding a large tumbler of whisky, his face red with a combination of high blood pressure and too many drinks.

'Mick,' Alfie said. 'Thanks for hosting. It's a great party.'

'No problem. Anything for my little girl.' Mick nodded at the terrace. 'Going out?'

'Could do with a bit of fresh air.'

'Too warm in here?' Mick glanced at the window. The moon was visible, still low in the sky. 'It's dark out.'

'It's fine in here.' Alfie smiled. 'I was just thinking of taking a walk. But I don't have to.'

Mick held up a hand. 'No. You do whatever you want. I was only asking. I did want to talk to you, though.'

'Oh?' Alfie said. Mick and he had never been close. They had probably had no more than two or three one-on-one conversations since he and Claire had met. Mick was not the kind of father who warmed to the men who were sleeping with his daughter. No doubt he had fantasies of taking Alfie shooting and accidentally unloading both barrels on him. Alfie didn't mind. He'd had the same thoughts himself. He couldn't stand the old bastard.

He liked his money, though.

And the money he'd given to Claire. There was at least a couple of million in various investments, moved into some kind of trust in her name to avoid inheritance tax. Claire didn't like to talk about it, but Alfie knew it was there, because Mick had tried to make him sign a pre-nup.

Well, he'd tried to make Claire make Alfie sign one. When she mentioned that her dad thought it might be a good idea, Alfie had agreed.

If you think it's necessary, darling. I wouldn't want it to come between us. I trust you totally.

She was visibly uncomfortable. *I trust you too. But Dad's insisting.*

Then you should do it. Your dad obviously doesn't think we're going to last, and maybe you share his opinion.

She didn't do it. She told Alfie a few weeks later there wouldn't be a pre-nup, and she never mentioned it again. It was at least two months before Mick spoke to him again, and when he did Alfie loved it. Mick didn't like losing; Alfie liked winning.

Mick coughed. 'I wanted to say that I was touched by your song. It's not the kind of thing I would ever have done – or anyone I know, for that matter – and I have to say I found it a bit bloody much, but Claire liked it. And that's all that counts.'

It was clear the words were hard for him to say. He would have preferred to have been congratulating Alfie for scoring a hat-trick of tries or his first test century or landing a particularly hard left hook, but a romantic – soppy – song would have to do.

'Thank you, Mick,' Alfie said. 'That means a lot.'

'You probably guessed this,' Mick said. 'But I didn't think much of you when I first met you. I thought you were a bit of a chancer, if I'm honest. I thought you lacked drive, and ambition, which is why I wanted the pre-nup. And maybe I should have insisted, but you make Claire happy. I've realized it doesn't matter whether you're the kind of man that *I* think is right for her. All that matters is whether she thinks you are. I'm glad she's found somebody she can have the life she wants with.'

He was, Alfie realized, quite drunk. Perhaps it was deliberate. After all, it was the only way he would ever be able to force the words he'd just said out of his mouth.

'She makes me very happy too,' Alfie said.

'Good.' Mick was clearly not interested in how Alfie felt. 'And now you need to give her what she really wants.' He grinned wolfishly. 'I never thought I'd say this to any man about my little girl, but it's time to get busy! She wants a baby, and there's no point in wasting time.'

His little girl, Alfie thought, *who liked, on occasion, to be handcuffed to their bed and blindfolded.* She was an annoying bitch, but in the right mood, she was good in bed. He wondered what Mick would think if he knew. Perhaps some photos could find their way into his possession so he could see what his little girl got up to.

'We're working on it,' Alfie said. 'Hope to have news soon.'

Mick's eyes narrowed. Alfie realized he had said too much. Claire, evidently, had not mentioned they were trying.

'Is everything OK?' Mick said. 'Are you having problems?'

'No,' Alfie said. 'No problems. It's early. That's all.'

'OK. Good luck.' He reached forward and patted Alfie on the shoulder. 'And take care of my girl.'

'I will,' Alfie said. 'You can count on it.'

Claire

Claire finished her glass of champagne. She looked around the room for Alfie; after his song and her dad's speech he'd disappeared. It had been a while – maybe twenty minutes – and she wondered where he'd gone.

She was glad he'd gone, as it happened. She'd kissed him and whispered a *Thank you, that was beautiful* in his ear when he had finished singing, but in truth she wasn't exactly sure how she felt about it. She veered between thinking it was a beautiful and touching gesture, and thinking it was a bit – well, a bit *embarrassing*. She knew he was soft and romantic and she loved that about him, but the song had been a little *too* soft and romantic – not to mention too public – for her.

She sometimes wondered whether Alfie misunderstood her. She loved his kindness and generosity but she got the impression he thought she was fragile and needed to be handled with kid gloves. She wasn't; she might have lived a life of material privilege, but she'd lost her mum as a teenager and no amount of holidays and clothes and cars could take away the hard edge that had left her with. It rarely came out in her private life, and almost never in her marriage, but Claire was known at work as a tough-minded and serious professional. Alfie never really talked to her about work. She got the impression he thought it was just something she did for fun, but it was far from it. She would explain it to him one day.

She walked towards one of the waiters for a refill. She'd already had three – or maybe four – glasses, but more champagne was the only way she would get through the party. As she reached him, she felt a tap on her shoulder.

She turned around. A guy called Hugh was smiling at her. He was wearing red trousers and a designer cardigan. His thinning hair was cut short and his eyes were glassy. She'd known him for as long as she could remember; his parents were friends with her mum and dad, and he had been invited to family events – birthday parties, weddings – over the years. He was a few years older and for a while their parents had harboured ideas that they might get together when the right time came, ideas that Hugh had clearly shared; on her fifteenth birthday he had tried to kiss her and, when she twisted away, had grabbed her breasts with both hands. She froze, and he took advantage of her shock by thrusting his hand up her skirt and into her underwear.

As soon as she realized what was happening, she ran downstairs, intent on telling her dad what Hugh had done, but when she got there he was standing with Bill, Hugh's dad, laughing about something. She hadn't seen him laugh much since her mum died, and she stopped, suddenly unwilling to do anything to upset him.

So she said nothing. And she'd said nothing ever since. But every time she saw Hugh she felt sick.

'Hi,' he said, his hand running down her arm to her elbow. 'Nice party.'

She shrugged his hand away. 'Thanks for coming.' Her voice was cold.

'Don't be like that,' he said. 'We've not seen each other for ages. Since the wedding, I think?'

'Could be,' Claire said.

'What have you been up to?' Hugh asked.

'This and that.'

'Have I caught you in a bad mood? You can tell me. We go back forever.'

'No,' Claire said. 'I'm looking for Alfie. He's gone missing.'

'Alfie,' Hugh said. 'The lovely Alfie. I must say, it was *quite* a song. Quite a . . . scene.'

Claire looked at him for a while before she answered. She realized she was no longer embarrassed by Alfie's song. It represented everything that was good about him, everything that was genuine and decent and honest. Everything that made him different to Hugh.

'Yes,' she said. 'It was. It was wonderful.' She smiled. 'Very few men could do something like that, Hugh, don't you think?' She didn't wait for an answer. 'I have to go. And hopefully it'll be another three years before we meet again.' She sipped her drink, then added, 'Or maybe longer. A *lot* longer.'

She walked across the room, not sure where she was heading but simply glad to be away from Hugh. She saw her dad walking into the living room. He caught her eye and gestured to her to come over.

'You got a second?' he said.

'Of course.'

'I was just chatting to Alfie,' he said. 'Telling him I'm glad you two are happy . . . '

Claire raised an eyebrow. That kind of conversation was not the norm for him and his son-in-law.

'I know, I know,' he said. 'I'm getting soft in my old age. Anyway, he mentioned something about trying for a baby.' He looked at her, his eyes fixed on hers. 'Is everything OK?'

Claire nodded, then, after a second, shook her head. 'It's been a while,' she said.

Her dad pointed to a man standing by the fireplace. He was tall, with neat grey hair. 'That's Tony Scott. He's a friend of mine, and a doctor. I asked him for the name of a good fertility specialist—'

'Dad!' Claire said. 'I don't want everyone to know.'

'They won't. He's a doctor. He'll keep it to himself. And he gave me a name. Dr Singh, in Harley Street. Call him and say that Tony Scott gave you his name. He'll see you.'

Claire shook her head. 'We'll be OK. It's not time for a doctor yet.'

'Don't be daft,' her dad said. 'See him, get checked out. If there's nothing wrong, it'll put your mind at ease.' He put his hands on her shoulders. 'OK? You going to do it?' He smiled a sad smile. 'Your mum would want me to do whatever I can to help. She loved you, Claire. I know she had her problems, but she was a good mum. All she wanted was for you to be happy. That's all *I* want.'

'I am happy, Dad,' Claire said. 'And I'll do it. Thank you.'

Her dad nodded and headed off towards the waiter. Claire watched him go. He was as good and loving a father as anyone could wish for. Between him and Alfie, she had the best two men possible in her life.

Alfie

Alfie sat on the stone bench and sucked on his cigarette. The house was at least fifty yards away and he was hidden from view by a pergola. He looked back at the house, watching for anyone coming towards him. He could easily put out his cigarette and vanish into the bushes, if he needed to.

It was ridiculous, hiding out to smoke a cigarette. He was a grown man. But it was typical of his wife: she had gone on and on at him about quitting since what felt like the day they'd married.

I know I'm nagging, Alfie, but it's only because I love you. I can't bear to see you harming yourself. And what about òur kids? I don't want them to be deprived of their father.

Over and over and over again, until in the end he'd given in and promised to stop, a promise he had no intention of keeping, so now he had to do it in secret.

It was the perfect symbol of how trapped he was by his stupid bitch of a wife.

They had met at a house like this, at the ostentatious wedding of some school friend of Claire's. It was quite a party – magicians working the crowd, a mini-fairground, all the booze you could drink. The champagne fountain alone probably cost more than Alfie earned a month. Three months.

Not that he was drinking from it. Claire was there as a guest. Alfie was the help.

Specifically, he was in the band, playing bass. Alfie was a recent, part-time member. The band had been mildly successful – a few top twenty hits – in the early 2000s, but had been playing smaller and smaller venues as their popularity dwindled, until they ended up doing cover versions of bigger hits than theirs at expensive weddings. Over time the line-up had changed until only the singer and drummer remained. To fill the gaps they brought in jobbing musicians and Alfie was merely the latest.

He noticed Claire early on. At first he wasn't sure why, but something set her apart. It wasn't the way she looked – she didn't particularly stand out from the other expensively dressed, tanned, yoga-bodied mid-twenties women. It was amazing what expensive clothes, professional make-up and a flattering haircut could do. All of them, whether naturally pretty or not, looked like models. The kind of models you'd see in a Land Rover advert at any rate.

Alfie found them both fascinating and repellent. He hated the way they took all this for granted, as though this kind of party, this kind of wealth, was simply how the world was. They had no idea how other people – people like him – lived, and they didn't want to know. They kept to their own set, gave their kids names that marked them out as belonging, as being 'one of us'.

Yet at the same time he couldn't keep his eyes off them. He was jealous, and hated that too.

But more than anything he hated the fact these people would never accept him.

Strangely, though, it was that which drew him to Claire.

She seemed vulnerable, a little apart from her friends. Watchful. Later he'd find out it was because her mum had died when she was young and she had lost the ability to trust – other people, her future, the world in general, or so her therapist had told her – but looking at her from the stage at that moment he didn't care why it was.

He cared that she turned away from the braying City boys who grabbed at her hand in an attempt to get her to dance, and then watched them, almost wistfully, as they turned their attention to someone else. He could see she was glad they had left her alone, but also disappointed. All she needed was the right one, one who understood her insecurity, who knew how fragile she was.

He could see she needed someone who wasn't threatening. Well, he could be that. He could be whatever she wanted, if it meant he got to come to these weddings as a guest.

Not to mention all the other benefits that went with life as someone like Claire's boyfriend. Smart address, smarter holidays, no money worries ever again. So, yes, whatever she wanted, he would be.

Midway through their set, the band took a break. He declined their offer of a joint behind the stage, and walked to the bar, where Claire was getting a drink.

Water please, he said, then nodded at Claire. *Hi.*

Hi, she said. *Are you in the band?*

Yep. Hope you're enjoying it.

Up close she was very pretty. Unlike most of the other guests she didn't need the expensive grooming.

You guys are great! I loved your song. You know – the one – she blushed as she realized she didn't remember the name of the band's hit. Alfie smiled.

Don't worry. I wasn't in the band then. At the moment I'm helping them out.

Is that what you do? Help out bands?

32

I'm a musician, yes. If that's what you're asking. I do all kinds of stuff.

Wow, Claire said. *I wish I could play an instrument.*

You could, if you tried.

You're very kind, but I don't think so. I'm tone deaf. She laughed. *You should hear me singing.*

I'd like to. And anyone can learn.

Not me!

The barman handed Alfie his water.

Not drinking? Claire said. *I thought you musicians were wild?*

I have to drive home. I have work tomorrow.

Another wedding?

Alfie shook his head. *Tutoring. It's hard to make a living from royalties alone.*

Royalties? Claire's eyes lit up. *Have you released records?*

Quite a few. At least, I've been on quite a few.

Anything I'd have heard of?

I doubt it.

Her smiled faded. *Are they alternative indie things that only the arty kids listen to?*

They're certainly things kids listen to, but I'm not sure about the alternative indie part.

Come on, then. Tell me one of them.

Well, Alfie said, *the most recent one was a ballad. It tells the story of a worm who lives at the bottom of a garden, and whose name is Wiggly-Woo. The one before you might remember from your infant school – I played piano on 'The Dingle-Dangle Scarecrow'.*

Claire burst into laughter. *You sing children's songs?*

I do. What's so funny? Music is an important part of childhood development.

I know, but – it's just – well, I had an idea of sex and drugs and rock'n'roll and that's a bit more—

33

Nappies and wet wipes and singalongs? I know. Not exactly living the life. He shrugged. *But I enjoy it. And it pays the bills. And I do think it's important for kids to have access to quality music from an early age. It might only be 'Twinkle Twinkle' but it doesn't have to be bad.*

I agree, she said. *And I admire you. It's very impressive.*

He glanced at the stage. The rest of the band was re-emerging. He grabbed a napkin and took a pen from his pocket.

Here, he said, and wrote his number down. *Give me a call sometime. I'll play you some of my back catalogue.*

He handed it to her and headed back to the stage. *She'll call*, he thought. *She'll call because she feels superior to me. Stronger. Because I'm a kids' entertainer and anyone who does that is safe. Weak. Not going to leave her. And that's what she wants.*

So that's what he'd be. He made a mental note to buy some kids' music CDs the next day. He'd never played on a kids' CD in his life, but he'd tell her he was on them. She wouldn't know any different.

Back on stage, he picked up his bass as the band played the opening bars of 'Wild Thing'. He glanced at her. She was talking to a friend who had her back to the band, but as he watched she looked up at him. He gave a little wave. She waved back at him.

He knew then this was a done deal.

And it was. They went on dates, ate meals Alfie couldn't afford in places he'd never known existed. He met her friends and their husbands, listened to how they spoke and matched his accent to theirs, modelled his behaviour – confident, charming – on the way they acted. She fell in love with him, head over heels. He fell in love with the life she offered him.

It was a life he could get no other way. He worked, on and off, but he didn't get very far. It wasn't his fault; he was as able as anyone else but he had the wrong background. He'd managed to get into a marketing firm at one point but had got sick of seeing graduates with RP voices and degrees in art history from Warwick and Durham and Oxford show up and take all the promotions. He hated them, hated taking orders from a fucking idiot who just happened to have been to the right school and the right university and whose dad had the right connections and whose mum had the right clothes and gave head to the right fucking people.

And there was nothing he could do about it. He had nothing and he was going nowhere.

But Claire fixed both his problems. She had money, and she had connections, and at first he had quite liked her, which was, for Alfie, as good as it got. He didn't *really* care about anybody – he certainly didn't love anyone in the way other people claimed to; in fact, it seemed absurd to him that anyone could ever be so dependent on someone else – so why not Claire? And what wasn't to like? She was pretty, quiet, and, if he was ever getting too bored with talking to her there was always sex. Like most new couples, they did that a lot.

But it had all changed now. Now he *hated* her.

He finished his cigarette and put his lighter and cigarettes back in his jacket pocket. As he did, his fingers brushed the phone he kept with the illicit tobacco. It wasn't his iPhone; that was in the back pocket of his trousers.

It was his *other* phone, a pay-as-you-go Android device he'd bought in a backstreet electronics shop.

He took it out and glanced at the screen. There were four missed calls and three messages. He swiped and read them.

The first was from that morning.

Hey! I'm missing you! Give me a call. It's been a week! Pippa x

Then, a few hours later:

Are you ignoring me? Only kidding. But call! Pips.

Then a new arrival only a few minutes old:

Henry! What's going on? Get in touch. Please?

It was the 'please?' that did it. He'd sensed she was getting too attached and this was confirmation. Besides, he was getting bored with Pippa Davies-Hunt anyway. Most of the thrill with her had been in the chase. She knew how to play hard to get, understood that once she let him screw her the mystery would be gone, the novelty would have worn off.

And she was right. *All* the thrill was in the chase. She was well educated and rich and lean and pretty but she was a disappointment in bed. She was stiff and unresponsive; compliant, yes – in order to try and keep himself interested he'd suggested some light bondage the third time they'd slept together and she'd gone along with it, not complaining when he choked her hard enough to leave her gasping – but it was the dumb compliance of a farmyard animal. She seemed to take no pleasure in it, seemed to think it was a grim necessity, the price paid for a boyfriend, the thing boyfriends and girlfriends did. It was like she was acting, and Alfie – Henry – was bored of her.

Yes, Henry was bored of her. Henry Bryant – handsome and elusive doctor, frequenter of the websites where people like Pippa went to meet men, owner of the Android phone in Alfie's pocket – was no longer interested in her.

And there was only one way to deal with it. He had to rip the plaster off. Put an end to it, immediately and irrevocably. It might as well be now. She didn't know it, but this had been coming from the start. As far as she was concerned, he was Henry Bryant, a doctor, single, and devoted to his work, which was why he would often be out of touch for a few days. She had no idea he was married and called Alfie Daniels and about to shatter her dreams.

Sorry, he typed. Been busy. I've been thinking too. I'm not sure this is working out. I think it's better if we call it a day. Sorry to do this by text, but I'm a bit of a coward.

Nice touch of humility at the end there, he thought. *Bit of humour too. Should soften the blow.*

The reply was immediate.

Are you fucking SERIOUS??! We need to talk, Henry. You can't end it like this.

He chuckled. There was no point being gentle with her. This was the last he'd have to do with her and so he might as well leave her thinking he was an arsehole. It'd help her get over him.

I can, and I just did. Sorry. It's over. Please don't contact me again.

He hit send and took a mint from his pocket. He slipped it into his mouth. Time to go back in.

The screen lit up with a message. Pippa, again. Fucking hell. She needed to get the message and fuck off.

You bastard. You absolute bastard. You can't do this to me! I won't let you. I love you, Henry! I need to see you one last time so we can talk about this. I'll come to your hospital at a time that suits you. OK?

Shit. She wasn't going to give up easily. It didn't matter, though. She had no idea who he really was, and if she did show up at the hospital he'd told her he worked at, they'd inform her there was no Dr Henry Bryant on the staff. He smiled at the thought of it. She really would be shocked then. Anyway, it made no difference to him. He was done with Pippa Davies-Hunt. He deleted her message and headed for the house.

Claire

Jodie, Claire's oldest friend, was walking towards her across the living room. She was with a man Claire vaguely recognized – perhaps a university acquaintance – and as she reached Claire she gestured at her companion.

'You remember Trevor?' Jodie said. 'I think you may have met at Bunny's wedding last year?'

Trevor shook her hand. 'Sorry to crash your birthday party. But I was out with Jo this afternoon. Happy Birthday, by the way.'

Claire smiled, and glanced at Jodie. No one called her Jo. Jodie rolled her eyes slightly, in a look that said *I can't get rid of him.*

'No problem,' Claire said. 'Nice to see you.'

'Where's Alfie?' Jodie asked.

'I'm not sure. Maybe getting a drink? He's around.'

'That was quite the . . . performance earlier,' she said.

'It was sweet of him,' Claire said. She felt defensive, especially after Hugh's comments. 'You know Alfie. That's how he is.'

'God, I totally agree,' Jodie said. 'I didn't mean anything negative, but not every guy sings songs at his wife's birthday, you know? I actually thought it was amazing.'

'He has a really good voice,' Trevor said. 'It was . . . impressive.'

'He was in a band,' Claire said, looking at Trevor. 'That was how we met.'

'He picked you out in the crowd?' Trevor said.

'Not exactly. They were playing at a wedding and he was on his break. I know – it sounds like a cliché, but he wasn't the band guy looking for groupies at all. He was so nice. So relaxed. He told me about his career singing children's songs. He wasn't embarrassed, like some guys would be.'

'He sings children's songs?' Trevor said.

'He used to,' Claire said. She was aware there was a hard edge in her voice, but she was getting sick of people thinking Alfie was some kind of beta male because he didn't run about thumping his chest and downing pints of lager. 'But sadly not any more.'

'Well,' Trevor said, finding it hard to know where to look. 'It'll – er – it'll be a useful skill when you have kids.'

Jodie caught Claire's eye. She knew they had been trying – unsuccessfully – and she changed the subject.

'Great party,' she said. 'I saw Derek Pritchard. He's back from Australia. Isn't he the—' Jodie was interrupted by her phone ringing. She looked at the screen. 'God,' she said. 'I have to take this. It's a friend. She's been having a tough time.' She lifted the phone to her ear.

'Pippa?' she said. 'Are you OK?'

Claire watched as her friend's eyes widened.

'The bastard,' she said. 'That is so awful.' She looked at Claire and Trevor and shook her head. 'Pips,' she said. 'It's noisy in here. I'm going to call you back, OK? Give me five seconds.'

'Everything OK?' Claire asked.

'Not exactly,' Jodie replied. 'Her boyfriend dumped her by text. I think you met her once – Pippa Davies-Hunt?'

'Yes,' Claire said. She had a vague memory of a tall woman with very long hair. 'Maybe at someone's Christmas do?'

'Dave Chapel,' Jodie said. 'She was dating him for a while. Anyway, she was convinced this new guy was the one, but I had my doubts. He came and went, you know? Blamed it on his job. He's a doctor.'

'Did you meet him?' Claire said.

'No. But I got a bad impression from the way she talked about him. Anyway, now he's dumped her, and she's distraught. The thing is, Pippa is a little bit' – she pointed her finger at her temple and twirled it – 'and she doesn't take this kind of thing well. She wants me to come over. I ought to.'

'No problem,' Claire said. 'You need to leave now?'

'Maybe in half an hour,' Jodie said.

'Great.' Trevor grinned. 'I'll grab some more drinks. Champagne?'

They watched him walk away. 'Is he—' Claire began. 'Are you?'

Jodie shook her head. 'He called out of the blue and asked if I wanted to meet for coffee. I remembered him from Bunny's party and I figured it couldn't do any harm, but now I can't get rid of him. I told him I was coming to your birthday party and he invited himself along.'

'At least you'll be able to tell him you need to be alone with Pippa.'

'Right,' Jodie said. 'Not that *that's* going to be great fun. She's really upset.'

'I'm not surprised. Dumping someone by text is pretty harsh.'

'Not something you'd have to worry about,' Jodie replied. 'Alfie's not going anywhere.'

'No,' Claire said. 'I doubt he is. It's such a relief to be with someone who makes you feel secure. In every other relationship I was always wondering whether whoever it was really

41

loved me, and if they did, why, what it was about me that they loved. It was a constant search for proof so I could relax. But with Alfie – I know he loves me. We connect on some deep level. It's like we were made for each other. And it's such a lovely feeling.'

'You really are lucky,' Jodie said. 'I hope I end up in the same boat.'

'But not with Trevor.'

'No, not with Trevor. And I know it's not going all that well right now, but you'll be pregnant soon, and you two will be the perfect parents. Your kids will be the luckiest kids around.'

Claire didn't want to say so, but she agreed. It was part of what attracted her to Alfie. She knew their kids would grow up with a dad who showed them how to be affectionate and loving, taught them it was OK to cry and show emotion, hugged and kissed and cuddled them long after they were babies. She had an image of her and Alfie and two children camping in the Lake District or riding bikes in a forest or eating popcorn on a family movie night. It was all she wanted – all he wanted, too – and the thought that it might not happen was unbearable.

'I hope so,' Claire said. 'I'm not sure what I'd do if it didn't work out. And Alfie would take it hard. I think he's more desperate than me for kids.'

Jodie gestured to Trevor. He was walking towards them with a bottle of champagne. 'Well,' she said. 'There is one saving grace about not being pregnant. You can have another drink.'

Alfie

Alfie headed back to the house. There was a group of people smoking on the terrace. Perfect. He could stop for a chat and then if Claire detected any lingering smell of smoke on him he could blame it on them.

'Hi,' he said. 'Nice evening.'

There were five of them, four men he didn't know and a woman he vaguely recognized. Her face was flushed and she was a little glassy-eyed. No wedding ring and probably no boyfriend, which was why she was out here smoking with a bunch of men who were no doubt hoping she'd leave them so they could talk about football or rugby or the other women at the party. He looked at her for a few seconds longer than was polite. She was starting to put on weight she would never get rid of and was on the cusp of losing the youthfulness that gave her what little appeal she had. She knew it, too; there was something desperate about the way she smiled at the men and laughed too loudly at their jokes.

He felt a twinge of lust. He found that kind of vulnerability irresistible. He'd have to behave himself, though. He could hardly go chasing women at his wife's birthday party.

'You want a ciggy?' one of the men said. He was tall and had thick red hair and a thin, irritating voice.

'No thanks,' Alfie said.

He walked across the terrace to the house. Through the window he saw Claire. She was clinking champagne glasses with Jodie and some tall guy. Did Jodie have a boyfriend? He'd be jealous if she did. He looked at her for a moment. He would have loved to fuck her. Two summers ago they'd gone for a weekend in St Tropez with her. She had a white bikini and he'd spent the entire time staring at her from behind his sunglasses, and then thinking about her while he was having sex with Claire.

Claire. It was getting worse. As soon as he was in there she'd ask where he'd been, and he'd say *nowhere, just a walk*, when what he wanted to say was *none of your fucking business*. He hated the feeling he was being watched the whole time. It made him feel trapped, like a wild animal that had wandered into a house and was now being kept as a pet. He couldn't look at her without feeling a deep and mounting anger.

Because there was no escape. Worse, by acting so in love with her from the start he had set a precedent, which left him with things like singing that awful song. He shook his head. It was so humiliating. But he had no choice. If he didn't totally overdo it he was worried the mask would slip and she would see his true feelings, and then it – all of it, the cars and houses and holidays and money – would be gone. And he had no intention of letting that happen, especially not now when he'd had a taste of it. All he needed was an escape.

Which was where Henry Bryant came in. It had started with a fake email address. It was amazing, really: all he'd had to do was open a gmail account in the name Henry Bryant and pop! All of a sudden, he existed. He could communicate

44

with people, log into chat rooms, post underneath newspaper articles, get Facebook and Twitter accounts.

Which he did for a while. He got involved in conversations in chat rooms and comments sections, and one of them – he'd forgotten which one – had led to an app which brought people who were looking for illicit, extra-marital affairs together.

You posted a photo, your age, some interests, and the app proposed some matches. You messaged back and forth, and, if you both agreed, you met up.

The first woman did not look like the photo she had posted at all. In the photo she looked in her early thirties and in reasonable shape; in reality she was ten years older and about three stone overweight.

Alfie didn't care. He would not have been attracted to her under normal circumstances, but that was the whole point: these were not normal circumstances, and he was not Alfie Daniels.

The second candidate he chose was a blonde, stick-thin mother of three in her late thirties. It was a clinical transaction; afterwards, Alfie asked her if she wanted to meet again. She didn't. The third one did, though, and she wanted to learn more about Henry Bryant.

So Alfie gave her more to learn.

It became a kind of game, to see how far he could take it.

And he had taken it much, much further than he had thought possible.

He got an address – a PO box number – and used it to get a bank account. With that, a bank account and then a credit card and a PayPal account. With his PayPal account he could buy and sell on eBay, which provided Henry Bryant with an income. The fact that the things he sold – first editions of books, rare vinyl, other collectables – were things Alfie bought was neither here nor there. None of his customers would, or could, ever know. He just needed a way of getting some money to Henry Bryant.

And with the money came – all acquired illegally and incredibly cheaply on the dark web – a birth certificate, passport and National Insurance number. Which meant Henry Bryant was real in every meaningful way possible. He could buy a house, get a job, cross international borders. He could do anything he wanted.

He just happened not to exist.

It had been perfect for Alfie. It offered him everything he wanted: a release from his life with Claire, the thrill of illicit sex with a variety of women, and most of all, a sense that he was beating the system, outsmarting everyone around him. And there was no link to him. The phone, bank account, everything – it all led to Henry Bryant.

It was odd: the longer it had gone on, the more he had started to feel that he and Henry Bryant were different people. When he was with some woman he'd met online in the corner of a pub in a part of London where Claire and her friends would never go, he *was* Henry Bryant. He didn't really feel guilty, but the slight misgivings he did have were eased by the thought that it wasn't him doing it.

It was Henry Bryant.

He even developed *Bryantisms*; mannerisms and affected patterns of speech – a pursing of the lips and drawing out of vowels – that he only did when he was being Henry. In some ways – and this was worrying – he *preferred* Henry. He was funnier, more relaxed. Moreover, he didn't have to be the soft, unthreatening little bitch that Alfie Daniels pretended to be.

He could be whatever he wanted, and he was. He cancelled at the last minute (on the occasions when it was too risky to go), drank hard when he wanted and was rough in bed. Most of all he didn't apologize, didn't simper and coo, and didn't sing any fucking stupid songs.

It was wonderful. And it was the only thing that was keeping him sane.

He became aware of a tapping on the window. He looked up. Claire was beckoning him inside.

Christ. He'd almost forgotten. He glanced at Jodie's buttocks; she was wearing a pair of very tight jeans. He pictured peeling them off, revealing some expensive underwear, an image which allowed him to force a smile on to his face. He waved at Claire, then blew her a kiss; she mimed catching it and planted it on her cheek.

It was sickening.

Inside, he kissed Claire for real, then hugged Jodie, enjoying the press of her breasts against his chest. She gestured at the guy standing with them.

'This is Trevor.'

Alfie shook his hand. He had a fixed, goofy grin. If this idiot was fucking Jodie he didn't think he could take it.

'We were on our way out,' Jodie said. 'I have to go and meet a friend. She's not doing so well.'

'Oh,' Alfie said. 'Everything OK?'

'Boyfriend troubles.' Jodie took out her phone. 'Quick photo before I go?'

She handed the phone to Trevor, who looked put out she didn't want him in the picture. Alfie thought it might be deliberate. Maybe he wasn't getting any with Jodie, after all.

The three of them lined up and Trevor took a few snaps. When he was done, he gave the phone back to Jodie.

'Nice to see you,' Alfie said. 'And good luck with your friend. I'm going to grab a drink.'

As he walked away, Henry Bryant's phone buzzed in his

47

pocket. Pippa, again. Obviously, despite how clear he'd been, she hadn't got the message. He'd reply later and get rid of her once and for all, before she became a problem.

Henry Bryant would never let her become a problem. He dealt with things, decisively. He would never have put up with what Alfie put up with. He would have found a way to deal with Claire.

And Alfie needed to. He just had no idea what to do.

Claire

Dr Singh sat opposite Claire and studied his notes. He looked to be in his sixties and had small, precise features. She had googled him and, as her dad had said, he really was an expert in the field of fertility; he had pioneered a number of treatments with spectacular results, which probably explained the fee her dad was paying.

It was the second time they had met that day; in the morning he had asked her a bunch of questions and discussed her goals, and then he'd sent her into the room next door where a nurse had drawn blood and performed an ultrasound scan, along with some X-rays.

We'll have the results shortly, he said. *But you'll have to see when Dr Singh is free to take you through them.*

Dr Singh was free that afternoon, and Claire had left work to come and meet him. She'd had to move a couple of meetings around, but as a partner she had that flexibility. Besides, she had been thinking about it all day, unable to focus on anything other than what the doctor might tell her.

'Well . . . ' He smiled. 'So far, it's good news.'

'What do you mean "so far"?' Claire said.

'I mean the tests we did showed no abnormalities, but

there are more procedures we can do. However, I'm not sure they're warranted, at this point. I see nothing wrong.'

He pulled a piece of A4 paper from a file and handed it to her. 'These are the results of your Hysterosalpingography – that's the fancy name for the X-ray we took of your uterus and fallopian tubes. As you can see, nothing showed up.'

She studied the paper. There was a lot of text, but her eyes settled on the only words that mattered to her.

Abnormalities: None

'What about the other test?' she said. 'The one about the eggs?'

'The ovarian reserve test,' Dr Singh said. 'That, too, was fine. You have a normal egg supply, and they are of good quality.' He laced his fingers together and leaned forwards. 'As far as I can tell, there is no problem with your fertility. We could do further imaging, or even a laparoscopy.'

'What's that?'

'It's a procedure to take a look inside the uterus. We make an incision in the navel and put a camera in there. If there was anything going on – endometriosis, scarring – it would show up. But, like I said, there's no reason to believe there is anything.'

Claire met his gaze. 'Then why can't I get pregnant?'

'Sometimes it takes a while,' Dr Singh said. 'And the stress caused by worrying about it can make it more difficult. If you can relax, take your time, that would probably help.'

She already knew this. Every one of the myriad of websites about pregnancy and childbirth mentioned it. *Make sure you stay relaxed. The body is less likely to conceive when under stress. A relaxed body is a body ready to have a baby.* All very well; the problem was that when you tried to relax the trying got in the way of the relaxing. It was like telling somebody not to think of an elephant; as soon as you said it an elephant popped into their mind.

'It's hard,' she said. 'I can't stop worrying that something's wrong.'

'There's nothing that I can see.' Dr Singh twirled his pen in his fingers. 'At least, not with *you*. There is, however, one other avenue to explore.'

'Which is?'

Dr Singh took off his glasses. 'Has your husband had his sperm tested?'

Claire nodded. 'A couple of months ago. It was fine.'

When she hadn't got pregnant after the first few months of trying, Alfie had declared that he was going to take a test.

I don't want to waste any time, he said. *If there's something wrong, I want to know so I can fix it.*

She had asked if he thought she should get tested too.

Not yet. You'll need to go to a doctor. I can do a home test. It's easy. And I want peace of mind that everything's OK with me.

And it was. She was at work when he did it, but when she came home he was beaming: sperm count was normal. She was pleased for him, but it only made her feel worse. If there was a problem then it was with her, and not him.

'Where did he have it done?' Dr Singh said. 'If you don't mind me asking. You don't have to say, of course.'

'It was a home testing kit.'

'Ah.' Dr Singh pursed his lips. 'Those kits are perfectly accurate, if correctly used, but there is scope for error. Do you know if he kept it?'

'I doubt it. I think he threw it away. I've never seen it.'

'Well, it's only something to consider, but maybe you could suggest that he come and see me. We can do a more comprehensive fertility test, so we're absolutely sure.'

'You think there's a chance it was wrong?'

'There's always a chance. Faulty test, or maybe user error. Think about asking him to come in.'

'There's no need to think. He'll want to do it. Can I book it now?'

'Are you sure you don't want to check with him first?' Dr Singh asked.

Claire shook her head. Alfie would be on board, she had no doubt about that.

Alfie

Alfie turned into their street – they lived in a double-fronted Victorian villa halfway down the street – and walked slowly towards the house. It was a few minutes past seven p.m.; he'd been to a showing in Battersea. He normally tried to avoid showings as much as he could. After he and Claire got married he had felt he needed some kind of job, but he had no idea what to do, so, when Mick suggested becoming an estate agent he had agreed. Mick had helped him to find a post at a different agency – he claimed he didn't want to mix family and business, but Alfie was convinced it was because Mick thought he was incompetent and didn't want him near his business. As it was, it had turned out to be an inspired choice of career.

He was, if he did say so himself, *fucking* good at it. People seemed to want someone with a big smile to convince them that whatever property they were looking at was the perfect place for them, and Alfie was happy to oblige. Even when he knew the neighbours were noisy and annoying and there was a problem with cockroach infestations in the summer he looked them in the eye and said they'd be *so* happy there. Not giving a shit about them made it easier, of course.

The other benefit – and this was huge – was that he could come and go as he pleased during the day and, even better, the agency had the keys to all kinds of empty properties all over the city which he could use when he met people online.

Claire had texted – *Doc says everything OK!* – so he had bought a bottle of champagne to celebrate.

'Hey!' he called out as he opened the door. 'Are you home?'

'In the kitchen,' Claire replied.

He walked in, making sure there was a wide smile on his face. 'I got your text. It's *wonderful* news. I'm so glad the doctor didn't find anything.'

'I know,' Claire said. 'In one way it's a relief, but in another it's frustrating – and worrying – because if there was a reason then at least the doctors could fix it, and if they couldn't we'd know for sure and could make other plans. As it is, all I – we – can do is wait.'

'It'll happen,' Alfie said. 'Eventually. Lots of people have been in this exact situation.'

Claire seemed about to say something but she hesitated. She looked a little sheepish.

'Everything OK?' Alfie said.

'He did ask about one other thing.'

'Which was?'

'Your test. The one you took at home.'

'What about it?'

'He wondered whether you should take another one.'

Alfie was, for a moment, lost for words. He had not been expecting to hear that. He'd taken his test – or so he'd told Claire – and he'd assumed the whole sperm-count question was settled. The last thing he needed was anyone else interfering. 'Doesn't he think they're accurate?'

'He didn't say so. Not exactly, anyway. All he said was, there's some margin for error. Maybe you didn't get it right.'

Alfie laughed. 'It's not tremendously hard to do. You just – you know, point and shoot – on the test and a line pops up in a window.'

'Still. He said there are other, more reliable tests he could do.'

'And get paid for.'

'I don't think he was trying to drum up business, Alfie. I think he was making a suggestion. Being helpful.'

Alfie held up his hands. 'I'm sorry. I was only being cynical.'

'So will you do it? Go and see him?'

Alfie weighed it up. He could say yes, and then simply put it off. Find reasons to cancel appointments. Eventually she might forget.

'Sure,' he said. 'I don't think it'll come to much, but why not? If it helps, I'll do it.'

'I knew you wouldn't mind.' Claire smiled. 'So I made the appointment. It's for seven a.m., this Thursday.'

Seven a.m. *this Thursday*? The stupid fucking bitch. What had she done now? This was typical of her. She had to *fucking* interfere. He'd told her his test was OK, but did she believe him? No – she went jabbering on to her private doctor that Daddy paid for because the NHS wasn't good enough for her and then she went and actually *made an appointment* for him, an actual goddamn *appointment* that he would have to attend. There was no way he had something going on at seven a.m., and she knew it.

But he couldn't attend. Any half-decent doctor would see immediately that he didn't have a low sperm count; he had no sperm at all. And then they'd see the vasectomy scar – it was small but they'd know exactly what it was – and he'd be screwed.

Totally screwed.

He'd wake up on Thursday and say he was ill. But then she'd reschedule.

He was trapped. Shit. Shit. Shit. He needed a way out. And fast.

'Are you all right, Alfie?'

He smiled at her and took out his phone – his iPhone, not his Henry Bryant phone, Henry Bryant who would have told her to go to hell, he'd already done the test and she'd better believe what he damn well said – and opened the calendar.

'What day was it?' he said, his voice calm and even. He grabbed her glass of wine and took a sip. He fought the urge to chug the whole thing.

'Thursday at seven a.m. Dr Singh said he'd open early for you.'

He nodded. He'd have to go. He'd simply have to find another way to deal with it. This was a real problem.

Unless. Unless he could find a way to nip it in the bud. He had the beginnings of an idea. Perhaps there was something he could do after all. He felt himself relax.

'I'll be there,' he said.

Claire

Claire swayed as the Tube train pulled out of the station. She glanced at her watch. Alfie should be with Dr Singh now. She'd wanted to go with him but she had a meeting with a client at eight. They were working on the product launch of a new flask, and they still hadn't settled on the design. It was getting late in the project so they had fired their original designers and come to Claire's firm. Part of the problem was the brief; they wanted something urban and sleek, but rugged and tough. It wasn't immediately obvious how to incorporate all those things, but she had some ideas.

She got off at her Tube stop and her phone rang. It was Jodie.

'Hi,' she said. 'What's up?'

Jodie didn't answer. Instead she made the sound of someone blowing out their cheeks in frustration.

'*That* good?' Claire said. 'Fill me in.'

'It's Pippa. She's driving me nuts.'

It took Claire a moment to place the name, but then it came to her. Pippa was the friend whose boyfriend had broken up with her by text. 'What's she doing?'

'She's moved in. She can't bear to be alone. And all she talks about is Henry fucking Bryant—'

'He's the guy who broke up with her by text?'

'The very same, and I never want to hear his name again. I didn't get to bed until one a.m. last night. She was telling me how she loved him and she'd been convinced he was the one and she didn't know what she'd done wrong, she simply *couldn't* understand how he'd changed from one day to the next, and didn't I think it was weird? And maybe there was something else going on with him because he hadn't been answering her texts or calls; he could have been taken ill or something bad had happened to him which was the *real* reason he'd dumped her and so maybe there was a chance they could get back together after all.' Jodie paused and took a deep breath. 'I get it, Claire, I really do, and I feel sorry for her. It's horrible to be dumped – we've all been there – and you get trapped in a cycle of wondering if you messed up in some way or other, but this is extreme. I mean, if she's like this it's no wonder he wanted out.'

'Or that he did it by text,' Claire said. 'He probably knew how she'd react. Not that it's an excuse. He should have told her to her face.'

'Yeah, he should. But that doesn't help me. She was up at five this morning, which meant I was too, ready for another few hours of speculation about why Henry Bryant had broken up with her. What am I going to do?'

'It'll pass. She'll get over it.'

'But in the meantime it's torture.'

'Take her out. Meet some new guys.'

'I'd feel bad inflicting her on them.'

Claire laughed. 'Then you'll just have to get her to move out in a kind and gentle way. Tell her she's welcome to stay for a while longer but you're busy at work and you need your space. Don't do it by text, though.'

Jodie gave a sardonic laugh. 'Maybe I should. It might work. Or I'll tell her I'm going on a business trip and come to stay with you guys.'

'Sure. Do whatever you need.' Claire checked the time on her phone. 'Anyway, I have to run. I have a meeting.'

'OK. And thanks for the advice, although I'm not sure I'm much closer to a solution. I feel better for venting though. By the way, I've got some good photos of us at the party. I'll send them over.'

They hung up and, a few seconds later, Claire's phone buzzed. Jodie had sent two photos from her birthday party: one of her and Jodie and Alfie standing together and one of Alfie singing the song he'd written, with her dad in the background looking at him in mild disgust.

Here you go, the message said. Look at your dad! Not sure what he thinks of the song! I'm sure he likes Alfie, but they're so different. Anyway, thought you'd get a kick out of this.

Claire laughed and walked towards the office. As she turned on to Haymarket there was a busker singing 'Father and Son'. She stopped to listen. She'd forgotten about Alfie but the song reminded her where he was. It was a good omen, a sign the appointment was going well. She smiled and reached into her bag for some change. All she had was a twenty-pound note. For a second she hesitated, but then she bent down and threw it into the guitar case. She had to. She had a sudden sense that it was all linked and she couldn't ignore the fact there was a busker singing a song about a father right at the point Alfie was with Dr Singh. She had to give to receive.

The busker looked at the note lying among a scattering of coins. He grinned at her.

'Thanks,' he said. 'And good luck.'

She turned away and headed up the street, smiling so much it was almost painful.

This was it. This was the day it all fell into place.

Alfie

Dr Singh folded his arms and looked at Alfie. He had a puzzled expression on his face.

'So,' he said. 'I have some results. Before we discuss them, I must say I am a little surprised.'

Alfie had no doubt that he was, but he frowned, then widened his eyes as though he was worried. 'What kind of surprise?'

Dr Singh sat back in his chair. 'Mr Daniels,' he said. 'Your sperm count is zero. There are no sperm.'

Alfie let his mouth drop open. 'But,' he stammered, 'but I took a test. It was OK.'

'I don't know how. Unless you read it incorrectly. Tell me, did you refrain from sex and masturbation for forty-eight hours before coming here?'

Alfie nodded. He'd made a big thing of it, telling Claire how hard it was to resist her.

'Then there can be no doubt. You are not producing sperm.'

'I can't believe it,' Alfie said. 'I really can't believe it.'

The doctor's bedside manner could use some work, Alfie thought. He'd just blurted out the news that a man would never be a father. He wasn't to know Alfie was perfectly aware of that already. For all Dr Singh knew, Alfie's devastation was genuine.

'I want to discuss something else with you,' Dr Singh said. 'There are some other avenues we could explore.'

'Oh?' Alfie said. 'Please. Anything.'

'Normally we would do two or three tests to get a good sense of the quality and quantity of sperm being produced over a period of time, but since there are no sperm at all I'm not sure it makes sense.'

'I get it,' Alfie said. 'If there are none then I have no chance.' He looked down, focusing on his fingernails. 'I can't believe it's come to this. It seems so hopeless.'

'Maybe not,' Dr Singh said. 'I'd like to do further tests. It's possible there is a blockage which is stopping the sperm from getting from the testes into the ejaculate. In fact, since there are no sperm at all, I'd like to check for this.'

'How would you do that?'

'We could do an ultrasound as a first step. We can do it now, if you like? We'll have results right away.'

Alfie looked at the doctor. He felt a violent hatred for him but he bit it back. He had to stay calm. If he let the doctor do this then it would be obvious he had had a vasectomy. It would be equally obvious he had lied about it. That said, Dr Singh would have to keep quiet – he couldn't reveal anything to Claire because of confidentiality. Still, it was better not to have anyone know.

He shook his head. 'There's no point,' he said. 'I'll know more about why I have no sperm, but it won't help.'

'Oh, it will,' Dr Singh said. 'It'll make all the difference in the world.'

Alfie straightened in his chair. 'Oh? How so?'

'Because if there is a blockage then that means you may well be producing plenty of healthy sperm. We can then either fix it, and you'll be able to get pregnant in the traditional fashion, or we can harvest those sperm and use them for IVF, or other such treatments.'

'I'm not sure,' Alfie said. 'It might be better to let it be. Accept the situation.'

Dr Singh frowned. 'Mr Daniels! This is a very simple procedure and it could change everything. You should at least discuss it with your wife. I'm sure she would be keen to pursue this option.'

'She wouldn't need to know, would she?' Alfie said. 'I mean, you can't tell her any of this, can you?'

Dr Singh did not reply for a long time. When he did, his voice was low and guarded. 'No,' he said. 'I can't.'

'Good. Then I'd like it if you didn't.'

'May I ask a question, Mr Daniels?'

Alfie nodded.

'Do you intend to tell your wife that everything is *normal* with your sperm test?'

Alfie thought for a moment. 'Yes, I do. But you can't say anything.'

'No,' Dr Singh said. 'I can't. But I will have no choice but to stop treating her.'

Alfie looked at him. That could be a problem. 'Why?' he said.

'Because I will know – even though I will say nothing – that the real cause of her not conceiving is your sperm. Knowing that, I cannot continue to act as though the problem might be her, not to mention the ethics of charging for treatment I know will be ineffective.'

'What will you tell her?'

'That an ethical concern has arisen and I can no longer be her doctor.'

'She'll want to know why.'

'I'll tell her I can't say why.'

Alfie nodded, slowly. He shouldn't have said he was going

to tell Claire his sperm was normal, but then Singh would have felt he could have discussed it with her, since Alfie had already told her. And he had to keep it from her.

So he'd had no choice. And now it was obvious what would happen: when the doctor told her there was some ethical concern, Claire would think something was badly wrong and would go immediately to another doctor. She'd make Alfie go with her, and she'd insist she was there at every appointment. That doctor would discover his zero sperm count and suggest a scan to look for a blockage, at which point the vasectomy would be revealed and his marriage, and the lifestyle that went with it, would be over.

The problems would pile on top of each other until the whole thing came crashing down, and that left him with only one option. The option Henry Bryant would have taken.

'OK, I'll tell her the truth. I have no sperm.' Alfie tapped the desk. 'Then what will you do?'

'I'll say it is true you have no sperm, but I don't know why, and since you do not want further treatment there is nothing more I can do to help at this point.'

'Well,' Alfie said. 'Let me tell you – patient to doctor – why I have no sperm. It's because I had a vasectomy. And before you ask, Claire doesn't know about it, and she's not going to find out. So here's what's going to happen: I'm going to tell her I have no sperm, and then, if she asks you about it, you're going to say it's true. And that's it. You're not going to say another word.'

Dr Singh's eyes narrowed, and he pointed his index finger at Alfie's chest. 'I'm not intimidated by you, Mr Daniels. I will keep your secrets, but I will not treat—'

Alfie's hand snapped out and he grabbed the doctor's finger. He stared at him and slowly bent it back. Dr Singh flinched in pain. 'Listen to me,' he said in a low voice. 'Listen to me, you filthy little Paki. You're going to tell her there's nothing

63

more you can do to help me and she's going to leave here feeling sad, and you'll never see her again. And if you don't, you won't need to worry about breaking doctor–patient confidentiality. You'll need to worry about me breaking your disgusting brown neck.'

'I'll call the police,' Dr Singh said, through gritted teeth. 'This is assault.'

Alfie shook his head. 'No, you won't,' he said. 'There's no evidence of any assault. And when they get here I'll say you fondled me when you examined me. I'll tell everyone. And they'll believe me, because people believe that kind of thing.'

He tightened his grip and lowered his voice to a whisper. 'And I *will* kill you. One night, when you're all alone, you'll wake up and wonder what the noise in your house was, whether there even *was* a noise, and then you'll look up and I'll be in your bedroom and it'll be the last thing you ever see. Understand?'

He could see fear in the doctor's eyes. He relaxed. This was going his way.

'I asked you a question,' he said. 'Answer it, you piece of immigrant shit. Do. You. Understand?'

Dr Singh nodded, his lips pressed together to suppress the pain.

'I understand,' he said.

'Good,' Alfie replied, and let go of his finger.

Claire

Claire's phone buzzed and she glanced at the screen. It was a text from Alfie. The meeting was in full flow, but she had to read his message.

Can you call?

Her stomach balled up. There was something about the text message which didn't seem right to her. He'd have his results by now. She'd been expecting a breezy *no problem* or *all fine down below*, but not this. Not a request to call her. She started to type a reply – *call you back soon* – but before she could finish it, she became aware that the room was silent. She lifted her head. Vicki Turner, the senior partner and founder of the firm, was looking back at her.

'Claire?' she said. 'Your thoughts on the last question?'

Claire swallowed. She had no idea what the last question was.

'Sorry,' she said. 'I didn't catch the question.'

Vicki Turner – tall, late-fifties, hair groomed into a static pile, pencil skirt and expensive jacket – looked pointedly at Claire's phone, and then spoke slowly.

'The question,' she said, 'was about the relationship with the client. If we have a strong relationship then maybe we can resolve the matter without pursuing legal action. Since you manage this contract, I was wondering whether you might be able to provide an opinion on the matter.'

'Right,' Claire said. 'Of course.' She searched for something to say but her mind had gone blank. She felt the heat rise in her neck and cheeks, felt herself flush. It was ridiculous; she was a grown woman, but here she was, her mind frozen.

'It's . . . ' she began, 'it's fine, I think. No, it's better than that. It's good.'

Vicki nodded. 'Do you think we may be able to resolve this payment dispute without going down the legal route?'

'I'm not – well yes, maybe.' Claire smiled. 'Maybe I can talk to someone there. Test the temperature.'

'OK,' Vicki said. 'Let's do that. Perhaps by the end of the day, if possible?'

'No problem,' Claire said. 'End of the day it is.'

Back at her desk, she picked up her phone and called Alfie. He answered on the second ring. She could tell immediately it wasn't good news.

'Alfie,' she said. 'What happened?'

There was a long pause. 'It turns out,' he said eventually, 'the problem is me.'

'What do you mean?'

'Well,' Alfie replied. 'I have a very low sperm count.'

'But you took that test! It was fine.'

'I know. That's what I thought. But it must have been faulty.'

'OK,' Claire said. 'It's not the end of the world. There are things they can do even if you have a low sperm count. We can try those.'

'Not in my case,' Alfie said. He sounded worse, flatter and more exhausted, than Claire had ever heard him sound before. 'I have *no* sperm, Claire. None at all. It's impossible.'

'No,' Claire said. 'It can't be! I'll talk to Dr Singh. See if—'

'Claire!' Alfie's voice was almost a shout. 'Please don't make this any worse than it needs to be. It's time to move on.'

She was about to argue, but she caught the words on her lips. Now was not the time. And besides, Alfie had no doubt explored all the possibilities with Dr Singh, and so if he said it was impossible it must be. He wanted this as badly as she did; there was no way he would leave any stone unturned.

'OK,' she said. 'I'm sorry, darling. I feel for you.'

'I don't care about me. It's you. This is your dream. You deserve better.'

'There is no one better,' Claire said. 'And this test result doesn't change how I feel about you one bit. I love you as much – more – than I ever did. This will only bring us closer.'

'Thank you,' Alfie said. 'Thank you for saying that. It means a lot. I love you.'

She looked at her watch. It was ten a.m. 'I'll see you tonight. What time are you home?'

'I don't know. I'm a bit behind. But I don't want to be too late. I need to see you.'

'Get back as soon as you can. We can have a drink and talk about how to deal with this. OK?'

He agreed and she put her phone on her desk. She pushed it away from her, then rubbed her temples. So there *was* a reason she couldn't get pregnant, and it was this. Although she'd wanted him to go and see Dr Singh she hadn't really thought there was a problem. It was more for peace of mind than anything else. But now this had happened.

And as it started to sink in tears came to her eyes.

She shook her head. She could cry about it later. For now

she needed to get her thoughts straight. Firstly, Alfie would be devastated, so she needed to be sensitive to him. Secondly, there were still avenues they could explore. If she wanted to have her own baby then they could use a sperm donor, or they could adopt. She'd often thought that, after she had a couple of her own and built a family home, she would like to adopt a child. There was something about the idea of sharing what she had with someone in need that appealed to her.

Well, maybe that was going to happen sooner than she'd thought.

She closed her laptop. She needed a coffee. As she got up, Jodie called.

'Hey,' Claire said. 'How're things?'

'Good,' Jodie replied. 'You? Want to meet up tonight?'

'I can't. And I thought you were locked into Pippa world.'

'I was. But, amazingly, she's going out tonight. We were supposed to be watching a movie, but she called and said she had plans. She sounded quite happy, actually. Maybe she got asked out on a date. Either way, I thought I'd take advantage and see if you were free.'

'Sadly not,' Claire said. 'I have plans with Alfie. But I'm glad Pippa is off your hands, for a night at least.'

'Me too. See you soon.'

Claire put her phone in her bag and headed for the main doors. She needed to get some fresh air. She could get her coffee somewhere nearby.

As she left the building she noticed that the busker was gone.

Alfie

Alfie put his phone down – his Henry Bryant phone – and stared out of the office window.

He was in trouble. *Big* trouble.

Just before he'd given Claire the bad news, Pippa had sent him a text message – We need to talk – which he'd ignored, as usual. He hadn't been able to ignore the next one she sent, though, since it contained his name. His *real* name.

You'll have to answer this one, Henry, it read. Or should I say, Alfie?

She knew who he was. How, he had no idea, but she knew. And if *she* knew, then others might. She was right; he had to answer, so he had called her.

Well, well, she said. *Nice to hear from you, Henry.*

She put a heavy, sarcastic emphasis on the 'Henry'.

Look, he said. *I can explain.*

Can you? she replied. *I doubt it. Although I suppose you're trapped in an unhappy marriage and Henry Bryant was your way out?*

Yes, he said. *I know it's a cliché but it's true. And this is true, too – I was falling for you too deeply and I knew that*

69

if it carried on I'd be in trouble, which was why I had to end it.

You texted *me*, she said. *You didn't even have the decency to call.*

I knew if I did you'd persuade me. I'm weak, Pippa, when it comes to you. I would have heard your voice and I would have been unable to do it.

She paused and he sensed her soften. He was telling her what she wanted to hear. It was amazing how easily people would believe you when you did that.

Pippa, he said. *I knew that if we stayed together I'd eventually have had to choose between you and my marriage, and I'd have chosen you. But that's impossible. My wife is vindictive. The divorce would have been messy and she'd have made sure I was left with nothing. And that's not all . . . she's violent. There's no telling what she would have done. So I couldn't let it come to that.*

I'd have helped you, Pippa said. *We'd have been OK together.*

You couldn't stop her. No one could.

It wouldn't have mattered. As long as we had each other, everything else would have been irrelevant.

Oh, Pippa, he said, injecting real longing into his voice. *I want to see you. Can we meet? Tonight?*

I don't know, she said. *You hurt me.*

Now she thought she was in the driving seat, she was playing hard to get, but that was all it was.

Please, he said. *I miss you.*

I miss you too, she replied, her voice almost a whisper.

Will you meet me? he begged.

Yes. I'll meet you.

Tonight?

Tonight.

And so they had arranged to meet later. Claire would be

expecting him home, but he'd have to come up with some reason he'd stayed out later. For now, Pippa was the priority. He had no idea what he was going to do, but he knew he had to find out how she knew, who else she had told, and then he could start to figure out how to fix this.

He took his car from the office car park and drove to Barnes, where they had arranged to meet in a pub. They hugged and he was struck by how, even at an emotional reunion, there was a limpness and passivity in the way she embraced him. A shudder of disgust ran through him.

They ordered two glasses of wine and sat at a corner table.

'So,' he said. 'It's great to see you. How've you been?'

She looked at him, her eyes wide, almost fearful. 'Not good,' she said. 'I was going a bit crazy.'

'Me too. But I'm here now.'

'And you're not Henry Bryant,' she said. 'You lied to me.'

'Only about that. Not about how I felt about you.'

'How do I know that? It's going to be hard for me to trust you again.'

Going to be, he noted. *In her mind, they were already back together.*

'I'm sorry,' he said. 'Truly I am. And not that it matters now, but how did you find out?'

She smiled a sly smile. 'A friend.'

Shit. So someone else knew. This was getting worse. 'Which friend?'

'Jodie.'

He froze. If Jodie knew then it was only a matter of time before she told Claire. They were best friends. He was surprised she hadn't called already. 'How did she find out?' he asked.

'She didn't. Not exactly.'

'Then what happened?'

'She was showing me some photos on her phone, and one came up of her with you. And your wife. Who I've met, by the way, a while ago. There was another photo of you singing a song. A romantic one, I assume. Of course, I was more than a little surprised to see you, so I asked who you were and she told me. Alfie Daniels, husband of the lovely Claire.'

'She isn't so lovely.' He shook his head. 'And it wasn't a romantic song.' There was an important piece of information he needed. The *most* important piece. 'You told Jodie about us?'

Pippa shook her head. 'No. I wanted to speak to you first.'

Alfie fought to stop himself shouting in relief. 'Did you tell anyone?'

'No. Like I said, I wanted to give you a chance to tell me your side of the story.'

'Thank you,' he said. 'That's very fair. And it's one of the reasons . . . it's one of the reasons I love you.'

She blinked. There they were, the three little words that made all the difference.

I.Love.You.

'Oh my God,' she said. 'I love you too, Alfie Daniels.'

Hearing her words also made all the difference to Alfie, but not the 'I love you'. It was hearing his name.

It reminded him that she knew who he was, and that she held his fate in her hands as a result. And it made everything clear to him. He knew exactly what he had to do.

'Let's go,' he said. 'I have my car. We can book into a hotel. I can't wait any longer.' He took her hands in his and stared into her eyes. 'And then I'm going to tell Claire it's over. Tonight.'

She blinked rapidly, her lips pressed together. 'Do you promise?' she said.

Alfie nodded. 'I promise.'

He told Pippa there was a hotel he had in mind in Tunbridge Wells, a hotel that was special to him and that, although it was a long drive, was worth it for what was, after all, a special occasion. He had no intention of going to a hotel there, but it sounded good. It was the kind of place where girls like Pippa imagined illicit assignations took place. He switched off his iPhone; he had a plan for what he would tell Claire later and it involved her being unable to get in touch with him.

As they approached Tunbridge Wells he turned on to a B road heading east. Pippa glanced at him.

'Is this the right way?' she said.

'Yep. It's a quiet little place. It's in the countryside. Hardly anyone knows about it.'

Which was all true. Hardly anyone did know about their destination. The only thing he had failed to mention was that it wasn't a hotel.

Ten minutes later he pulled into layby. It was on the edge of a dense forest. He switched off the engine, then put his hand on her knee. Her jeans were soft and expensive. He ran his hand up to her crotch.

'Alfie,' Pippa said. 'What are you doing?'

'I'm getting desperate,' he said. 'I can't wait any longer. I want you. Now.'

'How far is the hotel?'

'Not far. But I thought' – he turned and placed his hands on her cheeks and pulled her towards him – 'we could get started early.'

She twisted in her seat and kissed him. As she did, he put

his hands on her cheeks and held her face. She gave a slight moan and, for a second, he hesitated.

Then he slid his hands down her face and around her neck, and began to squeeze.

'Alfie,' she gasped. 'What are you doing?'

He squeezed harder, and she squealed as the pressure increased and her windpipe began to narrow.

'You silly little girl,' he muttered. 'Did you really think I was in love with you? Then you're more stupid than I thought. But that's good for me, because it made this *easy*.'

He looked at her. Her eyes were beginning to bulge in their sockets. Strangely, he felt nothing. Just a deep calm. He pressed harder, felt the flesh yield.

'I couldn't have you wandering around knowing that Henry Bryant and Alfie Daniels are one and the same,' he said. 'You understand that, right?'

In her eyes he saw that she knew she was going to die. She grabbed his wrists and tried to pull them away. She was surprisingly strong. He supposed she was desperate.

He focused on putting as much pressure on her throat as he could. Gradually, her attempts to pull away his hands grew weaker – he had some scratches which would need some explanation – until they stopped entirely. Slowly, he relaxed his grip, ready to tighten it at the slightest sign of movement.

There was nothing. He examined her face. She was wide-eyed, her mouth slack and open.

She was, without question, dead.

And Alfie felt *great*.

Claire

Claire looked at the call log on her phone. She'd tried Alfie eleven times since she'd got home from work. Eleven calls, none of them answered. She'd been expecting him home, expecting a quiet night together as they talked through their options.

She had not been expecting an empty house and eleven unanswered phone calls, or the intense and deepening worry. She imagined everything that could have possibly happened to him: hit by a car, mugged, stuck at work.

Suicide.

It was this that brought her out in cold sweats. He was a sensitive, caring man who had found out he couldn't have his own children, which was what he wanted more than anything else. He hadn't ever said much about his childhood, but she got the impression it hadn't been all that happy even before both his parents had died. She thought that was part of the reason he wanted to be a father so much; like her, he wanted to put right some of what had gone wrong in his own life.

So it was entirely possible he had killed himself. She loved him, but she knew he was not the strongest of men, and that made this situation all the more worrying.

She picked up her phone and glanced at the time. Nearly midnight. That was it. She'd call him one more time, and if he didn't pick up she was calling the police.

It turned out there was no need to call the police after all. Five minutes later he was back, assuming that it was him stumbling around in the hallway.

The door to the living room opened. She watched Alfie walk in, the top two buttons of his shirt open. His hair was dishevelled and his face was red. The harsh smell of whisky came off him in waves.

He stared at her, his mouth an unhappy line. He looked close to tears. Claire felt her anger – along with the worry – melting away.

'Where the hell have you been?' she said, her tone much softer than she'd been imagining it would be for the last few hours.

'Went for a drink,' Alfie said. His words were slurred and indistinct. He was not a big drinker and she had never seen him like this.

'On your own?'

He nodded.

'Where?'

'Bunch of places.'

'Why, Alfie?'

He shrugged. 'Why do you think?'

'You should have called. I was worried.'

'I'm sorry.' He looked away from her, his gaze unfocused. 'I couldn't face you. I feel like I've let you down.'

'Alfie!' Claire said. 'That's the last thing you've done! This isn't your fault. It's *nobody's* fault. It's just one of those things. It's sad – of course it is, I mean, I'm devastated – but I don't *blame* you. And I don't think any worse of you. You're my husband and I love you. Remember the vows? For better or for worse? Well, this is the "for worse" part.' She smiled at him. 'I stick by my vows, Alfie.'

He started to cry. 'Thank you,' he said, in a quiet voice. 'Thank you.'

She held out her arms. 'Come here. I need a hug.'

He walked towards her, staggering slightly, and sank on to the sofa. She pulled him into a tight embrace and he buried his face into her shoulder.

'How much did you drink?' she said. 'You really smell.'

'A lot,' he said.

'Did you leave the car at the office?'

He shook his head.

'Alfie! You didn't drive?'

'Left it somewhere.'

'Jesus,' Claire said. 'Where?'

'In Fulham, I think.'

'Why did you drive at all?'

He didn't answer. His eyes were starting to close and his breathing was getting deeper. She kissed his forehead. He was sweating, an oily, alcoholic sweat. She would have liked to go to bed with him so they could hold each other, tell each other everything would be OK, but it looked like that would have to wait. He had passed out on the sofa.

It was unlike him to be so selfish. She understood that he was sad, but she was too, and she was disappointed he had chosen to leave her alone while he went off and drowned his sorrows. It was a side of him she had not seen before. She supposed it was the price of his sensitivity.

She stood up and turned him on to his side, in case he was sick in the night. She'd forgive him this time, and in the morning they could talk about their options.

She was awake before five and at the breakfast table sipping a coffee by six, which was when he shuffled into the kitchen.

'God,' he said, his voice a rasp. 'I feel like shit.'

'You don't look much better. You were in quite a state last night.'

'I'm sorry,' he said. 'So sorry. It was selfish of me. But I felt like I'd let you down. I couldn't face you.'

Claire shook her head. 'You haven't let anyone down. I told you last night, although you probably don't remember, and I don't want to hear it any more, Alfie. It's not true, and it doesn't help. And I forgive you for last night. But please don't do it again anytime soon.'

'I don't plan to.'

'You going to work today?'

He shook his head. 'I think I'll call in sick. I wouldn't be much use anyway.'

'I don't have a meeting until eleven, so we can spend some time together this morning. Coffee?'

'I'd love one. But maybe some water first.' He opened a cupboard and fished inside for a small white pill bottle. 'And some ibuprofen. My head's killing me.'

'So,' she said. 'Things aren't going as planned for us.'

'No. And I'm so sorry.'

'Alfie.' She raised a hand. 'No more apologies. This is not your fault. Not in any way and by any stretch of the imagination. I don't want to hear you say sorry again. Deal?'

'Deal. Thank you.'

'All I want to do now is focus on what we do next. We still have some options.'

He sipped his coffee. The smell mingled with the harsh odour of the whisky that clung to him. Claire felt a vague, momentary nausea. She looked at him and, for the first time, wondered what it would be like if she left him.

Find a man who's a bit tougher. And who can have kids without all the stuff we're going to have to go through.

She checked herself, shocked she had even thought it. Alfie

deserved better and besides, she loved him. So they would have some challenges; she could hardly complain when they were so fortunate in the rest of their lives.

'I'm not sure what options we have,' he said. 'That's why I felt as bad as I did.'

Claire shook her head. 'Of course there are options! There are always options. We can try other medical avenues—'

'Like what?' Alfie said. 'I told you – I'm not producing any sperm. None. There's nothing we can do.'

'We could adopt,' Claire said. 'Or—' She wasn't sure this was the right time to raise this, but she reminded herself it was Alfie she was talking to. He'd be open to anything that might allow them to start a family.

'Or what?' Alfie said.

'Or we could try using a sperm donor. Maybe I could get pregnant that way.'

He stared at her, his mug paused halfway to his lips. 'A sperm donor,' he said. His voice was flat.

'It's just an option. I'm not saying we have to do it. But it's a possibility.'

He nodded. 'I guess it is. I hadn't really thought about it, but it is a possibility.'

'So you'd consider it?'

'Of course I would,' he said. He gave her a thin smile. She could see that it was forced, and the effort it took him made her appreciate it all the more. 'I'd consider *anything* for you.'

She'd known he would, but it was still good to have it confirmed. Even after last night, she was lucky to have him.

She moved closer to him and put her hand on his hip. He needed cheering up. He gave her a puzzled look.

'You really want to?' he said. 'With me in this state?'

She nodded. 'Although why don't you brush your teeth and have a shower first?'

Alfie

It was good sex, he had to admit that. He was in the mood for it, too. It was odd how the morning after a heavy night sex seemed so appealing. Hangover horn, he'd heard it called.

When he came out of the shower she was lying on her side of the bed, her head propped up on her elbow. He was struck by how he saw her almost as a different person; when he was talking to her in the kitchen he felt nothing but contempt for her, but now she was naked on the bed he felt totally different. He still didn't like her, but she had something he wanted.

He walked towards her. She sat up and pulled off his towel, then started to give him a blowjob. She cupped his testicles in her hands and massaged them gently. For a second her fingers paused on the thin ridge of the vasectomy scar, then they moved on. It was a good job she didn't know what she was feeling. It wasn't the first time he'd thought that, but it seemed more important now than ever.

When they had finished, he watched her dress and leave for work. The sex had been a welcome distraction, but he had a problem.

And his problem was *options*.

Alfie couldn't believe she wanted to talk about fucking *options*. He'd been expecting her to suggest adoption but he hadn't been too worried about it. It took a while and he was pretty sure he could have found a way to avoid it – maybe get arrested for some minor crime or develop a drug habit. He hadn't considered that she would want to use a sperm donor.

Christ, did she really think he would agree to bring up some other man's brat? She seemed to, which was a measure of how little she knew him, how well he had concealed his true self.

And since it appeared that *was* what she thought, he'd had to say he'd consider it, which was the same as saying he'd do it. Spoiled little bitches like Claire were used to Daddy saying *I'll consider it* and knowing what he meant was *yes*.

There was a glass of water by the bed and he picked it up – his mouth was disgusting, the sour taste of whisky still coming up from his stomach and making him feel like retching – and drank it down.

He'd thought he was done with this a long time ago. He'd thought the vasectomy had put paid to any chance of having children, but then she had gone and forced him to see Dr Singh. He had dealt with that, but now she was causing a different problem. If he refused to go along with it she'd make his life a misery. So he'd have to. Or he could divorce her, but her old man would make sure he got nothing.

Which he did not want either.

So, eventually, a sperm donor it would be, and then pregnancy, and he'd end up with an even bigger problem.

A kid. A fucking kid ruining his life and tying him to her forever. It could not happen. It wasn't just that being married stopped him doing what he wanted – that was bad enough but maybe he could have managed it, with some help from Henry Bryant – it was being married to *her*. He *hated* her. Hated the sight of her, hated everything she said and did and read and watched. Hated how she loved him and wanted his attention, and hated how he'd created a situation in which he had to keep giving it to her.

Most of all, though, he hated how she thought he was weak. Fragile. Of course, he'd made her think that, so he only had himself to blame, but that somehow made it worse.

So he was stuck. He looked out of the bedroom window. In comparison, Pippa had been easy to deal with.

Very easy. As soon as she'd said that no one else knew, it had been clear what he had to do. Those few words had been her death warrant.

He could kill her and no one would find out. For a moment, when he put his hands around her throat, he'd wondered whether he could do it, whether he could take a life. What it would be *like* to take a life. It had been shockingly easy, and quite fascinating to watch the light leave her eyes, to feel her body go slack, to release her when she was no longer breathing.

No longer alive.

More than fascinating. Enjoyable. Intoxicating, even. He almost couldn't believe he'd never done it before. He certainly wanted to do it again.

And it had been so simple. Even disposing of the body was easy. Pippa was now at the bottom of a disused, flooded quarry, wrapped in a tarpaulin – a cash purchase at B&Q – with only some heavy stones for company.

He remembered the boom she'd made as she hit the water. There'd been a big splash, the ripples spreading across the greenish-grey water, but the surface was calm again within seconds, and Pippa was gone.

Just like that.

82

No doubt Pippa's friends would wonder where she was. They might even know the name *Henry Bryant*, but they'd never find him. She'd told no one that she had discovered he was really Alfie Daniels, and no other link existed.

That was how Henry Bryant solved his problems. Decisively. He could, because no one could ever find him. That was the benefit of not existing.

Alfie couldn't deal with Claire in the same way, though – much as he'd absolutely fucking love to – because the first person the police would suspect would be him. It was far too risky.

Which was frustrating. He knew the solution to his problem. Kill her.

But he couldn't.

He couldn't be like Henry Bryant.

He looked at the ceiling.

Unless.

Unless there *was* a way. An idea emerged slowly. He turned it over in his mind, examining it from every angle.

He smiled. It was a *brilliant* idea.

He'd have to think it through more fully, but at first blush it seemed like it could work.

And if it did, it would solve all his problems.

Claire

Sitting at her desk, Claire answered her phone. It was Jodie.

'Morning,' Jodie said. 'How are you? Did Alfie show up last night?'

'He did. Eventually. He was *very* drunk.'

'That's not like him.'

'He'd had some bad news.'

There was a pause. 'Oh? What happened.'

'I'm not sure I should tell you this,' Claire replied. 'I think Alfie would be OK with it, but I have to swear you to secrecy, just in case.'

'Of course. I'm assuming it's to do with babies?'

'It is. He went to the doctor. His sperm are – well, they're not there. He has none.'

'Really? I thought he'd done a test?'

'He did, but it looks like it was faulty in some way. Dr Singh re-did it, and he has no sperm.'

'None?'

'None. He was very upset.'

'I'll bet,' Jodie said. 'I feel so sorry for him. For you *both*.'

'You know,' Claire said. 'It's not that bad. We talked about other options and he's open to them.'

She was telling the truth. Despite the disappointment of the sperm test, she was happy. The world seemed suffused with a warm glow. It was like her memories of Christmas as a child: everything warm and light and peaceful.

It was because she knew how fortunate she was. Some men would have been threatened by the idea of a sperm donor, their male ego unable to take the idea of their wife becoming pregnant by another man, even if it did not involve him having sex with her. They'd prefer to adopt, or even remain childless. And she had seen something of that in Alfie, but he had put it aside and agreed they could look into it. It didn't mean they would do it, but she was sure, when the time came, he would agree.

That was how he was. Selfless, thoughtful, committed to their marriage. When she'd left that morning he had hugged her and thanked her for being so understanding, for forgiving him for coming home late. There he was, a man who, a matter of hours earlier, had been given some devastating news, and his first thought was to thank her. He was amazing, he really was.

She'd googled *Sperm Donor* and read the results. It was very easy. In essence, you selected the sperm based on the characteristics of the donor and then it was inserted, either at the clinic or at home.

She wondered what characteristics you got to choose from. Height, race, eye colour? Or was it also IQ, sporting ability, social class? She decided she didn't care. Whatever the choices were, she would pick the ones that most closely matched Alfie. That way they would get a child as close to the child they would have had on their own. She wouldn't look for someone any different to him, wouldn't seek an upgrade. There was no need: he was perfect already.

And maybe there was a way of her being artificially inseminated with his sperm. There were probably other tests Dr

Singh could do, other procedures that might allow him to get some of Alfie's sperm. Maybe the sperm donor would be unnecessary. Either way, there were possibilities, and she had a husband who was open to whatever it took. Despite everything, it felt good to be moving forward.

The door of her office opened. It was Claudia, one of the partners, who had left a message earlier to say she was looking for her.

'Hey,' she said to Jodie. 'I have to go. Talk more later.'

Alfie

Alfie sat on the sofa. He had a bowl of raw broccoli and chickpeas in one hand – he was starting to feel better but he still needed to cleanse after all the alcohol he'd drunk – and Claire's laptop in the other. She had a sleek new MacBook which she had treated herself to a few months back. At the time, Alfie had read that it had vastly more computing power than the Apollo moon-landing mission had used, but as far as he could see all Claire did was waste time on it watching the inane videos her friends posted on Facebook.

Did people really feel moved by a video in which some bearded hipster sneaked a twenty-dollar bill into a New York tramp's backpack? Did they not have any idea that the money would immediately be turned into crystal meth or cheap vodka, a transaction which was not shown in the video? If they didn't, then it was no surprise they were so easily manipulated by people like him.

And it was easy. Early on he'd decided he didn't want to work – he couldn't, simply couldn't – in some bullshit job where his time was not his own and his shitty pay bought him a tiny flat in Clapham; so he'd found a way not to. He'd seen Claire and seen the opportunity and taken it. Now he had a life in which work was optional. He only did it so that her father didn't think he was a slacker, but he didn't have to try and get promoted and he didn't have to worry about what he got paid. The flat, the car, the holidays all came from her old man.

Which was something he took great pleasure in. He *loved* spending the old bastard's money, loved watching him fall for Alfie's act just as much as his stupid daughter had done. Mick thought Alfie wasn't up to much, but the irony was – and it was a delicious irony – Mick had no idea that was exactly what Alfie wanted him to think.

The price though, had turned out to be too high. He'd underestimated how much he would grow to hate Claire. But now, he had a solution.

Henry Bryant.

He flipped open Claire's laptop and typed in her password. She shared her passwords with him – *I have nothing to hide from you, darling*, she'd said – which was another example of how things like trust only made you vulnerable.

He opened a web browser and navigated to a website. It was one he was familiar with, one he had used many times before, although not as Alfie Daniels.

It was where Henry Bryant went to find women who were looking for an illicit encounter.

Where Henry would find *Claire*.

First, though, he needed to create an email account in Claire's name. He considered something anonymous, like *DIRTYFLIRTY77@whatever.com*, but it was out of character for her – as, he was aware, was looking for hook-ups on the internet, but there was nothing he could do about that – so he settled on an outlook account with her initials, *CHD*, and a string of random numbers.

He picked a photo of her, tanned and slender, in a bikini on their last holiday. She was standing in the shade of an olive tree, looking to her left. Her face was barely visible, which was perfect. It was typical of the photos on the website and would get plenty of attention.

He created her profile – she was thirty, interested in men, 25–49, no strings attached – and submitted it. Then he closed the website and deleted it from the internet history.

That would remove it from the computer. At least, that was what someone like Claire would think. She would be under the mistaken impression that all you needed to do was delete the history and all traces of the website would be gone from the computer.

Someone who knew better would know where to look, though.

They would look for, and find, cookies. Cookies wouldn't tell you much, but they'd tell you enough. They'd tell you that someone had been on a website they shouldn't have been on.

And when the time came that would be all he needed.

Claire

Claire called Dr Singh's office. The receptionist, a tall, red-haired guy in his early twenties called Asher who was trying to make it in the acting world, picked up.

'Hi,' she said. 'This is Claire Daniels.'

'Hey,' Asher replied. 'Mrs Daniels. How can I help?'

'I was wondering whether I could make an appointment?'

'Sure. When were you thinking?'

'As soon as possible. Ideally sometime this week?'

'Hmm.' Asher said. 'I don't know. He's pretty booked up.'

'It wouldn't take long. I only need to have a conversation. I have some questions I'd like to ask him.' She hesitated, and lowered her voice. She hated to do this, but she had caught him looking at her when she had been in the office and she suspected he had some older woman fantasies about her. 'It would be *really* helpful, Asher. I'd really appreciate *anything* you could do.'

There was a long pause. 'Well,' he said. 'I might be able to fit you in for fifteen minutes on Friday afternoon at four.'

There was unmistakably a flirtatious tone in his voice. Claire felt bad for leading him on, and a little sorry that his fantasies – of her, at least – were going to be dashed. To her surprise, she did, for a moment, consider it – it would be a way to get pregnant, after all, and he did have a relaxed confidence that was very sexy. But she wasn't interested in him. She wouldn't – couldn't – do that to Alfie, to a man who was so devoted to her, so devoted to *them*, to their marriage.

'Thank you, Asher,' she said. 'I'll see you then.'

As she hung up she saw she had a message from Jodie.

Want to meet tonight? Pippa's off with her boyfriend. Seem to be back together. At any rate she hasn't been here since the date.

Good for her, Claire thought, and typed a reply:

Sure. See you later.

OK. I'll text later with time and place. Everything OK with Alfie?

Yes. Feeling a bit better now.

Poor guy. I feel for him.

I know. We talked this morning about the other options. I think he had some hesitation but he was OK with them. Fill you in later. Have to run. I was in late and I'm behind.

She put her phone down. She was glad for Pippa. She only hoped it worked out. She wanted everyone to be as happy in their relationship as she was.

Alfie

Alfie walked into the estate agency. He still had the last vestiges of his hangover, but he needed to come into the office. He didn't want to do this from home, not now it was getting serious.

'Alfie,' Victoria, the receptionist, said. 'I thought you were off sick?'

'I started to feel better,' he said. 'How are you?'

She smiled at him, evidently pleased he'd asked after her. That was who he was: humble, great to work with, unthreatening. He didn't want your job or your project or your wife. He just wanted to be nice and do the right thing for the company.

He walked through the main office to the rear. The junior agents sat at desks near the front door. Alfie and Rachel, the other senior agent – she'd earned it, rather than having her father-in-law arrange it for her – had offices in the back corner.

At his desk he switched on his Henry Bryant phone. For a second he expected a flood of desperate text messages from Pippa, but then he remembered. She was at the bottom of a flooded quarry, so she was in no position to be sending messages.

He opened the dating app, and then searched the profiles for someone in Claire's age range and location and scrolled through the people that came up. There were hundreds. A majority of them listed themselves as married, a fact that had amazed him at first. He'd never have guessed all these people were looking for a bit on the side, living their cosy domestic lives, kissing their wives or husbands goodbye in the morning and dropping the kids off at school and then, unbeknown to anyone, logging on to a website where they could arrange some dirty sex.

People had all kinds of secret desires and, given a chance to satisfy them without getting caught, they took it.

He clicked through the profiles. There were a few that interested him – a tall blonde whose photo showed off a pair of enormous fake breasts; a woman who looked like a bodybuilder, which would be a new experience for him – but he ignored them. There'd be time for that later. For the moment he – Henry Bryant, that was – had a specific target in mind.

And there she was. Claire. In her white bikini. He had to admit that she was – without question – one of the most attractive women on the site. Henry was going to have some competition.

He allowed himself, for a moment, the fantasy that Claire had set up the profile herself and he had stumbled across it, a husband who had found out his wife shared his penchant for extra-marital sex. It was quite a thrill; he was surprised to discover that he found the idea of his wife fucking another man, maybe with him in the corner of the room watching, a real turn-on.

He snorted. Claire would never do that. She viewed sex as a spiritual transaction, as a symbol of the union between one person and another, as a holy act that led to the gift of a child. She would no more betray her beliefs than she would betray Alfie himself.

Not that anyone looking at her photo would know that. They'd assume she was just another desperate wife trapped in a mundane life and looking for something, anything, to spice it up, to stop her turning to the numbness of whatever medication the doctor would throw at her to keep her from slitting her wrists.

He clicked on her profile. A message box came up.

Hi, he wrote. *What an amazing photo. Would love to get to know you more. A bit about me: I'm a doctor, early thirties. Unmarried. I work long hours but when I'm not at work I like to enjoy myself – good food, the theatre, walks in the countryside, and, I'll admit it, meeting up with women like you. Anyway, would love to hear from you. Henry B.*

He sent the message, then put the phone in his desk drawer. He'd learned from the experience with Pippa that he had to be careful. He'd made a mistake with Pippa, let Henry Bryant come too close to Alfie Daniels, and it wasn't going to happen again. Which meant that nothing of Bryant's – he found that he really thought of him as a different person – would be at the house. No more keeping the phone hidden in his work bag or a jacket pocket. It would stay here.

Along with the other one he'd need to get. The one for Claire – or for him posing as Claire – to use.

But first he needed her to reply to Henry, and for that he needed her laptop. He looked at the clock; it was lunchtime. There was a door at the back of the office which led out on to a terrace. He could leave that way.

He took a key from his coat pocket, locked his desk drawer, and headed out.

At home, he went to the desk in their bedroom and opened Claire's computer. It was a thirty-minute trip from the office so he'd be back before anyone noticed he was gone – not that they'd care. They'd think he was at a viewing, as they always did.

He logged in to her account. There it was. Henry Bryant's message, along with seventeen others.

Seventeen. Was that how it was for all the women on here? Were they all inundated with messages from men? He read a few and shook his head in disgust.

Some were clearly stock messages, sent out in bulk.

> Hi, I'm a professional male, clean, forty-three but with a youthful outlook on life. Would love to meet. Message me?

Others were desperate:

> Looking for a soulmate who can understand me. I think that might be you. Please get in touch.

Others were downright crude.

> Hi, sexy. Want to play? You're a hot bitch. I'm 8 inches, uncut and open to any kind of fun.

It was appalling. Henry Bryant was selective in his targets, judicious in his approach. He thought about what to say, about how to appeal to a specific person, but it appeared these people just sent out filth at random. The world really was full of awful people.

He deleted – on Claire's behalf – all the messages apart from two. The one from Henry, and one from a married fitness instructor who seemed half-decent. Then he composed her reply:

Henry B. Thanks for getting in touch. You sound very interesting and I'd love to get to know you more. This is my first time, as it happens. How does it normally work?

He hit send. This was going to be easier than he had thought.

Claire

Claire put the contract down on the table. She placed her pen on top of it then folded her arms.

'This isn't exactly what I was expecting,' she said. 'I have two comments. First, the price is lower.'

Doug, the owner of the firm – an innovative engineering company she had been working on landing for months – shook his head.

'Not lower,' he said. 'Spread out differently. We pay when certain operational metrics are met. If your design work supports that—'

'Doug,' Claire said, 'I understand what the contract says, and I also understand that you've set those metrics up to be impossible to prove or disprove, which means when the time comes you'll say we haven't met them, and we won't get paid. Like I said – the price is lower.'

'I disagree. The price is the same.'

'It looks like we have a difference of opinion,' Claire said. 'So let's move on to my other comment.' She glanced at Erin, the graduate trainee who was shadowing her. Afterwards she'd tell her this was the key moment. 'My other comment is that, price reduction or not, this isn't what we agreed.'

'Not everything is signed,' Doug said. 'This is a negotiation.'

'No,' Claire said. 'It's a contract review. We've done all the negotiating. I agreed to do some work for your company and you agreed to pay for it. Now the price has changed but the work hasn't. You're getting – or trying to get – more for less. And I'm afraid I'm not prepared to do that.'

Doug shrugged. 'Then we don't have a deal.'

'It would seem so.' She let the words hang between them. Doug held her gaze, then picked his phone off the table.

'It seems a waste,' he said. 'To let all this work come to nothing.'

'All that work led to an agreement,' Claire said. 'Which I took as a commitment. And I stick to my commitments. I expect my business partners to do the same.'

'Well . . . ' Doug got to his feet. 'It was nice to – nearly – do business with you.'

'Likewise.'

'You know,' Doug said, as he turned to leave. 'A reputation for being inflexible is not a good thing.'

'Maybe not,' Claire said. 'But a reputation for being honest is invaluable.'

When he had left, Erin stared at her. 'You're going to let him walk away?'

'Yes,' Claire replied. 'Either he'll be back, because he knows the original deal we had was good for both of us, or he won't. If he's not then that's fine. There are more clients out there, Erin. And you have to be able to trust the people you work with.'

She could see on Erin's face that she was impressed, and she wished Alfie was there to see it. If she had a complaint about him it was that he sometimes gave her the impression he thought she was soft, spoiled by a life of ease and luxury. She wasn't; she'd built a career in an industry unrelated to the one her dad had been so successful in, and she was good at her job. Dedicated, knowledgeable, honest and with a hard edge when necessary. Ironically, she would have excelled in the rougher world of real estate and construction. She was her father's daughter, but Alfie didn't ever see that. Maybe she'd have a chance to show him one day.

Claire's phone buzzed. There was a message from Jodie.

Got some news. Still on for a drink after work?

Claire replied:

Sounds intriguing. 6pm at Piccolino's?

So Jodie had news. It could have been any number of things – a promotion, a big lottery win, a decision to run a marathon – but if Claire had to bet, she'd have laid her money on it being something to do with a new man in her life.

She picked up her phone and sent a message to Alfie.

Out tonight after work with J. Won't be late. Home by nine. Is that OK? Love you.

The reply came immediately:

Of course. Have fun. Love you too. A xxx

Alfie

Alfie read his wife's text message. She was out tonight, leaving him home alone.

It was great news. First, because he didn't have to see her. He could do whatever he wanted; on another occasion he might have swiped on someone's profile and arranged a meeting, but not at the moment, not while he was being careful. Tonight, he'd content himself with some porn.

The ease of access to hardcore pornography was, as far as Alfie was concerned, the most welcome development of the internet age. As a kid, getting hold of porn was a struggle. You had to either steal it from under the hawk-like gaze of some newsagent, or get lucky and find it in the darker corners of some municipal park. Even then, it would be pretty tame compared to what was available now at the click of a mouse button. There was anything you could think of. Alfie's favourite were the videos in which the woman was humiliated, picked up, used, and discarded on some roadside. He *loved* that stuff.

And second, it was great news because it fitted exactly with his plan for her. She said she was out with Jodie, but he didn't know that for sure. All he had to go on was her text message. The truth was she could have been *anywhere*.

Maybe meeting someone she shouldn't have been meeting to do something she shouldn't have been doing.

He took Henry Bryant's phone from his desk drawer and opened the app. He found Claire's profile and tapped on it.

> Hi. I know this is short notice but I'm going to be free tonight. If you happen to be around, we could meet up? Would love to see you in the flesh. Henry.

He needed her laptop again. It was early to leave the office, but that didn't matter. He stood up and headed for the door. As he reached it, he hesitated. Although he could put a stop to all this later on, now was the moment when it became real. From this point forward, it would take on a life of its own.

No. He would not hesitate. Henry Bryant had not hesitated when he needed to deal with Pippa. He'd *acted*. That was the lesson Alfie had learned from him. When opportunities arose, you took them.

And this was an opportunity. He opened the door, and smiled.

An hour later he was at the desk in the bedroom, Claire's laptop open.

He typed a reply.

> I'm meeting a friend for a drink after work but will be available (just to say hi – not for anything else, unless you're very lucky!) after 8. We could meet at The Standard in Battersea? Let me know. Cx

It was a good message. Alfie was quite proud of it; precisely the right mix of flirtatiousness and primness. Very Claire.

He hit send and sat back in his chair. The pieces were all

101

moving, sliding silently into place, but the only person who had any idea was him.

It was a *thrilling* feeling.

It was a little after nine when he heard the door open. She came into the living room and sat next to him on the sofa. He kissed her – she tasted of wine – and watched her take off her shoes and rub her feet.

'I'll do that,' he said. He took her feet and put them in his lap. 'You relax.'

'God no,' she said. 'My feet are disgusting.'

'I don't mind,' he said. 'I love your disgusting feet.'

'OK. If you say so.'

He started to massage the large muscle below her big toe. She tipped her head back and closed her eyes.

'That feels amazing,' she said. 'Thank you.'

'My pleasure. And . . . I get a great view.'

She opened one eye and looked at him. 'Are you looking up my skirt?'

'Of course I am. Do you think I actually *want* your sweaty feet in my hands? There has to be something in it for me.'

He ran a hand up her leg to her knee and parted her thighs.

'Now I see,' she said, her breath short. 'And I thought you were just being a loving husband.'

'I am being a loving husband,' he said. 'But not *just* a loving husband. Also a husband with an ulterior motive.'

'I think I know what your motive is.'

'Are you sure? Let me show you anyway.'

Afterwards, they lay on the sofa. Claire had her head on his shoulder, her eyes closed.

'So,' Alfie said. 'Where did you go?'

'To Piccolino's,' Claire replied. 'It was packed.'

'How's Jodie?'

'She's good. She has some news.'

'Oh? Anything exciting?'

'Fairly exciting. She has a boyfriend.'

'Who?'

'A guy called Josh King. He's a lawyer. She met him online and they've been on a few dates. She didn't mention anything. You know Jodie, she keeps herself to herself– but it seems it's more official now.'

'Great. But a lawyer? Is she sure?'

'They're not all bad,' Claire said. 'She seems keen on him. You know, I think it's so brave to go on a date with someone you met online. You don't know anything about them – they could turn out to be a mass murderer. It's not like us. We met by chance and I had the opportunity to weigh you up before we met alone.'

'So you think. You could have weighed me up wrong. I could have had sinister plans for you.'

Claire shook her head. 'No. You told me you were a musician on CDs of kids' music. That's not exactly the way a killer would go about their murderous business. They'd pretend to be a hedge fund manager or an international business superstar.'

Or a kids' musician, Alfie thought, *if they knew that was the kind of unthreatening man the woman wanted*. Henry Bryant would have been proud of him. He'd seen the opportunity, and taken it. He'd had to lie, had to get hold of some kids' songs and play them to her, claiming he was on the recording, and after he did she'd laughed at him, the condescending bitch.

He remembered it well. She'd laughed, and then caught herself and said she didn't think it was funny, she thought it was unusual and she really, really liked it, but she had *laughed* at him.

Which was, much as he hated it, what he'd wanted. What he'd *needed*.

'You're right,' he said. 'Most people would never admit to being the guitarist on "The Wheels on the Bus", far less make it up. They might pretend to be a lawyer, though.'

'Exactly my point.'

'Jodie better watch out.'

'Don't say that!' Claire groaned. 'Now I'm worried.'

'Why don't you invite them over for dinner this weekend?' Alfie said. 'That way, if he is up to no good, we'll have met him. It'll be much harder for him to strangle her and throw her in a quarry if we've actually seen him in person.'

'God,' Claire said. 'What a horrible thought. I wasn't thinking of inviting them because of *that*.'

'Saturday evening? I'll cook.' Alfie kissed her. 'By the way, what happened with her friend? Is she still living with her?'

'Pippa? No. Jodie's not heard from her. She thinks she's got back together with the guy she was seeing, but she hasn't tried to get in touch in case she moves back in.'

'Oh,' Alfie said. 'Good. I'm glad that all worked out.'

Claire

Claire looked at the profile.

Danny Bond.

Balding, slightly overweight, standing on a beach somewhere holding a bottle of beer. From his posts he seemed to be into football, motor racing and videos of people playing dangerous pranks on each other. He also had two daughters and a wife called Kellie.

Danny Bond, the only name Alfie had ever mentioned as a friend from his childhood.

It wasn't like she could look on Alfie's Facebook account for any others. He wasn't on Facebook. A while back Claire had suggested he sign up, but he had shaken his head.

Not my kind of thing, he said. *I can see it's useful, but it's not for me.*

There was very little of him online. When they'd met she'd googled him – *Alfie Daniels* as well as *Alfie Daniels, Luton*, the town he said he was from. There was more or less nothing: no Facebook, no Twitter, no local news articles. His name cropped up in relation to the band who'd been playing at the wedding, but that was it. It was almost as though he'd tried to keep his online presence to a minimum. She'd said as much to Jodie, who'd claimed it was a red flag – *What's he hiding?* she'd said – but now she knew it was just Alfie. He wasn't hiding anything; he was low key.

She wondered whether there was some trauma in his past, something more than the death of his parents. They'd died a year apart, his dad of a heart attack, his mum of breast cancer, and not long after that he'd left Luton for good.

He never spoke about them, but she knew their names – Martha and Ian – because she'd found his birth certificate in a filing box he'd brought to the house when they'd moved in. The box contained the only records she'd seen from his past, and there wasn't much there. Along with the birth certificate there were a couple of baby photos, a certificate from a spelling competition when he was eight, a handful of school reports and a newspaper cutting about an act of vandalism at a school in Luton in which some dogs had been killed and left to rot in the school over the summer. She'd wanted to ask why he had that cutting, but she didn't want him to know she'd been snooping, so it remained a mystery.

Which left Danny Bond. He'd told a couple of stories about him and Danny; she assumed that when he'd left Luton days after his mum died he'd lost touch with him.

Claire thought he might like to see him again, especially if he became a dad. Whoever Danny was, he was part of Alfie's past and Alfie might want to share that with his child. She'd been thinking about it for a while, searching for something she could do for him that wasn't a fancy watch or new car or other material gift.

Me and Danny used to hang around together, he'd said. *We thought about starting a band once, but he gave up playing guitar.*

Maybe it was time for them to get the band back together. Alfie never complained about it, but Claire thought he needed a close friend. He had no one to share things with in the

106

way she could with Jodie. It might not be a problem now, but in the future he might need it.

She wanted to show him she *cared* about him, that she listened to what he said and thought about how to make his life as good as it could be.

And maybe Danny Bond was the answer.

Claire imagined him and Alfie meeting up, introducing their kids to each other, sharing a drink. Alfie glad to see him, grateful to his wife for arranging it.

Or unhappy with her. Angry that she was meddling. She wasn't sure what to do. She wasn't even sure this was the right Danny Bond.

Well, that could be easily fixed. She could send him a friend request and ask him. He might tell her he and Alfie hadn't been friends, really. Or he might tell her he didn't want to see Alfie.

Either way, she wouldn't be committing to anything. All she'd be doing was finding out whether this was even an option, and there was no harm in that.

She tapped on her phone, and started to write an introduction.

Alfie

Alfie walked, head down, along a quiet street. A faint odour of sewage mingled with the smell of fast food. It was safe to say that this part of East London had not yet felt the gentrifying effects of the wealth sloshing around the City.

Which was precisely why Alfie was there.

He paused outside a shop window. It was dirty, the items on display barely visible, but he could make out a series of outdated electronic goods: televisions, DVD players, computers. That wasn't why he was there, though. He and Claire had a state-of-the-art B&O entertainment system with individually zoned and controlled speakers in each room.

He was there because they sold phones. Specifically, pay-as-you-go smartphones, full of credit, sold for cash with no questions asked and up and running in minutes. There was no CCTV on this street, and although the shop owner no doubt had his own for the sake of security, he was the kind of small business owner who had a strong aversion – an allergy, almost – to the forces of law and order. If asked whether a man answering to Alfie Daniels' description had bought a phone from him, he could be counted on, out of sheer hatred for the police, to say *No such man ever entered my premises, Officer. Cross my heart and hope to die.*

Not that the cops would ever show up there. They had no way to link Alfie or Henry to this shop, and in any case, this phone wasn't for either of them.

It was for Claire.

After their first meeting – at least, after the meeting that their messages suggested had happened earlier in the week – Henry had sent a message via the dating website.

Claire, that was amazing. Good food, better conversation, and then simply fantastic sex. I'd love to do it again, whenever suits you. But here's an idea – if you want to meet then let's stop using this website to communicate. You don't want to have it on a laptop your husband might see. You should get a phone. Go to a shop and buy a pay-as-you-go smartphone. Once you have it running, text me. We can keep in touch that way from now on.

So now Alfie was getting the phone. He could have gone to Boots or Asda or somewhere else –which was what Claire would have done, if she was actually doing this – but he didn't want to set up an account. He needed – in the event it was ever discovered – the phone to be traceless.

He pushed the door open and walked inside. A squat man with a shaven skull glanced up at him. He studied him for a second, and then, nodded, apparently happy that Alfie did not represent a threat he couldn't deal with.

'All right, mate,' he said. 'What can I do you for?'

'Phone,' Alfie said. 'Simplest you have. I need it to do text and email.'

The man reached behind his head for a plastic case. 'This should do it.'

'No,' Alfie said. 'I want one that's already set up.'

The man nodded slowly. 'What for?'

'Some business.' Alfie put his hand in his pocket and took out five twenty-pound notes. He put them on the counter. 'I need one that costs about this much. You got anything like that?'

'I might have.'

'Maybe you know someone who does?'

'You're not a cop, are you?'

Alfie shook his head and met the man's gaze. 'No. I'm not a cop.'

The man looked him up and down, once, then twice. 'You don't look like one. Too well dressed.' He sniffed and tapped his nose. 'And I don't smell bacon. I got a good nose for bacon.' He put his hand on the pile of twenties. 'Twice that,' he said. 'Bargain. About the price of them shoes you're wearing.'

Alfie took another five twenties from his pocket. He knew better than to get out his wallet.

'OK,' he said. 'But that's it.'

The man nodded and took the cash. He turned and walked through a door behind him. Alfie listened as a metal drawer opened, then shut. The man appeared in the doorway. He was holding two phones. He put them on the counter.

'Take your pick,' he said. 'Fifty quid credit on each. When it's gone, the phone's useless.'

Alfie took one. He didn't care which. He wouldn't need it for long. He switched it on and the screen lit up.

'It works,' the man said. 'Comes with my standard warranty.' He grinned. He was missing both his front teeth. 'Zero days' cover and don't ever show up again.'

Alfie waited until he was sure the phone was working, then nodded.

'Thanks,' he said, and left the shop.

* * *

110

He had parked nearby. When he was back in his car, he glanced at his watch. It was midday. He'd have to hurry; he was on the hook to cook dinner that night and he was supposed to be out buying the ingredients. He was planning to drop off the car and the phones at the office and then head to Borough Market to get scallops, oysters and venison, which was what he always cooked. He'd told her he was a good chef when they met – it was a lie, but it was useful as it confirmed her opinion that he was the kind of guy who she could trust, unlike the hedge fund types who were used to being cooked and cleaned for.

The problem was that he could barely boil water, so he'd told her he was one of those cooks who did a few things well, which allowed him to perfect one recipe before he cooked for her. He'd chosen things that people didn't have often – like venison – so they wouldn't really know what to expect, and things where the ingredients spoke for themselves and all you had to do was not ruin them, like oysters and scallops.

Before he went, though, there was something he needed to do. He took out the new phone and tapped out a message.

Henry, it's Claire. Let's meet asap. I have a dinner on Saturday night, but could get away on Sunday afternoon? A is going to play golf.

Golf. It was a very useful sport. It was the perfect excuse to disappear for a few hours so he could get away from Claire and get up to no good. Now it turned out that it gave her the opportunity to do the same thing.

He hit *send*, and in his pocket another phone buzzed.

Henry Bryant had a message.

Claire

When Claire and Jodie were younger they had developed a set of secret signals, which they used to communicate when they were out in bars and clubs and men were chatting them up. There was the brush of the left eyebrow, which meant *This guy's bugging me so say you need the loo, and I'll come with you*, there was the brush of the right eyebrow which meant *Let's get them to buy us a drink and then we'll get rid of them*, and there was the tug on an earlobe which meant *He's hot.*

As they finished the venison Alfie had made – it was so great to have a husband who cooked, such a relief that he didn't think it was the 'woman's place', like so many of her friends' husbands did, despite their claims to be modern men – Claire looked at her friend over the dinner table and reached up to pull on her earlobe. Josh King was a great guy. Jodie gave a slight nod.

I know.

Claire was glad that her friend's relationship was going well. Josh was relaxed and at ease with her and had a constant smile on his lips. They kept looking at each other, their gazes holding a fraction longer than necessary, as though they didn't want to break away. Claire had the impression that, if she and Alfie hadn't been there, Jodie and Josh wouldn't have bothered with dinner, at least not until they'd satisfied a more urgent hunger.

It reminded her of when she'd first met Alfie. They hadn't been able to keep their hands off each other. Sometimes they had spent entire weekends in bed, waking up late on a Saturday morning and finding no good reason to do anything other than lie there and have sex and talk and have more sex and eat and talk and have more sex, before going to sleep and repeating the following day. When Monday came the intrusion of the real world was a shock. They resented having to get out of bed and put on clothes and go and spend valuable hours in the office, hours which were mostly occupied with thinking about how soon they could get back to each other.

It had been intoxicating. She had had boyfriends before, had thought she was in love with them, but whatever that feeling was it was a shadow of what she had with Alfie, and she had known it from the start. If you had asked her whether she would be interested in a slightly goofy musician who played in wedding bands and on kids' CDs she would have said that was the last thing she was looking for. But then she'd met him and found out that that was *exactly* what she was looking for, and it had changed her life. It was almost as though he had been made for her.

And now she saw the same thing happening for Jodie.

Claire ate the last of the venison and looked at Alfie. 'That was delicious,' she said.

'It was.' Josh sipped his wine. 'You've got a talent, Alfie.'

'No,' Alfie said. 'I'm good at following recipes. And I always cook the same things, so I get better and better at them. Don't ask me to bake a soufflé or clarify a consommé – I'd have no chance.'

'You should try,' Claire said. 'You might surprise yourself. Discover a side you didn't know you had.'

'That's what I'm scared of,' Alfie said. 'You might see me for who I really am.'

'And what's that?' Jodie said.

'A guy who's trying to fake it till he makes it,' Alfie said. 'Right now you think I'm being modest, but if I served you some flaccid, tasteless soufflé you'd be thinking yeah, he really *isn't* a chef. I don't want to break the illusion. I've worked hard on building it up!'

'It's not modesty, Alfie,' Claire said. 'It's false modesty. You just want us to say how great you are.'

Alfie held up his hands. 'You got me. I admit it.'

'Either way,' Josh said, 'the meal was wonderful. Thank you.' He picked up Jodie's plate. 'I'll help clear the table.'

Alfie picked up Claire's. 'I'll join you. And I'll grab another bottle of wine.'

They walked towards the kitchen. As they left the room, Claire heard Josh ask Alfie where he had bought the venison.

'Borough Market,' Alfie said, and then started to explain which vendor he went to.

'Well,' Claire said. 'He's a nice guy. A *lovely* guy.'

'He is,' Jodie said. 'Internet dating is a bit of a lottery but I got lucky.'

'When did you meet him?'

'Two weeks ago.'

'You kept it quiet.' Jodie normally filled Claire in on the details of her dates – most of them amusing, some downright disastrous – but she hadn't mentioned Josh until a few days ago.

'I know,' she replied. 'I had a feeling he might be more of a keeper than the others and I didn't want to say anything in case I jinxed it.'

'Well, it seems to have worked.' Claire leaned forwards. 'Have you guys – you know?'

Jodie nodded. 'We can't stop. You're lucky we got here on time. Put it this way – I didn't have much time to get ready.'

'I remember those days,' Claire said. 'They're still here, a bit.'

'You know something,' Jodie said, 'it might be a bit early to be saying this, but I have a feeling he might be the one. I don't know what it is, but I can see it. I can picture us together, married, raising kids. I've never had that before.'

'That's how it was for me and Alfie,' Claire said. 'I knew from the start. I could see it all – marriage, kids, the whole thing – and it's worked out that way. It's not exactly happening on the baby front, but we'll get there. And I can't complain. Alfie's great.'

'It *will* happen.' Jodie squeezed Claire's hand. 'Either with Alfie, or a donor, or by adopting, but it *will* happen.'

'I hope so,' Claire said. 'And I hope it's easier for you, when the time comes. I can't wait to be mums together. Maybe Alfie and Josh'll be friends, take the kids out for walks in the park.'

'Can you imagine?' Jodie said. 'If that happens? If Josh was the father of my children?'

They were interrupted by Alfie walking into the room.

'Bit early for that, isn't it?' he said. 'Don't let Josh hear. It'll scare him off.'

'Just thinking out loud,' Jodie said. 'That's all.'

'I feel I ought to let him know. Warn him he's got a stalker who wants his babies.'

Jodie's eyes widened in mock anger. 'Don't you dare! I'll kill you.'

'All right,' Alfie said. 'Your secret's safe with me.'

'Where is he?' Claire asked.

'Powdering his nose.' Alfie gestured to the bathroom. 'So how's everything else, Jodie?'

'Fine. Work's the same. My boss is still as creepy as ever.' She sipped her wine. 'I am a bit concerned about Pippa, though. I haven't heard from her since she went on her date.'

'When was that?'

'Thursday.'

'It's only a couple of days,' Claire said. 'And if he's the one for her she might be otherwise occupied.'

'Probably. But I'm getting worried, to be honest.'

'What was the guy's name?' Claire said.

'Henry something. Hang on a sec. I have it in a text from a while back.' Jodie took out her phone and scrolled through the messages. 'Henry Bryant,' she said. 'He's a doctor.'

'Google him,' Claire said. 'If he's a doctor, he should show up.'

Jodie tapped on her screen. After a few seconds she frowned.

'That's weird,' she said. 'There's a few Dr Henry Bryants. But they're all in the US. I don't see any over here.'

'Maybe he's not on the internet,' Alfie said. 'Not everyone is.'

'No,' Jodie said. 'I suppose not. But still. You'd think there'd be *something*.' She put her phone down. 'It seems a bit odd. Tomorrow I think I'll ask some other friends of hers if they've heard from her.'

As she finished, Josh walked in. He was holding a bottle of white wine. 'You left this in the kitchen,' he said. 'Top-up, anyone?'

Alfie

Alfie opened his desk drawer and took out his Henry Bryant phone. Claire had gone to an exhibition at the Tate Modern with Nicole, a friend from university whose parents were rich enough, and willing enough, to indulge her fantasies of being a sculptor. Alfie had been to an exhibition of her work once. She held it at her studio, presumably because no gallery wanted to associate itself with the shapeless lumps of junk she produced.

Alfie had to force himself not to collapse into giggles as she took them around, describing how her creations were abstract representations of different aspects of human experience. He had nodded, and murmured how beautiful they were and how talented she was. On their way home, Claire had expressed some doubts over Nicole's prospects for success, but Alfie – despite thinking they were the kind of garbage that talentless nobodies produced and called art – had said he liked them.

It's not simply about commercial success. She's realizing her artistic vision, and that's what counts. I admire what she's doing. She's got a real talent.

Even at the time, he'd wondered where he got such bullshit from, but it had the effect he wanted.

That's what I love about you, Claire replied. *You're so uncynical. So generous. You see the best in everyone. Most of us view success in traditional terms – selling well or getting a big exhibition or becoming a doctor or a lawyer – but you don't think the same way as everyone else.*

That last statement was certainly true, but not quite in the way Claire thought, which was why he was in his office at ten a.m. on a Sunday morning.

The dinner party had sucked the life out of him. Josh was thoroughly tedious, a middle-of-the-road member of the chattering classes with a mind as yet unsullied by an original thought. They had stood in the kitchen and he had talked about the government and public sector pay and social justice and how great Jodie was until Alfie had considered strangling him and walking into the dining room to tell Jodie and Claire that there'd been a terrible accident and Josh had choked on his own self-righteousness.

Of course, Claire *loved* him. He was exactly the kind of table-clearing, nappy-changing, peace-loving, sensitive guy she thought Alfie was.

He needed a break, so he told her he had to get some work done in the morning so he could play golf with a clear conscience in the afternoon.

He was going to do neither.

He'd decided not to meet anyone new until he'd dealt with Claire, but he needed some excitement. Some colour. Something that wasn't Claire and Jodie and Nicole and all the dull, uninspired tedious people like them mistook for a life.

Like the Tate Modern, for God's sake. If you had asked a thousand people to design a temple to self-obsessed mediocrity they would never have been able to come up with something that fitted the bill as perfectly as the Tate Modern. Alfie knew he didn't get the art there, but he also knew that the reason was there was nothing to get. It was a scam

118

perpetrated on people too worried about what people thought of them to admit they found it unintelligible and boring.

He opened an app. His username for this one was Johnny Cowen; it was one of the sketchier apps, and the people who used it were unashamedly looking for sex, which was exactly what he wanted.

He scrolled through the users. He paused on one. Yes, she was perfect. Older than him, pinched expression, smoker's skin further damaged by a fake tan. Rougher than usual, but perfect: she'd be easy, grateful for the attention.

They met in a pub near Victoria station. She was there when Alfie arrived, sitting at a table in the corner drinking a large glass of white wine. Some kind of horrendous cheap chardonnay, probably.

'Hello,' Alfie said. She was older than he had guessed from the photos. Late forties; maybe even early fifties. 'I'm Johnny. You must be Katinka.'

Which was a bullshit name if ever there was one.

She looked at him. He could see that she had been expecting someone different, that the people she normally met were not young, handsome and in good shape.

'Yeah,' she said. 'You having a drink?'

He looked at the barman. 'A ginger ale, please.'

'Ginger ale?' she said. 'That's not a drink. Put a whisky in it.'

'Bit early for me,' Alfie said. He smiled at her. 'But you get stuck in. Nice to meet you.'

'You too.' She sipped her wine. 'You do this often?'

'Often enough.' He could smell the cigarette smoke on her breath. He found it strangely arousing. This was exactly what he needed. 'You?'

'From time to time.' She glanced at his wedding ring and nodded. 'I see. You like a bit on the side. No risks.'

'That's about the size of it,' Alfie said.

'Already talking about the size of it,' she said, and laughed, in a real smoker's cackle. 'You youngsters are very forward.'

She was really quite disgusting. For a moment he had a strange feeling that she was almost a different species to him, an animal of some sort. Less than an animal; at least a dog was what it was supposed to be. She was a degraded version of a human being, a sordid, drink-soaked insult to people like him. For a second he considered what it would take to kill her. Not much – a blow to the head, or his strong hands around her wrinkled neck, like Pippa. It had been a thrill, that first time, and he was eager to try it again.

He could do it at her house, leave the body in the bathroom. No one would trace it to him.

He gave a shake of his head. He could do it, but he wasn't going to. She was not his next. That was reserved for someone else. Someone special.

'Everything OK?' she said, a look of concern on her face. She'd thought his head shake was a sign he was changing his mind.

'Yes,' he said. 'Just thinking about work.'

'Well put that from your mind,' she said. 'We'll find something else to keep you occupied.'

'I hope so.' Alfie put a hand on her knee. It was bony, the muscles wasted. 'You want to stay here? Or go somewhere else?'

'Where did you have in mind?'

Alfie patted the keys in his pocket. He'd chosen a furnished apartment that they had for rent and grabbed the keys on his way out of the office.

'My place is nearby,' he said. 'Want to go?'

Claire

Claire had managed to get an appointment for Wednesday morning. It was the earliest Asher could do, despite her brazen flirting. Now she was here and it was not going well.

Dr Singh did not seem pleased to see her.

He tapped his fingers on the edge of his desk. He looked at Claire, then looked at his computer screen.

He's nervous, Claire thought. *No – not nervous. Uncomfortable. On edge.*

It was odd; he was normally so composed. Every time she had seen him before, he had greeted her at the door of his office, gestured for her to take a seat and then listened, her file on the desk in front of him.

'So,' he said stiffly. 'How can I help you?'

'Well,' she replied. 'Alfie told me about his fertility test and I wanted to talk about other options.'

'Hmm.' The doctor nodded three or four times. 'I see.' There was a long pause. 'And what kind of options were you thinking about?'

Claire was starting to feel uneasy. 'Adoption,' she said. 'But obviously you couldn't help with that. Maybe a sperm donor. Which you *could* help with.'

'Have you spoken with your husband about this?'

'Yes, briefly.'

'And he is in agreement?'

Claire nodded. 'I think so. I mean, we haven't reached a final decision, but he didn't have any objections.' She sat back in her chair. 'I don't really know much about this – which is why I wanted to talk to you – but I imagine this can be a hard thing for a man to accept.'

Dr Singh nodded. 'Yes. The fragile male ego, and all that.'

'Right. But what you have to understand about Alfie, Dr Singh, is that, even if he felt his ego was threatened by this, he's the kind of man who would put it aside. He wants us to have a family as much as I do and he'll do anything to make it happen.' She shook her head. 'He was devastated when he got the news. *Devastated*. I've never seen him like that before. I felt so sorry for him.'

Dr Singh folded his arms. 'Mrs Daniels. I am afraid I am not in a position to give you advice on this matter.'

'I understand,' Claire said. 'Alfie's state of mind is not for you to discuss. It's not a medical matter – at least, not a fertility matter. But that's not why I'm here. I'm only looking for some initial thoughts. What the process is, risks, that kind of thing.'

'That's what I'm saying,' Dr Singh replied. 'I'm unable to advise you.'

Claire was baffled. What was he talking about? 'Why not?'

'I'm afraid I am not able to tell you.'

Claire shook her head. This was becoming ridiculous.

'I don't understand. What reason could you have for not telling me about the process of sperm donation? Why can't I know about it?'

'You can. But I'm not the right person to consult about it. I can give you the name of a colleague. You will be in good hands with her.'

122

Claire didn't reply for a while. This was beyond weird. He'd been so open with her, and now he was shutting her out. Something must have happened, and she could only think of one thing.

'Dr Singh, if you don't want to treat me for some reason – maybe you have a moral or religious objection to this – then that's fine, although I find it odd you'd be a fertility doctor in the first place if you did have those kind of objections. But please tell me what the reason is. Surely I deserve that?'

'I have no objections on those grounds,' Dr Singh said. 'If I had, I would tell you.'

'Is it something about me, then? Is there a medical risk? To me or the child?'

He shook his head.

'Then what is it?'

Dr Singh looked up at the ceiling, as though deep in thought. Claire had the distinct impression he was on the verge of saying something but couldn't make up his mind whether to do so. She waited for him to speak.

'You are aware,' he said in a quiet voice, 'of doctor–patient confidentiality?'

'Of course.'

'It is something I take very seriously,' he continued. 'It is critical to my work. My patients need to know they can trust me. Unless I suspect a serious criminal offence, I would never breach it. If word spread that I had, my practice would be irreparably damaged.'

'Right,' Claire said. 'I get that, although I'm not sure I understand what's going on any better.'

'What I am about to tell you,' Dr Singh said. 'Is the most I am able to share, so please do not ask for any more information.'

'OK,' Claire said. 'I won't ask.'

'All I am going to do is share with you some medical information which is related to the field of male fertility. What conclusions you draw from this are entirely your own. Likewise, if you were to take any action – related to your husband – on the basis of it, that would also be on your own account. I want to be clear: I am not breaching any confidentiality requirements, and I want you to agree that you will not claim later that I did.'

'I won't.' Claire held her hands in her lap to stop them from fidgeting. Whatever this was about, she doubted it was good news. 'Please just tell me, Dr Singh.'

'What I want to tell you,' Dr Singh said, 'is that if a man had had a vasectomy, but had not told anyone, it would be easy to discover this. All one would have to do is look for a small scar on the side of the testicles.'

Claire looked at him. 'Why would you want to tell me that?'

He shook his head. 'That is a good question,' he said. 'It is the *key* question. But you will have to answer it yourself. I can say nothing more.' He folded his arms. It was clear the appointment was over.

It was also becoming clear what he was suggesting.

He was suggesting that Alfie had had a vasectomy.

She walked towards the Tube station. She was on auto-pilot, her mind replaying the times she and Alfie had had sex.

The times she had given him a blowjob. There was, she recalled it clearly, a ridge at the side of his balls. She hadn't paid it much attention – she'd been focused on other things – but she remembered it.

And it could have been a scar.

And if it was, Alfie had had a vasectomy.

And if he had – it was hard even to think that – then Dr Singh would have found out pretty quickly. He would have discussed it with Alfie, who would have told him, since it was obviously something he was keeping secret, not to say anything. The doctor would have been conflicted about it, and would have found a way to tell her.

And that would explain all of this, apart from one thing.

Why had Alfie done it? And why lie about it? Her stomach lurched. If he'd been lying about the vasectomy, then he'd been lying about everything. The test he'd taken at home. The test he'd taken at Dr Singh's.

His desire to have a kid *at all*.

Their entire relationship.

It couldn't be true. It went against everything she knew about Alfie, against everything their marriage stood for. He would have to be an entirely different person from the man she loved, and she couldn't believe that was the case.

There must be a mistake. Dr Singh had got something wrong.

That was it. This was all a misunderstanding. She just needed to talk to Alfie to find out exactly how.

Alfie

Alfie sat at his desk and sipped a tiny, bitter espresso. On his screen was a new listing, a four-bedroom terraced house in Wandsworth. It needed work, but it was still the best part of two million pounds. It was ridiculous. Thirty years earlier it would have been teachers and nurses who lived there, but now it was bankers and lawyers and oligarchs washing dirty money. Anyone who didn't have either an outsized income or family money had no chance of buying a place like that.

Not that he cared. He would have if he'd been one of the teachers and nurses, but he had Mick's money.

And thank God for that. Without it, he'd be nowhere. His parents – still alive, as far as he knew, although he'd told Claire they'd both died when he was in his twenties because the last thing he wanted was her meeting them – had no money. His mum had been a cleaner in his school, a job that bestowed on her the name 'Scrubber' amongst the feral pupils who ran riot at his shit-house comprehensive, and left him with the nickname 'Son of Scrubber'.

He'd hated school, hated every second of every day. Hated the name and the laughter and the way he couldn't stop himself from responding, from getting angry and shouting at them to *shut up!* Of course, the appeal only made them laugh harder and shout the hateful nickname louder.

His dad was no help, but then that was no surprise. He was the most useless man Alfie had ever met; he was almost always out of work – not because there weren't jobs around, but because every time he managed to fall into one, he was fired as soon as his employer realized he was totally incompetent. He turned up late, or at the wrong place, and, when he was there, he misunderstood his instructions or broke the equipment. He didn't even have an excuse – he wasn't a drinker and he had reasonable health – he was just a fool. In centuries past he would have been the village idiot.

Alfie was amazed he'd managed to father a child. Sometimes he wondered whether he had, or whether he was the issue of a brief moment in which his mum had succeeded in finding pleasure with some other man.

A man, Alfie liked to think, like Henry Bryant.

Either way, he had been condemned to be the butt of jokes all through his school years. Day in, day out, right up until he walked out at sixteen with a handful of worthless qualifications and a resolution never to go back.

And he never would. As soon as the summer holidays came he had escaped, well and truly, and before he did he had taken his revenge, made sure that Davie Andrews and Arnold McFadden and Ian Porter would wonder, for a long time after he left, whether it was something more than a coincidence that all three of their family dogs went missing at the same time he did.

They would have found out it was no coincidence later that summer, when the school caretakers smelled something odd coming from 5V's classroom and went in to investigate, only to find the rotting corpses of all three dogs.

127

He hadn't done much in the years afterwards, drifting from job to job and from town to town, getting by on the proceeds of the odd gig, petty crime, and the occasional more serious infraction – for a while he'd stolen from blind people, who were extremely easy to mug – until he had seen Claire at the wedding.

And he'd known she was vulnerable. Known what kind of a man she was looking for. And he had made himself that man.

It was amazing how her money changed everything. People looked at him differently, saw success, gave him respect. He was someone who could walk into an estate agent's office and discuss £2,000,000 houses in Wandsworth. No one called him Son of Scrubber. No one called him anything. People liked Alfie Daniels. They wanted him around.

And he couldn't let that be threatened.

Except it was. He'd made a mistake. A miscalculation. Since the day he'd met her, he'd found Claire irritating, but he'd assumed he could put up with it. When he was with her he would put on his mask, pretend to be a loyal, faithful husband, and when she wasn't around he could do what he wanted. The problem was that it had become *stifling*.

The irritation had become dislike and the dislike had become hatred.

And now she wanted kids. She'd keep going until she got one, via a sperm donor or adoption or some other fucking way, and that would ruin it all. He'd be trapped forever, the only way out a divorce which would leave him back where he started.

Back as Son of Scrubber.

Until now he'd had no solution, but Pippa had given him the idea. She had become a problem for Henry Bryant and so Henry had killed her.

And Henry could do the same to Claire. Now that they were lovers – according to their messages – if Claire disappeared it could be pinned on Henry. The connection would be made quickly. And, since no one knew who Henry Bryant was and there was no link to Alfie, all Alfie would have to do would be to play the grieving husband and keep her money. He would be the victim. People would *sympathize* with him.

So he was going to kill Claire. Maybe in the same way as Pippa. Perhaps he'd throw her in the same quarry. It didn't matter. If the bodies *were* found, people would simply assume that Henry Bryant – who would have disappeared – disposed of his victims in that way.

He'd realized another thing, recently: this had been his plan all along. Not to invent Henry Bryant – using him was merely another piece of opportunism – but to kill Claire. He hadn't been aware of it, but this had been the endgame since they met.

And now he had a way to do it, and it was brilliant.

He opened his desk drawer and took out the two phones. One, Henry Bryant's. The other Claire Daniels's. It was time for Claire to make the date – maybe for the coming weekend – which would be her last one. He put them in his pocket and headed out for a walk.

In the park, Alfie sat on a bench by a small pond. Two swans glided past. He'd heard that swans mated for life and if one of them died the other would pine so acutely that it would stop eating and waste away. He didn't know whether it was true or not – he suspected swans were not that stupid – but the fact people told the story as though it was admirable for swans to behave in this way baffled him. How could anyone – human or swan – allow themselves to become so bound up with someone else that they couldn't live without them? He could never have done it. One person was much like another. He didn't need any of them.

He took out the phones and typed a message from Henry to Claire.

Hey, lovely. Let's meet this weekend. I need to see you. Just tell me what works for you; I'll fit it in.

Claire's phone buzzed; after a pause, he used it to reply.

I need to see you too. What about seven pm on Saturday? I'll tell A I'm meeting an old friend. We can go to a hotel. I don't want to waste time at a bar.

Bryant replied shortly afterwards.

How about my place? It's more comfortable than a hotel. I'll meet you at Piccadilly Tube station and we can walk from there.

So that was it. It was *real*. This Saturday he would kill Claire. It was Wednesday now so a mere three more days. He could hardly wait. He pictured knocking her unconscious in the car and driving her to the same layby where he'd killed Pippa. He'd wait until she was awake – he was looking forward to it now, looking forward to her expression as his hands, tight around her neck, cut off her supply of oxygen, looking forward to telling her how much he hated her and how he was going to blame this on Henry Bryant – and get rid of her body.

After that it would be simple. Wait a day, and then start calling her friends and family asking if they'd seen her. When they hadn't, he'd call the police, and, with him guiding them

– and their technicians combing her laptop – they'd find out about Henry Bryant.

A name that would quickly be connected to Pippa.

Two women who met the same man online and both disappeared. It wouldn't be long before the assumption that they were dead hardened into fact.

Which would leave him, the grieving widower, all alone.

He smiled. It was good to have a plan. He stood up. It was time to go home to his lovely – and soon to be ex – wife.

Claire was at home when he got back. 'Hi,' she said. 'Good day?'

He nodded. 'Yes,' he said. 'I missed you.' He put his hand on her hip. 'I've been thinking about you all day.'

'I've been thinking about you, too. I was looking forward to a night together, but I have to go into the office.'

'No,' he said, relieved that she'd be gone. 'Not tonight.'

'I'm afraid so.' She reached for his belt and unbuckled it, then pressed her lips to his. 'But we have time for this before I go.'

As they kissed, she tugged his jeans down, then pushed him on to the sofa. She sat next to him, then bent over and took him in her mouth. Alfie closed his eyes and pictured Victoria, the receptionist at the estate agency, in Claire's place. She was high on his list of women to fill the post-Claire void.

He was starting to enjoy the fantasy when Claire stopped. He opened his eyes to see her sitting up, looking at him.

'I'm sorry,' she said. 'I need to stop.'

'Everything OK?' he asked.

'I'm not feeling all that well. And I have to finish some work.'

Alfie felt a surge of irritation, but he bit it back. He was not the kind of guy who complained about his wife interrupting a blowjob, and there was always porn when she left. He frowned in an effort to look concerned.

'You should stay home and make sure you feel better.'

Claire shook her head. 'It's fine. Just the start of a cold, or something. And I have to go in. It's important.'

'OK,' Alfie replied. 'Take care of yourself, darling.'

When he woke up the following morning – Thursday, the last Thursday of his life with Claire – she was already gone. He'd been asleep when she came home. There was a note by the bed.

HAD TO GET IN EARLY TO WORK. SEE YOU TONIGHT. TAKE-OUT? I'M EXHAUSTED.

He showered and dressed and had breakfast with a smile on his face. Now he had a final plan he had a feeling of lightness. He hadn't realized how much Claire had been getting him down. He'd grown so accustomed to the sensation of being constrained, of being unable to be his true self. Well, soon he would no longer have to worry about that.

And it felt great.

He frittered the day away in the office, unable to concentrate on work – not that he was bothered. He went to the park for a couple of hours after lunch, then came back to his office and watched videos on YouTube. That evening he was at his desk, packing up to leave for the day – he was still smiling, the prospect of freedom keeping his mood buoyant – when Claire called.

'Hi,' he said. 'How are you? Do you want me to pick up food? What do you want?'

132

'You choose,' she replied. 'That's why I'm calling. I have to go out. I've got a client dinner.'

'You didn't mention it.'

'I only found out an hour ago.' She exhaled sharply. 'It's the last thing I want to do, but the project is getting busy and I've got no choice. I have to get going. Don't wait up. It could be a late one.'

'I'm sorry,' he said. 'Don't let them keep you out.'

'I won't. Love you, Alfie.'

He smiled as he hung up. This was *perfect*. Almost *too* perfect. She was going out unannounced. Even though it had nothing to do with Henry Bryant, it all added to the image of a woman having an affair.

It *was* a late one. Nine p.m. came and went, then ten, then, at ten thirty, Alfie called her mobile phone.

It went straight to voicemail.

'Hi,' he said. 'It's me. Hope the dinner's going well. What time should I expect you?'

By eleven she had not returned his call. He sent a text.

Hey. Hope all's well. I'm going to bed soon. I'll have my phone on if you need me. Love you. Ax

This was unusual for Claire, but it was exactly what he wanted. It would help when he was talking to the cops in the days after he killed her.

She had *been going out more than usual. Only last Thursday she went out to a client dinner that came up suddenly. She came home when I was asleep. But I didn't think anything of it. I didn't think she was seeing another man.*

The police would speak to the clients she was at dinner with and they would confirm her story, but it wouldn't matter. What mattered was the impression it gave.

He lay down and closed his eyes. He hadn't fallen asleep this quickly in years.

He woke up slowly. The office didn't open until nine, and he rarely got there before half-past, so he didn't set an alarm. Claire was up earlier than him, so he used hers.

But hers hadn't gone off.

He looked to her side of the bed, and his eyes narrowed.

It was empty, and the pillows were still stacked neatly against the headboard.

It hadn't been slept in.

He glanced at the clock on the bedside table: eight a.m. He sat up and listened for the sounds of her making coffee or getting dressed.

There was nothing.

He picked up his phone. No missed calls, no texts. He tried her. Straight to voicemail.

Where the fuck was she? He scrolled to Jodie's number. Maybe she'd got drunk and stayed with her. It was unlike Claire – *very* unlike Claire – but it was possible.

He dialled the number. Jodie picked up immediately.

'Hey,' she said. 'What's up?'

'Have you seen Claire?'

'No. Why. Is she not at home?'

'She went to a client dinner last night. She didn't come home, and she isn't answering her phone.'

'Oh my God.' There was a note of alarm in Jodie's voice. 'I haven't heard anything from her.'

'Where else could she be?'

'I don't know!' Jodie said. 'I'll call some friends. She has to be somewhere. I'll let you know as soon as I hear anything.'

'OK,' he said. 'I'll call work. Thanks, Jodie.'

'Don't mention it. Keep me posted, OK?'

As he hung up, Alfie almost smiled. It was ironic. This

134

was exactly what he had been expecting to do: phone around asking after his missing wife and act concerned that she had not come home from a night out.

But he didn't smile. Not quite.

Because he hadn't been expecting to do it so soon. And he hadn't been expecting not to know where she was.

He'd been planning for her disappearance to be a smoke-screen.

But this was for *real*.

Interval

'Are you . . . Are you her?'

The naked woman did not answer her question. She stared into the distance, her hands covering her breasts and pubic hair in an attempt to hide her nudity. She needed a bath, her skin was streaked with dirt.

'You're . . . ' the driver paused, 'you're the woman who went missing, aren't you?'

The naked woman turned to look at her. Her eyes focused gradually, and she blinked.

'Yes,' she muttered.

'Well, you're OK now.' The woman glanced around to check they were alone. 'I promise. You're OK now. I'm Barbara. Take this.' Barbara shrugged off her jacket – a thin, cotton one she'd bought a week before from Burberry as a summer treat – and draped it over the naked woman's shoulders.

For a moment she considered calling the police and waiting where they were – there might be evidence they wanted or something like that – but she dismissed the idea. The woman needed to be in a safe, warm place where someone with experience in these situations could deal with her and, besides, she had an uncomfortable feeling that someone else might show up at any moment.

Someone who would not have the woman's best interests at heart.

'Let's go,' Barbara said. She led the hitchhiker towards the passenger side of the car and opened the door. The woman climbed in and Barbara leaned over her to fasten her seat belt.

She walked quickly to the driver's side and started the car. She checked the mirrors to make sure they were still alone, and then pulled away. She reached for her phone so she could call the police. Before she could hit dial, the woman spoke.

'Alfie,' she said, her voice a croak. 'I want to see Alfie.'

PART TWO

Alfie

Friday

i

Alfie's phone rang. He snatched it from the kitchen counter and looked at the screen. It had been an hour since he had woken up and realized Claire was gone, and he was still expecting her to call.

It was Mick.

'Hey,' he said. 'I saw your missed call. Missed *calls*. What's going on?'

'Have you seen Claire?' Alfie said.

'No. I'd have thought you'd be the one who knows where she is early in the morning. I'm just her dad. You're her husband.'

'Well I don't,' Alfie said. 'She didn't come home last night.'

There was a pause. 'What do you mean?'

'She went out to a client dinner. I went to bed around eleven. When I woke up she wasn't here.'

'Have you called her?'

'Yes,' Alfie said. 'Lots. It goes straight to her voicemail.'

Mick inhaled sharply. 'Fucking hell. Have you called the office?'

'Yep. No one's seen her this morning.'

'What about her assistant? Have you talked to her? You could find out who was at the dinner?'

It was a good idea. 'OK,' Alfie said. 'I'll do that now. I'll let you know what she says.'

Alfie hung up. He called the office and asked for Caroline, Claire's assistant.

'Hi,' she said, when he was put through to her. 'I hear you're looking for Claire?'

'Yes,' Alfie said. 'She was out with a client last night—'

'Which client?' Caroline interrupted him.

'I don't know. She didn't say.'

'Hmm.' Caroline hesitated. 'That's odd.'

'What is?'

'Well,' she said. 'I'll ask around and check, but I'm pretty sure there was no client dinner last night. At least, not that I know of.'

'Oh,' Alfie was finding it hard to think. Claire had been lying? 'There must be some misunderstanding.' He hung up before Caroline could reply, and stared at his phone as her words sank in. There had been no client dinner? So where had she gone? And why had she lied?

His phone rang again. It was Jodie.

'Have you found her?' he said.

'No.' There was a note of worry in Jodie's voice. 'I've called everyone I can think of. No one's seen her.'

'Shit.' He too had worry in his voice, and it wasn't put on for Jodie's sake. It was real. It wasn't because he was concerned about Claire herself – if she had been kidnapped and murdered that was fine by him. It was because something odd was going on and he didn't know what it was.

'What did she say?' Jodie asked. 'Before she went out?'

'She said she was going for dinner with a client. But when I called the office, no one knew anything about it.'

'Are you kidding?' Jodie said. 'She made it up? You think she was lying?'

'Maybe no one else at work knew about the dinner,' Alfie said. 'That could be it. I don't know if I'm ready to think she was lying yet.' He was ready to think *exactly* that. Claire had invented a reason for a night out – a clumsy one, as alibis go – and had not come home.

So where had she gone? Was she – of all things – having an *affair*? And even if so, why hadn't she come back?

'It doesn't seem like Claire,' Jodie said. 'She probably did have a dinner. If it was arranged late in the day, no one at the office would have known.'

'That could have happened. She hadn't mentioned it before yesterday.'

'Then that'll be it,' Jodie said. 'It must be.'

It was possible, but Alfie wasn't convinced. Claire's office was quite small and for the most part they all knew what the others were up to. Someone would have known; at the very least they would have had an idea who the client was and been able to check quickly.

And it didn't solve the other part of the mystery.

'Then where is she now?' Alfie said. 'And why's she not answering her phone?'

'I don't know,' Jodie said. 'But there'll be some explanation, I'm sure. She probably left it late and crashed in a hotel and her phone died. Something like that.'

'I guess so,' Alfie replied. 'But what if it's something else? Perhaps she got hit by a car or fell ill or she ran into someone who . . . into the wrong kind of person.'

'Alfie,' Jodie said, 'don't start thinking like that. We have to stay positive.'

'It's hard. My mind keeps racing in all directions.'

'Alfie . . . there is one thing. I don't know how much of this you wanted her to share, but she did talk to me about how you two were trying for a baby.'

'Right,' Alfie said.

'She mentioned you'd had some bad news.'

'About my sperm count, right?'

'Right. You probably didn't want her talking about it, but we're friends. She needed to talk to someone.'

'It's fine,' Alfie said. 'All I care about is finding her. Are you saying you think that has something to do with her going missing?'

'I think it *could*,' Jodie said. 'It's possible she reacted badly to the news. She really wants a child – I know you both do – and to find this out was a big blow. Maybe she needed to be alone to process it, so she went out for an evening on her own, and that wasn't enough so she checked into a hotel—'

'But why?' Alfie said. 'If that was what she wanted she could have told me. I'd have been happy for her to go for as long as she needed.'

'Because she probably didn't want you to feel like she was upset because of it. She knows it's hard on you too and she might have felt you would have thought she was being selfish.'

'You think so?' There was a certain logic to it. It was the kind of thing Claire might have done.

'I do. My guess is she's in a spa hotel somewhere getting a massage and she'll call later to say she's sorry she put you – us – through this, but she's on her way home now.'

'I hope so,' Alfie said. 'I really do.' He stayed silent for a moment. 'What happened with your friend, Pippa? Did she show up?'

'No,' Jodie said. 'It's been over a week now.'

'It's weird that they both disappeared. Did you call the police?'

144

Jodie took a deep breath. 'I didn't,' she said. 'But her parents did. I talked to them and they're freaking out. She's not been to work and she's not answering her phone. They told me the police put her on some missing persons list, but they can't really do anything until there's evidence of a crime. Perhaps she's with this guy, Henry Bryant, or on holiday somewhere. Either way, there's nothing to investigate.'

'What if Claire's the same?' Alfie said.

'She isn't. This is totally different. Pippa is . . . well, Pippa is flaky. This is *Claire*. It's different, Alfie. I promise.'

His phone buzzed. It was Mick. Fuck. He didn't want to speak to him, but he would only keep calling if he didn't.

'I've got to go,' he said. 'It's Mick.' He switched calls. 'Hi.'

Mick was abrupt at the best of times, which this wasn't. 'Any news?'

'There is,' Alfie said. 'There was no dinner. At least, not one they knew about at the office.'

'What the fuck? Then where was she?'

'Jodie has a theory. She thinks Claire may have wanted some alone time and—'

'I don't need theories,' Mick said. 'I need my daughter back.'

'Me too. We've called everyone we can—'

'And why would she want time alone? Is something going on I should know about?'

'No,' Alfie said. 'I'll explain later. For now—'

'For now,' Mick said, 'we need to get busy finding Claire. I'm sending somebody to see you.'

'What do you mean?' Alfie said.

'He's a former cop I know. He was a detective inspector. Paul Simpson. Got pissed off with the force and left.'

Shit. The last thing he needed was some busybody ex-detective poking about in this.

'Shouldn't we leave that to the police? And isn't it a bit soon?'

'We can't wait for the cops. And it's never too soon. If she walks in the door an hour after Simpson shows up, then no harm done.'

'Mick,' Alfie began, 'I'm not sure—'

'Simpson'll be there soon,' Mick said. 'Tell him everything.'

ii

Former Detective Inspector Paul Simpson accepted Alfie's offer of a cup of tea and took a seat in an armchair. He had an A4 pad on his lap and a red felt-tip pen in his hand. He had short, greying hair and a slack, expressionless face.

'So,' he said. 'Your wife is missing?'

Alfie nodded. 'As of last night.'

'Perhaps you could take me through what happened?'

'There's not much to tell.'

He explained how she had left, at short notice, for a client dinner, an appointment which had turned out to be a fabrication, and how she had not come home. Since then no one had seen or heard from her.

Simpson made notes as he talked. When he had finished, the detective tapped the end of his pen on the paper. 'Would your wife have any reason to leave home?' he asked softly.

'Such as?'

'Maybe you had an argument? Threatened her in some way?'

Alfie straightened in his chair. 'I have *never* threatened her,' he said. 'And I resent the implication.'

Simpson smiled. 'I'm not implying anything, Mr Daniels.

Please don't take it that way. I need to establish as many of the facts as I can. So everything was well between you?'

'Yes,' Alfie said. 'Although we had recently received some bad news.'

Simpson looked at him. His eyes were suddenly focused and inquisitive. 'Oh?'

'We've been trying for a baby. It wasn't working, and we found out that it was because I have . . . I have a very low sperm count.'

'I see. And you think she might have been upset by that?'

'She was upset by it. Her friend – Jodie – thinks she may have wanted to be alone.'

Simpson nodded. 'That is a reasonable hypothesis, in the circumstances. Although just a hypothesis, at this stage. There are others.'

'What kind of others?'

'I'm sure you've considered some of them. My job is to eliminate them. Speaking of which, do you have any thoughts about where your wife may have gone if she wanted to be alone? A favourite hotel? Or place? A lake or river or village that means something to her?'

'There's a hotel she likes near Bristol. And we've been a few times to a village in the Cotswolds that she always says she'd like to move to someday.'

'Could you give me the names?'

Alfie did; Simpson noted them down.

'I'll call the hotel,' he said. 'As well as possible places in the village.'

'You could check her bank cards. See if she's spent any money.'

Simpson raised an eyebrow. 'You overestimate what information I can access,' he said. 'But you could check. If you know her passwords.'

'We have a joint bank account,' Alfie said. 'So I can check

that easily. But she has her own credit card. I could try to guess her log-on details.'

The truth was he knew exactly what they were. He knew all her passwords – email, Facebook, Instagram, phone – and he checked her information often. He wasn't suspicious of an affair and didn't expect to find any evidence of that kind of thing, nor was he particularly interested in whatever he *did* find. He simply revelled in the knowledge he could look into her life any time he wanted.

'I'd suggest checking,' Simpson said. 'Any leads would be useful.'

Alfie stood up. 'I'll get my laptop,' he said.

He walked into the hallway and picked up his work bag. He took out his computer and walked back to the living room. As he did, he weighed the risks of showing this guy their bank account. He'd see their balance – it was pretty healthy – but that didn't matter. Simpson already knew they were rich. There was nothing else Alfie wanted to hide. Anything related to Henry Bryant was totally separate.

And what if there was a transaction from last night – a train ticket, or a cab fare, or a bar bill? Well, then it would give Simpson something to go and do and maybe he'd find Claire. Which would be, on balance, a good thing; Alfie was not enjoying the sensation that he was not in control of this situation.

No, there was nothing to hide. He walked into the room and put the laptop on the coffee table.

'Give me a moment to switch it on,' he said. When the screen came to life he opened the browser and logged on to their bank account.

There was nothing from the night before. He let Simpson study the screen. After a few moments, he nodded.

'Try the credit card,' he said.

Alfie looked at the ceiling, as though recalling information.

149

'It's a Barclaycard,' he said. 'Her username could be her email.'

He typed it into the screen, then put the cursor in the password field.

'Let's see,' he said. 'It could be—' He typed some random assortment of characters and hit enter. The message came back:

Password or username is incorrect.

'Not that. I'll try another.' He typed *lookatthisshithead*. Again, the message came back:

Password or username is incorrect.

He thought for a long time, then tried again, this time with what he knew was the correct password, and they were looking at her credit card account.

'Third time lucky,' he said. 'This is it.'

The last transaction she had made was lunch – a sandwich shop near work – the day before. There was nothing more recent.

'Hmm,' Simpson said. 'She could have another card, of course.'

'True,' Alfie said. 'But that would mean she'd been lying to me for a long time. I can't believe that.'

'I'm sure you're right,' Simpson replied. 'But it *is* a possibility. My job is to think through all angles.' He sat back in the armchair. 'I'll understand if you don't want to do this, but there is something else we could look at.'

'What's that?'

'I take it Claire has a work email. I'm wondering whether she has a personal one too?'

Alfie nodded. 'Of course.'

'Do you know the password?'

Alfie stared at him, forcing a look of outrage on to his face. 'I'm not reading her emails,' he said. 'That's private.'

Simpson held up his hands. 'Fine. Like I said, I understand

if you don't want to do it, but there might be something there.'

There wasn't, Alfie thought, but he'd log on and show the guy, although not before faking some serious reluctance.

'I don't think I want to,' he said. 'She's probably taking some time to herself. I can't violate her privacy like that.'

'OK. But we might miss some important information. In other cases like this, it's been useful.'

Alfie let the silence grow long. 'I don't know the password,' he said. 'So we probably can't anyway.'

Simpson gave a slight, almost triumphant, smile. 'Why don't you try, and if you get it we can glance at the emails and see if anything stands out. If there's nothing, we can shut it down right away, and when Claire's home you can tell her to change her password.'

Alfie nodded, slowly. 'OK,' he said. 'We can try.'

'Try the one you used for the credit card. A lot of people have one password they use for everything. It's a big security risk, but people do it all the time.'

Claire didn't, but Simpson didn't need to know that. Alfie typed in the correct details and watched as her emails came up.

'You were right,' he said. 'It *was* the same.'

'Then you can tell her you did her a favour. When she changes it, she'll be much more secure. Anything there?'

They bent over the screen.

There was something there, something Alfie was not expecting. Something Alfie would not have thought was even remotely possible.

Among the unread emails – one from the bank, one from Boden, one from Jodie, *Where are you!!!* in the subject line – was another email.

An email from the day before.

An email from *Henry Bryant*.

An email Alfie had *not* sent.

151

iii

Alfie stared at the screen in disbelief. There were three emails from Bryant, all from the day before.

Subject: Tonight?

Simpson interrupted him.

'You look surprised,' he said. 'Something I should know about?'

Alfie glanced up. The detective's head was cocked to the side and he was looking at Alfie with a growing interest. Alfie was about to say *No, everything's fine*, but he caught himself.

This would come out, and if he'd lied it would look suspicious. He had to tell the truth.

And then this would unfold exactly as he'd planned. Claire was gone in mysterious circumstances, the cops would find the evidence he had carefully planted and find out about her affair with Henry Bryant, they would draw the link to Pippa and then they would quickly make the assumption that both women had been murdered.

And then there would be a huge manhunt for Bryant, but

they would not find him, because there was nothing to find. Maybe Alfie would figure out a way to use Bryant's credit card in the Bahamas so they'd assume he had fled the country.

And everybody would feel sorry for poor Alfie, who would be free of Claire, as well as rich. It was perfect, and it was exactly what he had been meaning to do.

Except for one thing. It was supposed to happen this weekend, but it was happening now. Someone else was doing this.

And the thought of that terrified him, because he had no idea who. He would have to try to work it out later, though. For now, he had to deal with Simpson.

'I know the name,' he said. He pointed at the email. 'I never met the guy, but I know the name.'

'Who is he?'

'The boyfriend of someone Claire knows. Well, she's met her. It's her friend Jodie who knows her well. A woman called Pippa.'

'So why would he be emailing Claire?'

'I don't know. And it worries me.' Alfie looked Simpson in the eye. He held his gaze. 'Pippa disappeared about a week ago. She went out with Henry Bryant and no one's heard from her since.'

Simpson raised an eyebrow. 'You think this is linked? Who is Bryant?'

'Someone she – Pippa – met online. No one really knows who he is.'

Simpson held his hands up. 'Well, this is now officially out of my league. You need to call the cops.'

When Simpson had left – Alfie made him promise not to tell Mick what he had seen but to leave it to him – he sat at the computer and opened the most recent email. He scrolled to the bottom of the string to start with the first email.

From: Henry Bryant
To: Claire Daniels
Subject: Tonight?

Claire – sorry to use your email, but I'm having problems with my usual means of communication, and I can't bear the thought of missing a chance to see you – I'm free tonight. I had plans but they fell through and now I have a long, empty evening ahead of me. Can we meet? I'm aching to see you. XOXO HB

From: Claire Daniels
To: Henry Bryant
Subject: Re: Tonight?

I want to – you know that, I want to desperately – but I don't know if I can. Alfie's home and if I make up something suddenly he might suspect.

From: Henry Bryant
To: Claire Daniels
Subject: Re: Tonight?

Aaaargh! Please – if there's any chance? Maybe say you have a work dinner?

From: Claire Daniels
To: Henry Bryant
Subject: Re: Tonight?

OK. This isn't like me, but I'll do it. I can't stop thinking about you. 7pm at the usual place? I have to be back by 10.30 – 11 at the latest, though or I'll turn into a pumpkin.

From: Henry Bryant
To: Claire Daniels
Subject: Re: Tonight?

Wonderful! I'm thrilled you can come. Yes, 7pm and

I'll get you home before you turn into a pumpkin (although isn't it the carriage that does that?) I can't wait to see you. You're in my thoughts constantly, too. This is turning into something more than we bargained for. Henry

Alfie's mouth was dry. He was blinking rapidly and he felt nauseous. There *was* no Henry Bryant. He was Alfie's creation. He didn't really exist. Yet here he was, arranging to meet Claire, and she seemed to know him. They'd obviously met more than once. So who was it? Who the hell had Claire gone to meet?

He checked the email address. It was a new one – Yahoo mail – which explained why he had not received the emails. Henry Bryant – the new Henry Bryant – had broken free of Alfie.

So where was Claire now?

He took a deep breath. He had to focus. He had to approach this logically. Who *could* it be? Someone Claire had met and started an affair with who happened to be called Henry Bryant? No – it was too much of a coincidence. So who else knew about Bryant? Only Pippa.

At least, he *thought* only Pippa, but it was possible she'd told someone else. She could have told Jodie, but then Jodie would have told the police her friend had gone missing after going on a date with a man who was using a fake identity, a man who happened to be married to her best friend.

Which left Pippa. But she was slowly decomposing at the bottom of a disused and flooded quarry, and Alfie didn't believe in ghosts.

And that left – Alfie drummed his fingers on the desktop – that left no one. It was possible that Pippa had told a different friend but, again, why would they bother with this? Surely, like Jodie, they'd simply call the police too?

So the only alternative was that it was entirely random.

Someone – maybe on the hook-up website – had encountered Henry Bryant and worked out it was Alfie and was now using it to do what Alfie had done, while at the same time messing with him. He could see how someone could get a perverse kick out of that.

He shook his head. It seemed so improbable. It was always better to find the simplest explanation. It was normally the right one.

And the simplest explanation was someone who knew about Henry and had something against him.

Which brought him right back to Pippa, who was dead.

At least, he *thought* she was. She'd seemed dead, but he was hardly an expert in killing people. Was it possible she had tricked him? That she had played dead so he released the pressure around her throat? And then, somehow, had swum away when he had thrown her into the quarry?

No. He had wrapped the body in a tarpaulin, weighted it down, and tied it closed. There was no way she could have escaped.

Yet you read about stranger things, about people crawling out of the mass graves at Nazi concentration camps, or surviving at sea on a raft for a thousand days.

It didn't seem possible, but it would fit.

But then why would she have involved Claire? Why not simply go to the police? Even if she had escaped, impersonating Henry Bryant seemed so unlikely.

And she had not escaped. She was dead when he dragged her from the car on to the tarpaulin. He knew she was. He had seen her eyes grow dull, felt her body slacken. There was no way she had tricked him. He had watched her die.

That was why it had been such a thrill.

So there was something else. There had to be. And he would find it.

He glanced at his watch. It had been twenty minutes since

Simpson had left. He needed to call the police, then get in touch with Mick. If he delayed any longer, he might ask why, and Alfie did not need any awkward questions.

He picked up his phone.

iv

'What the hell do you mean?' Mick said. 'She was having an affair with someone?'

Alfie had called Mick and told him he had news and they needed to talk, but it would be better in person. Mick had tried to get him to spill the beans on the phone but Alfie had stuck to his guns.

Alfie gestured at the computer screen. 'I found this.'

'You read her emails?'

'Simpson – the guy you sent – suggested it. He thought there might be useful information there.'

Mick clicked on the most recent email and read the thread. As he did, his expression softened.

'Jesus,' he muttered. 'This is ridiculous.' He looked at Alfie. 'I'm sorry. I can't believe she's been stupid enough to do something like this. You deserve better.'

'Maybe, but I'm not thinking about that now. I just want her back.'

'Then you're a better man than me. Daughter or not, if this was my wife I'd never want to see her again.'

'I love her, Mick.'

'You must do.' He turned away from the screen. 'So you think she's with this guy Bryant?'

'It seems so.' Alfie stood up and paced the room. 'There's more, Mick. It gets worse.'

'Worse than this? What is it?'

'Henry Bryant was also seeing a friend of Jodie's. Pippa. Claire only knew her in passing.'

'Fucking hell,' Mick said. 'What is it with these women? It's like they're back in the sixth form.'

'That's not the bad part,' Alfie said. 'Pippa disappeared a week ago.'

Mick's head shot up. He looked at Alfie, his eyes narrowed. 'What do you mean?'

'I got this from Jodie, so I don't know the whole story, but Henry Bryant had broken up with Pippa at some point and she'd more or less moved in with Jodie. I gather she's a bit unstable.' He knew this was a detail Mick would like. 'But anyway, Bryant got back in touch with her and they went on a date – and she's not been seen since.'

'You think he did something to her?'

'I don't know. But I don't like the idea of Claire being with him.'

Mick rubbed his temples. He suddenly looked like an old man, the aura of uncompromising strength falling away.

'God,' he said. 'My poor girl. You said you called the police?'

Alfie nodded. 'They're sending someone over.'

'OK. You want me here when they come?'

'I think so,' Alfie said. 'That would be good.'

The police arrived an hour later: a woman in her fifties who introduced herself as Detective Inspector Wynne, and her colleague, another woman, maybe twenty years younger, who gave her name as Detective Sergeant Lawless.

'Funny name for a cop,' Mick said.

DS Lawless smiled a thin smile. Alfie guessed she had been told that on more than a few occasions. She looked at Mick, and Alfie took advantage of her attention being elsewhere to let his eyes move over her face and body. She was pretty, although she looked tired, and she clearly kept herself in good shape. Good body, nice backside. Under other circumstances, he might have been interested in a more intimate relationship with her, but not while he was supposed to be a worried husband.

He looked up to see DI Wynne watching him. He stared down at his hands.

'My dad was a judge,' DS Lawless said. 'Judge Lawless. I think the careers adviser had a sense of humour.'

DI Wynne leaned forward. 'So,' she said, her voice low and steady, her vowels flat. 'Your wife is missing?'

Alfie nodded. 'You're not from here?'

'Warrington,' DI Wynne said. 'I moved south. Temporary thing. They needed some reinforcements down here. But your wife? Could you walk us through what happened?'

Alfie explained it all: how Claire had gone out to dinner with some clients, and how she had not been there when he woke up.

And how he had found the emails from Henry Bryant, and how Henry Bryant had been going out with a woman called Pippa who had moved in with a woman called Jodie Pierce who was friends with Claire.

And how Pippa had disappeared and Jodie was – so Alfie had been told – freaking out about it.

DI Wynne glanced at DS Lawless. 'Do we have contact details for Ms Pierce?' she said.

DS Lawless nodded.

'We'll need to talk to her,' DI Wynne said. 'As soon as we've finished here.' She looked at Alfie. 'Did Mrs Daniels mention who the clients were?'

Alfie shook his head. 'She just said she had to go to dinner.'

'Would she normally do that? Or would she give the name?'

'She might,' Alfie said. 'But not necessarily.'

'You mentioned the dinner was arranged at the last minute?' DS Lawless said. 'Which was presumably out of the ordinary?'

'Yes,' Mick said. 'But there was no dinner. It was an excuse. We already know that.'

'We do,' DI Wynne said. 'But we're trying to go step by step. It helps us. I apologize for any inconvenience.'

'Fine,' Mick muttered. 'Carry on.'

'I think it might be time to look at the emails,' DI Wynne said. 'Could I see them?'

'Of course,' Alfie said. He gestured at the computer. 'Her account is open. There are three from Bryant. You can see Claire's responses if you open them.'

DI Wynne and DS Lawless read the emails. After a few minutes, DI Wynne moved the cursor to the Sent Items folder and clicked on it.

There was one more email, from Claire to Bryant. Wynne opened it.

From: Claire Daniels
To: Henry Bryant HenBryt1983@outlook.com
Subject: Re: Tonight?
    Yes, it is more than I bargained for. I think we may have to do something about it soon. Claire, XOXO

'Hmm,' DI Wynne said. 'Interesting.'

DS Lawless looked at her. 'Why so, boss?'

'Perhaps their relationship is more established than we thought. There may be a simple explanation, Mr Daniels. They may have gone away together – for a few days, weeks, months – and have decided to ignore any attempts to contact them.'

That, Alfie knew, was *not* what had happened, because Henry Bryant did not exist, but he could hardly tell DI Wynne that. 'What about Pippa?' he said. 'She disappeared too, and she had been seeing Bryant. If he was . . . ' He looked away. 'If he was in love with Claire, he'd hardly be seeing Pippa on the side.'

'Yes,' DI Wynne said. 'That is odd.' She got to her feet. 'I think we ought to talk to Ms Pierce.'

'Aren't you going to look around the house?' Mick said.

DI Wynne raised an eyebrow. 'Do you think Mrs Daniels is here somewhere?'

'No,' Mick said. 'But maybe there's some . . . you could get the forensic people in.'

'There's no evidence a crime has been committed here,' DI Wynne said. 'Unless you are suggesting that Mr Daniels may have something to do with your daughter's disappearance?'

'Not at all,' Mick said. 'I just want to be sure you lot are doing whatever you can.'

'We are,' DI Wynne said, and looked at DS Lawless. 'OK. Time to go.'

'I'll call Jodie and tell her you're on your way,' Alfie said.

DI Wynne shook her head. 'No,' she said. 'It would be better if you didn't do that, Mr Daniels.'

V

Jodie called ninety minutes later.

'Hey,' she said, slightly breathless. 'I had the cops here until five minutes ago.'

'Yes,' Alfie said. 'They were here first. What did they ask?'

Alfie was interested to know what they were thinking – whether they thought *he* was a suspect, or whether they were starting to come to the conclusion that Claire was in trouble. It was an odd feeling – it was as though this was a trial run and he was finding out whether his plan would have worked, whether he could have killed Claire and tricked the police into looking for the fictitious Henry Bryant. If he found out he could, though, there was little he could do with the knowledge, since this was *not* a trial run.

He had no idea *what* it was.

'I'll get to that,' Jodie said. 'But what's changed? Why are they involved? I asked, but they were very cagey. They said I should call you.'

'It's . . . it's not great, Jodie.'

'What's going on?'

'Claire was – it looks like she was seeing someone. I found some emails.'

'Oh my God,' Jodie said. 'I don't believe it. Alfie, I—'

'There's more. The emails were from Henry Bryant.'

There was a long silence. 'Pippa's Henry Bryant?'

'I think so.'

'What were the emails about?'

'Dates. And how their relationship was getting out of control. Their feelings for each other.'

'This is ridiculous,' Jodie said. 'I don't believe this. It explains what the police were asking me, though. They were interested in whether I thought Claire had been having an affair.'

'Did they mention Bryant?'

'No. They kept it more general. They wanted to know whether I thought she might have had any affairs during your marriage. I said no, Alfie. And I was telling the truth. She loves you, and she's been faithful. I know she has.'

'It doesn't look that way,' Alfie said.

'There's some other explanation. The more I think about it, the more certain I am.'

'What else did they want to know?'

'If you two had a good marriage. If Claire had ever talked to me about problems between you. Arguments, that kind of thing.'

'And?'

'And I said no. All she's ever said about you is how much she loves you and how lucky she is to have you. That's how I know she's not having an affair. She wouldn't have lied to me.' Jodie sniffed and Alfie realized she was crying. 'She's my friend, Alfie, and she hasn't been deceiving me – or you. She's not capable of it.'

'People aren't always what they seem,' Alfie said.

'Not Claire. No way. And they stopped asking about you and her. They moved on to Pippa. They became *very* interested in her. I told them what I know, which isn't much. I gave

164

them her laptop. I think they think Pippa and Claire are linked, and that can't be good. I'm getting really worried.'

'Me too,' Alfie said. 'Me too.'

Alfie sat on the sofa. On the television, a cricket match unfolded. He wasn't paying attention, but he liked the noise in the background. Without it, the silence was oppressive. Both Mick and Jodie had offered to stay with him but he had told them he wanted to be alone. As far as they were concerned, he was dealing with both a missing wife and the discovery that his wife had been cheating on him. It was no wonder he wanted some time to himself.

Which he did, because he had no idea what was going on and he needed to think. The problem was he didn't know what to think *about*. All he knew was that Claire was gone and someone was impersonating Henry Bryant, and Alfie could only think of one reason why.

It was, at best, the beginnings of an explanation, but it was all he had. It was possible someone was using a fake identity to target women, but, instead of inventing their own, they had simply stolen someone else's. It made sense; you could go on a hook-up website, find a profile that looked promising and borrow it. Then, when you met the women, you would use that name and no one would know who you really were. It was an easy way to hide your identity.

Yes, it was a coincidence that 'Henry Bryant' was the identity someone had stolen, but not *that* much of a coincidence. Henry was a good one to target – young, a doctor, the photo didn't show his face – so in a way it was no surprise.

At least he had a theory that worked. Someone was using Henry Bryant as a cover, and in doing so they had met Claire.

Now that *was* a surprise. He'd have sworn blind Claire was faithful to him and that, if she ever wasn't, it would be because she fell in love with someone. He would never have even contemplated the thought she would be looking for sex on the internet. But like he'd said to Jodie, people aren't always what they seem.

Just look at him. Everyone thought Alfie Daniels was a devoted, loving, slightly unimpressive, husband, when he was anything but. So yes, he had a theory.

The problem was, he had no idea what to do about it.

Saturday

i

He was awake early. The house was quiet. He smiled. He liked it like this. It was a glimpse of the future: him, alone in his big house, his bank stuffed with cash, the day waiting for him, the world his to do what he wanted with.

But not yet. First he had to get through whatever the fuck was going on.

After his shower, he shaved. The blade was blunt and he clicked it off into the bin. He wrapped a towel around his waist, pausing to glance at himself in the mirror – he really did have a great body – then went downstairs.

In the kitchen he brewed a pot of coffee. As he poured a cup, his phone rang. Alfie did not recognize the number. Normally he would have assumed it was some automated calling system selling cheap holidays and ignored it, but not now. Now every call could be vital.

It could be Claire.

'Hello,' he said. 'This is Alfie Daniels.'

'Mr Daniels. This is Detective Inspector Wynne.'

Alfie glanced at his watch. It was nearly eight a.m. 'Is everything OK?'

DI Wynne did not answer the question. 'Mr Daniels, we discovered something in relation to Pippa Davies-Hunt which might be of interest in your wife's disappearance.'

'What was that?'

'It's not something I can really share with you, other than to say it may be important.'

Alfie had a good idea what it was, but DI Wynne didn't need to know that. 'Then why are you calling?'

'Because we found it on Ms Davies-Hunt's computer, and we would like to take a look at your wife's to see if there is anything similar on hers.'

'What kind of thing did you find?'

DI Wynne paused. 'At this point, I'd rather not say. But we would like to examine your wife's machine as soon as we could.'

'I can be available in a few hours,' Alfie said.

'I was thinking of right now.'

Alfie opened the door and gestured to DI Wynne to enter. DS Lawless followed her in, along with a young man who looked like he should be in school. Alfie was about to ask whether the cops had picked him up for truancy when DI Wynne introduced him.

'This is Brad,' she said. 'He helps us when computers or other kinds of information technology are involved. I'm afraid that's not a skill DS Lawless or I have.'

'OK,' Alfie said. 'What can I do to help?'

Brad coughed. 'Could I look at your wife's laptop? If you have any passwords, that would be helpful. If not, I'll be able to do what I need, although I think you'll have to sign something authorizing it.'

'Of course,' Alfie said. 'Anything to help bring Claire back. It's through here.'

He showed Brad to the laptop. It wouldn't take long for him to find what Alfie had left there, but he took a seat as though settling in. DI Wynne and DS Lawless remained standing.

'Could you give me an idea of what you are looking for?' he said.

DI Wynne was about to say something – probably a refusal – when Brad interrupted.

'It's here,' he said. 'Same website as the other one.'

Alfie glanced at the computer tech, and then looked at DI Wynne. 'What website?' he said. 'What's going on?'

DI Wynne looked solemn. 'One minute.' She turned to Brad. 'What exactly did you find?'

'A cookie,' he said. 'Everything else has been deleted, but the cookie is there.'

'So you don't have any messages?'

'No. Not yet. But if we can get into the account we can get them. The company that runs the website would be able to provide them.'

'If we can get a warrant,' DS Lawless said.

'Which I'm sure we will,' DI Wynne muttered. 'Given what I think is going on.'

'Excuse me,' Alfie said, his tone indignant. 'But what exactly *do* you think is going on?'

DI Wynne sat opposite him. 'When we examined Ms Davies-Hunt's computer, we discovered she was a user of a certain type of website.'

'What kind of website?' Alfie said.

'A hook-up site,' DS Lawless replied. 'People meet on these sites in order to have affairs, if they're married, or to find casual sexual partners. That was what Ms Davies-Hunt was doing.'

'And in the course of this she met Henry Bryant,' DI Wynne continued. 'And it seems, from some of the emails we recovered, their initial meetings for sex developed into something more. Into a relationship. At least, that is what Ms Davies-Hunt thought. According to Ms Pierce, Henry Bryant broke up with her when it became clear she wanted more. And then, after arranging to meet him, she disappeared.'

'And you found the same website on Claire's computer?'

'A cookie,' Brad said. 'She must have deleted everything else.'

Alfie looked away, upset. After all, he should be: he had just found out that his wife had met Bryant – the man she had been having an affair with – on a hook-up website.

'I'm sorry, Mr Daniels,' DI Wynne said. 'I know this must be difficult. But it may help us to discover what happened to your wife.'

'And what do you think that is?' Alfie said, in a quiet, defeated voice.

'People – women in particular – who use these websites put themselves in a dangerous position,' DI Wynne said. 'They arrange to meet unknown men in secret. Often – for obvious reasons – they don't tell anyone where they're going to be. Yes, you can meet in public areas, get to know the person, assess the risks, but at the end of the day you're meeting a stranger, and that comes with a degree of vulnerability. For starters, you have no guarantee they are who they say they are. They might not want their real name to be known.'

Alfie shook his head. 'Are you saying . . . ' He left the question hanging.

'I'm saying,' DI Wynne replied, 'that Henry Bryant was involved with Ms Davies-Hunt, and she disappeared. He was also involved with your wife, and she too has disappeared. It seems – from the messages your wife and he exchanged and from what happened with Ms Davies-Hunt – that he likes to develop a relationship with the people he meets. Perhaps it makes them trust him.'

'You think he's taken her? Her and Pippa?'

'I think it's possible, and I think there may be others. Maybe not using the name Henry Bryant.'

'Oh God,' Alfie said. 'Claire. Poor Claire.' He looked up at the detective, his eyes wet with tears. 'Do you think – do you think she might – he might have killed her?'

'I don't know,' DI Wynne said. 'But we will find out. I promise you that, Mr Daniels.'

ii

He supposed he should have seen it coming. The story had everything: mystery, sex, a posh girl misbehaving, so it would be irresistible to the press. Still, he was surprised they had learned about it this quickly. Maybe there was a cop who leaked this stuff in exchange for a supplement to their income.

Either way, he had not expected to open the door to a woman in her thirties with a camera and a strong Newcastle accent.

'Alfie Daniels?' she said. 'I'm with the *Daily Herald*. I understand your wife is missing and she may have been abducted by a man who has done this before. Do you have any comment?'

'I'm sorry,' Alfie replied. 'I really don't know what to say.'

'Is it true your wife met this man on a sex website?'

'I don't want to talk about it. It's none of your business.'

'Was your marriage happy?' the reporter said. 'Were there any—'

Alfie shut the door. These people really were awful. Vultures. He'd been planning to go for a walk to try to clear his head.

He was on edge. He felt out of control, and he couldn't stand it.

And now, he was trapped in his house. He went into the kitchen and poured another cup of coffee, then logged on to see what the newspapers were saying.

The story was on the *Daily Herald* website an hour later.

SEX WEBSITE WOMEN DISAPPEAR

Reports emerged today that women who use websites to find partners for illicit sex may be putting themselves at risk of more than an unwanted trip to an STD clinic.

In the past two weeks, two women, Phillipa Davies-Hunt and Claire Daniels, have disappeared. Both women vanished after arranging meetings on the same website. There are indications, although the police have yet to confirm them, that they may have met the same man.

Davies-Hunt, 33, was last seen more than a week ago. Since then she has not responded to emails or phone calls. A friend, who did not give her name, said she was 'extremely worried. This is not like Pippa at all.'

Daniels, 30, did not come home after going out on Thursday night. She informed her husband, Alfie, that she was going to dinner with clients of the design firm where she is a partner, although it appears there was no such dinner.

Her husband said, 'I really don't know what to say. I just want Claire back.' He did not comment on the state of their marriage or his wife's use of sex websites.

Daniels' father, wealthy estate agent Mick Stewart, refused to comment. There is no indication that a ransom has been demanded.

Alfie smiled. He couldn't stop marvelling at the irony that this was exactly what was supposed to have happened. It was the script he had written, being enacted as he had laid it down, but with one exception.

He didn't know the final act.

An hour later DI Wynne called.

'Sorry to bother you again,' she said. 'I'm outside with DS Lawless. I was wondering whether you're free to talk.'

'Of course.' Alfie got off the couch and went to the front door. He opened it and let them in. 'Take a seat. Can I offer you a drink?'

'Not for me, thanks,' DI Wynne said.

DS Lawless shook her head. 'Me neither.'

DI Wynne looked around the living room. 'Nobody here with you?'

'No,' Alfie said. 'Jodie offered, but I'm OK.'

'No family? Friends?'

'Is this a social call? Are you worried about me?'

'No. But often people gather round at a time like this.'

'I don't have many friends,' Alfie said. 'And no family.' He was about to tell her his parents were dead, but he stopped himself. DI Wynne was the type who would check. 'Claire is all I have. Have you made any progress?'

'Not a lot,' DS Lawless said. 'Yet. Although we are viewing this as potentially a serious crime, so we have more resources available to us.'

'I see,' Alfie said. 'A serious crime.'

'Which doesn't mean we don't think we'll find her,' DI Wynne said. 'There's still every chance of that.'

'What about Henry Bryant?'

'No sign of him,' DI Wynne said. 'There are a number of people by that name and we're contacting them, but at this point we have nothing.' She leaned forwards. 'It's almost as though he doesn't exist.'

Alfie nodded slowly. 'We need to find him.'

'Yes,' DI Wynne said. 'We do.' She took out a notebook. 'Could you tell me where you were the night Ms Davies-Hunt disappeared?'

'I was out,' Alfie said. 'I'd had some bad news and I went drinking.'

'Where did you go?'

Alfie named some of the pubs he'd staggered into after killing Pippa.

'And what time did you return home?'

'Late. I don't exactly remember. I was very drunk.'

'Do you normally get drunk, Mr Daniels?' DS Lawless said.

'Rarely. But like I said, I'd had some bad news.'

'Would you be open to sharing the nature of that news?' DI Wynne asked.

'I found out I'm infertile. Claire and I had been trying for a baby. I was upset.'

'I'm sure she was, too,' DI Wynne said. 'But you left her on her own?'

'Yes,' Alfie said. 'And I'm not proud of it. I was selfish, but the last time I checked, selfishness was not a criminal offence.'

'It still isn't,' DI Wynne said. 'And I apologize, but I have to establish the facts. And it is a coincidence that you were out the night Ms Davies-Hunt disappeared. In my line of work, we have learned to take an interest in coincidences.'

'Well, this really was a coincidence. I was out in a bunch of pubs. Ask the bar staff. They'll remember me.'

'We will,' DS Lawless said. 'We certainly will.'

DI Wynne started to speak but he raised his hand to stop her.

'Am I a suspect?' he said. 'I'm sorry to be so frank, but I'd like to know.'

DI Wynne caught his gaze and held it. 'Should you be?' she said.

There was a long pause.

'No,' Alfie said. I shouldn't.'

'Then let's talk about Claire's movements.'

DS Lawless handed him a piece of paper. It was a list of Oyster card transactions. She tapped one from the Wednesday before. It was the name of the Tube station near Alfie's office.

'She came to see you at work?' Lawless asked.

Alfie shook his head. 'I don't think so. I didn't see her.'

'She was there.'

'Maybe I missed her. I was out of the office.'

'At a showing?' Lawless said.

'No. Taking a walk. There's a park near the agency.'

'Was it normal for her to come to your office during the day?' Wynne said.

'Not really. But we've been having a tough time. Maybe she wanted to see me.'

Wynne nodded. 'Maybe.'

Lawless pointed to another Oyster card transaction. It was from shortly after eight p.m. the same day.

'And this?' Lawless said.

'She went into work late that night,' Alfie said. 'That's the Tube station she uses.'

'So,' Wynne said. 'She came to see you even though she was so busy she had to work late, but didn't call you to check you were there?'

'Yes,' Alfie said. He shrugged. 'That's what happened.'

'Does it not strike you as odd?' Wynne asked.

'Not really. She probably wanted to see me. We're very close.'

Lawless nodded. 'Then that night she took a cab home

ten minutes before midnight. She put it on the company account.'

'They do that when they work late,' Alfie said. 'The firm pays for a cab.'

'Very generous,' Wynne said. She didn't look at the paper with the Oyster card transactions on it. 'Then she goes to work the following morning, early. Six a.m., in fact.'

'Right,' Alfie said. 'I was asleep. She left a note.'

'Oh?' Lawless said. 'Could we see it?'

'Of course.' Alfie went to the kitchen counter and picked up the pad. He turned to the page with Claire's note on it and brought it into the living room.

He handed it to DS Lawless and watched as she read it.

HAD TO GET IN EARLY TO WORK. SEE YOU TONIGHT. TAKE-OUT? I'M EXHAUSTED.

She passed it to DI Wynne, who read it and then put it in a plastic bag.

'So,' DS Lawless continued. 'We have her going to work early Thursday, and then going straight from work to dinner with a client.'

'Yes,' Alfie said. 'She called late in the day to tell me she had to go out.'

'And yet she didn't take the Tube that Thursday evening,' Wynne said. 'Or call a cab on the company account. My guess is she flagged down a cab and paid in cash.' She paused. 'Wherever she was going, it seems she didn't want anyone to know.'

'Right,' Alfie said. 'Because she was going to meet Henry Bryant, whoever he is.'

'So it seems,' DI Wynne said. 'And we have no trace of her after she left her office. What did you do that evening?'

'Stayed here,' Alfie replied 'What else would I have done?'

'You tell me,' DI Wynne said. 'You were here the entire night?'

'The entire night,' Alfie said.

'Alone?'

'Of course alone!'

'So no one can confirm you were here?' DS Lawless said.

'I guess not,' Alfie said. 'But can't you check my phone records? See where I was?'

'See where your *phone* was,' DS Lawless said. 'Not quite the same thing.'

'Look. I'm having rather a bad day. You might not have read it, but the press have got hold of this story – from one of your lot, I assume – and it's all over the place. My wife has been having an affair and is missing, and now you're accusing me of being behind it, as well as the disappearance of some other woman I've never even met. So you'll forgive me if I'm a bit pissed off.'

'My forgiveness is not material,' DI Wynne said. 'My job is to gather all the information that *is* material. And I think DS Lawless and I have done that. Thank you for your time. We'll be in touch.'

Alfie stared at her. 'I don't doubt it,' he said.

iii

By seven p.m. there were six or seven reporters outside his door. He didn't open it, but eventually he'd have to. Eventually he'd have to face them and their cameras and questions.

And Alfie didn't want to.

He didn't want his face in the papers, didn't want people studying it for signs of grief or guilt and then looking at the photos of Pippa and Claire and thinking, *Hmm, I saw that guy in a pub in Barnes with the first girl who disappeared.*

He needed to stop that from happening. He picked up his phone and dialled Mick.

'Alfie. Everything OK?'

'Kind of,' Alfie said. 'Apart from the reporters outside the house.'

'Those *bastards*,' Mick said. 'Splashing my girl's business all over the newspapers. Making out she's some kind of slut. It's none of their fucking business.'

'I know. But they'll stay here all night.'

'No they won't,' Mick said. 'I'll be right over.'

He was there an hour later. Alfie watched out of the bedroom window as he pulled up in a black cab – he hated Uber, he told Alfie once, couldn't understand why anyone used it – and climbed out wearing a pair of wine-red cords and a Barbour jacket. His face was red and he looked like he wished he had a shotgun to go with his country clothes.

One of the reporters noticed him and the pack turned, sensing fresh, vulnerable meat.

Alfie smiled. Mick was hardly fresh, and he was very far from vulnerable.

'Do you know Mr Daniels?' one of the reporters shouted, his camera aloft. 'Are you a relation?'

'I think it's the wife's old man,' someone else said, and he pushed towards Mick, intending to intercept him on the pavement.

Mick marched towards him.

'You lot can fuck off,' he bellowed. He grabbed the camera from the reporter's hand and snatched it away.

'Hey,' the reporter said. 'You can't do that!'

He tried to grab the camera back, but Mick held it away from him. He'd played rugby until his mid-thirties and, although he was carrying some extra weight, he was still, underneath it, a powerful man.

And an angry, determined one.

He threw the camera hard on to the pavement. The lens snapped off and rolled into the street. He kicked the body into the wall of the house. Alfie was no camera engineer, but he was pretty sure the damage was terminal.

'I just bloody did,' Mick said, and advanced towards another reporter. 'And I'll do it again'

The reporter moved aside. Mick walked to the front door and rang the bell.

Alfie went down to let him in. As he approached the door he could hear his father-in-law.

'You lot are a disgrace,' he was shouting. 'Do you ever think about that? A fucking disgrace.'

'You owe me a camera!' the reporter whose camera was now in pieces shouted. 'You can't treat me like this!'

'You don't like it?' Mick said. 'Poor you. You shouldn't be hanging around harassing people. And next time I'm bringing some of my boys along with me and you'll like it a lot less, you scumbags.'

Alfie opened the door. Mick raised his middle finger to the reporters and stepped inside.

His appearance belied his belligerence. He looked awful. His large frame seemed to have slumped and his eyes were sunken and red.

'Bastards,' he muttered. 'Hope that gets rid of them.'

'How are you holding up?' Alfie said.

Mick looked at him. His lip quivered and he started to cry. 'She's my little girl, Alfie,' he said. 'I want her to be safe. That's all I've ever wanted.'

His worry – grief, almost – was raw. Alfie saw that this was how people expected *him* to react. He'd have to up his game.

'I know,' Alfie said, in a low voice. He turned away as though overcome with emotion. 'I know.'

Mick stayed for the rest of the evening. By nine p.m., he was drunk, snoring on the sofa. Alfie put on his shoes and headed for the front door.

There were three reporters still hanging around. Two men, leaning against the bonnet of a Ford Focus and a woman, talking on her phone and smoking a cigarette.

He needed Henry Bryant's phones from his office. They had been on his mind all day, but he hadn't wanted to go in when his colleagues would be there.

But he didn't want to be seen by the press. He grabbed a baseball cap, put it low over his eyes, and headed for the back door. There was a gate at the end of the garden that opened on to a walkway, but they would probably be there, too.

181

He climbed the fence separating the neighbouring garden, then climbed another two. When he emerged on to the walkway, he saw a reporter by his back gate.

He walked past, eyes low.

The reporter tapped him on the shoulder. 'You know Alfie and Claire?'

'No comment,' he muttered, and walked on.

Once he was on a main road, he flagged a black cab. Like Claire had, he'd pay in cash. He didn't want a record of this trip, not that it mattered. If anyone asked, he'd say he'd wanted to take his mind off things by going into the office, but he'd prefer to avoid the conversation, if he could.

On the way, he read the news stories. Claire and Pippa were all over the internet. Someone had tweeted their photos with a message asking people to retweet to their followers.

#FindPippaandClaire! Retweet this!
If you see them call the police!

Now it was the highest trending hashtag on Twitter. Alfie took a deep breath. He needed this to die down as soon as possible.

But he feared it would only get worse.

The office was empty. He unlocked the door and headed for his desk. The phones were in the drawer, untouched. He put them on the desk, then grabbed a few files in case anyone asked why he'd been there.

He thought about the best place to dispose of them. The Thames, probably, but he didn't want to be seen throwing them off a bridge, especially since his face was increasingly well known.

Down a drain, maybe. Or in a skip.

No. He wanted them destroyed. He decided to take them home. When Mick was gone, he'd smash them into thousands of pieces with a hammer, then scatter the pieces all over London.

He picked them up and froze.

There was a text message on Henry Bryant's phone.

He stared at it, then clicked it open.

Miss me? it read. Miss you too. See you soon?

He dropped the phone on the desk with a loud cry, then read it again.

Miss me? Miss you too. See you soon?

It was a blocked number. Was it Claire? That would make sense, but why hadn't she signed it? And where had she got this number? More to the point, why would she have sent it?

He grabbed the phones and stuffed them into his pocket. He couldn't wait to destroy both of them.

iv

When Alfie got home, Mick was still sleeping. Alfie took a blanket and spread it over him on the sofa.

Then he took a bottle of whisky from the drinks cabinet – some kind of expensive Scotch his father-in-law had brought over – and poured a large measure.

He pulled an armchair to the front window and sat down, looking along the street. The reporters were gone, although they'd no doubt be back at some point. It was a normal night on a London street. A man in a suit was making his way home, laptop bag hanging from his shoulder, eyes fixed on his phone. Two women in expensive jeans and patterned tops were standing on the other side of the street. He watched as a cab pulled up and they climbed in.

Nothing out of the ordinary.

Except for the fact his wife was missing and in his pocket was a phone with a message from her – or someone pretending to be her – on it.

He sipped the whisky. He kept the glass at his lips and then sipped again, more this time. His mind was buzzing.

He sat, and drank, and watched the street.

Sunday

i

Alfie was woken by the doorbell ringing. He had no memory of going to bed; at around two a.m. he'd had a final whisky, but it had not made him sleepy. It had only made his heart race and given him the hangover now clouding his vision as he stumbled down the stairs to the front door.

He caught a glimpse of himself in the hallway mirror. He was dishevelled, his face dark with stubble and his eyes red with lack of sleep. At least today he did not need to act the part of a grieving husband. He looked exactly like people would have expected him to look.

He opened the front door. DI Wynne and DS Lawless were standing there.

'Apologies for disturbing you,' DI Wynne said, not looking in the slightest apologetic. 'We have some questions we were hoping you could help with.'

'Right now?' Alfie said. 'It's early.'

Wynne glanced at her watch. It was a 1980s Casio digital, which looked original.

'It's eight a.m.,' she said. 'We don't want to waste any time while we're looking for your wife.'

Alfie took the hint. It wasn't exactly subtle.

'Come in,' he said. 'I'll get dressed.'

When he came downstairs again, DI Wynne was sitting in the living room. DS Lawless was on her feet and Mick was sitting by the window, cradling a mug of strong tea in his hands. Alfie had no idea whether he had stayed on the sofa all night or made it up to bed in the meantime.

Wynne looked slowly around the room. 'Mr Daniels,' she said, 'I'd like to go over the night Ms Davies-Hunt disappeared. Could you perhaps walk us through what you did that evening?'

'I already told you everything,' Alfie said.

'I'd like it if we could go through it again. It's important to know the whereabouts of everybody concerned.'

'What do you mean, "concerned"?' Alfie said. 'I wasn't involved. I didn't know Pippa.'

'It's routine,' Lawless said. 'If you could bear with us, Mr Daniels, it would be appreciated.'

Alfie sighed. 'OK. I was upset that day. I'd had an appointment with Dr Singh and learned some bad news. We don't need to talk about it again, do we?'

'No,' Wynne said. 'What happened after the appointment?'

'I went for a walk. To clear my head.'

'Where did you walk?' DI Wynne asked.

'Honestly,' Alfie said, 'I don't remember. I know it sounds bad, but I was in a daze. I walked a long way. I bought a half-bottle of vodka somewhere and drank most of it.'

'Where did you buy it from?' Lawless asked.

'I don't remember. A corner shop.'

'Did you pay with a bank card?'

'Cash,' Alfie said. 'At least, I think so. I can check my bank records.'

He knew there would be no transaction, because there had been no vodka. He'd been on his way to meet Pippa in Barnes, in the car he kept in the garage of a house owned by some Russian as an investment. It was unoccupied; Alfie's agency had the keys and were named as the emergency contact.

'Do that,' DI Wynne said. 'We'd like to see those records, if we could. And after your walk' – she put a heavy emphasis on the word – 'you went to a series of pubs?'

'That's right.'

'We did talk to the staff at those pubs,' DS Lawless said. 'And some of them remember seeing you. You were quite drunk, by all accounts.'

'I'd had half a bottle of vodka, which is a lot for me.'

'The earliest time we have you identified is around nine p.m.,' Lawless said. 'Before that, we only have your word for your movements.'

Mick snorted. 'You need to stop wasting time on this and start finding Henry fucking Bryant,' he said. 'Get his bank accounts, passport, birth certificate. Find a photo and circulate it. Alfie has nothing to do with it. This is ridiculous.'

'Maybe,' DI Wynne said. 'And maybe not. We have to pursue every—'

Alfie banged his hand on the arm of the chair. 'I had *nothing* to do with Pippa's disappearance,' he shouted, with all the conviction and anger of a man who had not slept. 'Or Claire's! And I resent you suggesting that I do.'

'I don't doubt it,' DI Wynne said, her even tone unperturbed. 'But we need to establish everybody's movements. It's normal procedure. That's all we're doing.'

'Oh, for Christ's sake,' Mick said. 'Alfie had nothing to do with this Pippa woman. It was Henry Bryant. Alfie would

187

never do that kind of thing. Trust me, he loves Claire like a puppy loves its master. He had no reason to harm her, and even if he wanted to, he hasn't got the balls.'

He glanced at Alfie apologetically. Alfie looked away.

'Thank you all the same,' DI Wynne said. 'But we will come to our own conclusions.'

Alfie was about to suggest that she and Lawless leave when DI Wynne's phone rang. She looked at the screen and frowned.

'One minute,' she said, and lifted the phone to her ear. 'Wynne,' she said, then: 'Yes, ma'am.'

She listened, her face expressionless, then spoke.

'Did she say anything about where? And who?'

She looked at Alfie, then at DS Lawless. Something passed between the two cops.

'Yes. Of course, I'll pass it on.'

She hung up, then folded her arms. 'Well,' she said. 'It looks like I may have spoken too soon. It seems we won't have to come to our own conclusions after all.' She stared at Alfie. 'We found your wife.'

Alfie's eyes widened. His stomach contracted. He was about to find out what the hell was going on.

'Is she OK?'

'From what I was told, yes. I don't have all the details.'

'What happened to her?' Mick said. 'Where's she been?'

'It seems she was held captive,' DI Wynne said. 'And she escaped. She hasn't given many details yet. She's been asking for her husband. Apparently, she was very concerned to get a message to Mr Daniels. She wanted to make sure someone passed on these exact words: "Tell Alfie I love him."' The cop caught Alfie's eye. For the first time since he'd met her, she looked uncomfortable. 'And she said to tell him she's sorry.'

ii

Alfie walked into the police station alongside DI Wynne and DS Lawless. They had driven him there and on the way he had asked for whatever details they had been given. There weren't many.

Mick had followed in a cab. He said he had never been in a police car and wasn't going to start now; as they opened the door to the station, he pulled up.

Alfie waited for him. When they walked in, Wynne and Lawless were standing at the desk. A uniformed PC pressed a button and there was a buzz as a door unlocked. His gaze lingered on Alfie for a moment.

'Interview Room Three,' he said.

They followed the two detectives along a corridor. They stopped by a door, and DI Wynne turned to him.

'Ready?' she said, her hand on the handle.

Alfie nodded and she opened the door.

Claire was sitting behind a table, a female officer in a chair beside her. There were two mugs of tea on the table in front of them, one full, one – Claire's – empty. She was wearing a pair of jeans – not hers – and a loose-fitting navy-blue police sweater. Her feet were bare and very dirty. Alfie was carrying a small rucksack containing some of Claire's clothes and shoes. DS Lawless had suggested he bring it.

As he walked in, Claire looked up. Her skin was pallid and her eyes were puffy with lack of sleep, or tears, or both.

'Alfie,' she said, her voice low and cracked. 'Alfie. You're here.'

He hurried across the room and bent over, wrapping his arms around her body. She had a strange smell, rich and earthy, but not unpleasant. She hugged him back, her grip weak.

'Claire,' he said. 'I was so worried. I'm so glad you're safe.'

'Can we go home?' she said. 'I want to go home.'

Mick put a hand on her shoulder and Alfie stepped back so he could hug his daughter.

'Of course you can go home,' Mick said. 'You can do whatever you want.'

Alfie looked at the cop. 'Can we leave?'

The cop looked at DI Wynne. 'We took a statement,' she said. She handed her a folder. 'But you may have more questions.'

'I'll answer them,' Claire said, her voice strained. 'If it helps catch him.'

DI Wynne smiled. 'Thank you,' she said. 'The earlier we get information the better.'

'Can Alfie stay here? While we talk?' Claire asked.

'Of course,' DI Wynne said. 'If you'd like him to. Mr Daniels?'

'I'll stay.'

'Me too,' Mick said.

Claire shook her head. 'Just Alfie.'

Mick frowned, but he nodded and followed the officer out of the room. When everyone had left, DI Wynne opened the folder and scanned the paper inside.

'OK. Let's get started. The sooner we're done with this, the sooner you can get home.'

Alfie held up the rucksack he had brought. He thought Claire would probably be happy to get the questions over with, but he wanted a few minutes with her so she'd have a chance to tell him anything she wanted to without the cops there. He also wanted some kind of control over this mess.

'How about she gets changed?' he said. 'It'll be nice if she's in her own clothes.'

Claire nodded. 'Yes. I'd like that.'

'Of course,' DI Wynne replied, getting to her feet. 'Knock on the door when you're ready, and the officer will come and get me.'

When Wynne had left, Alfie handed Claire her clothes.

'So,' he said. 'How are you feeling?'

'OK. Not great. But OK.'

He hesitated. He wasn't sure how to ask this, but he needed to know. He needed to know what the hell was going on. 'What happened? . . . Do you want to tell me?'

'It was—' she said, and closed her eyes. When she opened them they were full of tears. 'It was awful.'

He didn't press her, despite how desperate he was to know who this new version of Henry Bryant was. One thing he did know, though, was that he was real. Someone, masquerading as Henry Bryant, had imprisoned Claire. She had, presumably, escaped somehow and now she was back.

But he was no nearer to understanding who it was and why they were doing it.

The door opened and DI Wynne came in. She sat opposite Claire. DS Lawless stood behind her.

'OK,' DI Wynne said. 'I've read your statement. I'll start with that, if it's OK?'

Claire nodded.

'So you left work to meet Bryant on Thursday evening

191

last week. You told your husband you were going to a dinner with some clients but you were in fact going to meet Mr Bryant?'

'Yes,' Claire said. She looked at Alfie. 'I'm sorry. So sorry. You deserved better.'

Alfie hugged her. 'It's fine,' he whispered. 'It's really fine. Whatever happened, we can work it out. I'm just glad you're safe. That's all I can think of right now.'

'Was this the first time you had met him?' DI Wynne said.

'No. We'd seen each other a few times before.'

'You met Mr Bryant on a website?'

'Yes.'

'Was he the first person you'd met on such a website?'

'Please,' Alfie said. 'What has this got to do with what happened? Claire and I can work through this together, but we don't need to talk about it now.'

'It's OK,' Claire said. 'I'll answer whatever questions DI Wynne has.' She brushed her lips with her fingers. 'He was the first person I met on a website. But he wasn't the first person I had an affair with. I had an affair with a colleague a few months back.'

Alfie groaned. He looked away. Claire put her hand on his knee. 'I'm sorry. Truly, I am. I was – I was feeling lost, Alfie.'

'But you did not meet that man – your colleague – online?' DI Wynne said. 'You don't have to stay for this, Mr Daniels.' She looked at Claire. 'If it makes it easier?'

'I want him here,' Claire said. 'If it's OK with you, Alfie?'

Alfie nodded. There was no way he was leaving. He needed to hear what Claire had to say. He needed to know what was going on.

'I didn't meet him online. He was from the office.'

'I see,' Wynne said. 'Let's move on to Henry Bryant. We will need details of all the places you went with him. We'll look for CCTV footage, speak to bar staff, talk to any cabbies who drove you around. We'll also be able to go through credit card payments and maybe get a card number for him.'

Claire gave a rueful smile. 'He always paid in cash. At the time, I thought it was because he didn't want any records for his wife to find, but it seems there was a more disturbing reason.'

'He's married?' DS Lawless asked.

'He said so,' Claire replied. 'He wore a ring.'

'Maybe a fake,' Alfie said. 'To make him look trustworthy.'

'Maybe,' DI Wynne said. 'Could you describe Henry Bryant?'

'Slim . . . slim, but very strong. Dark hair, wide-set eyes. Handsome. He looks a bit like Alfie, but taller. Maybe six one, or two.'

'We'll get an identikit drawing of him,' Wynne said. 'You can adjust it, although hopefully we find some CCTV pictures with an actual image.' She sipped her tea. 'Could you describe what happened the night he took you captive?'

'We met for a drink. In a pub in Holborn.' She looked away. 'I ordered a gin and tonic, but that's all I remember. I woke up in a room. I was' – she choked on the words – 'I was tied to a bed.'

'Some kind of drug,' DS Lawless said. 'It might show up in the toxicology report, but probably not. It's most likely out of your system by now.'

'Yes,' DI Wynne said. 'Do you recall anything about the room?'

'No,' Claire said. 'It was pitch-black.'

'No sounds? Smells?'

Claire thought for a moment. 'I did hear cars. And what sounded like a truck unloading. But I wasn't really concentrating on it.'

'Had Bryant assaulted you? Sexually?' DS Lawless asked.

'I don't think so.'

'Did he? Later?'

Claire shook her head. 'No. He didn't seem interested in – in *that*.' She blinked. 'I was there for a day or two, I think. Something like that. He came in and out. Brought water and some food.'

'Did he say anything?'

'No. He untied me from the bed and put a hood on me. He tied my hands behind my back and led me out of the room and down some stairs. I guess we went into a garage, because I heard the sound of a car door opening and he pushed me into the boot of a car. He tied my ankles together and then he left again.' She started to cry. 'It was terrible. It was hot and I was crunched up. I started to panic, banging my head against the lid of the boot. But he didn't come.' She glanced at Alfie. 'And then, of course, there was Jodie's friend, Pippa.'

'What about her?' DI Wynne said. 'Was she there?'

'No,' Claire said. 'But as I was lying there I remembered how she'd disappeared, and I wondered whether she'd gone through something like this. And then I remembered what Jodie had told me. About the guy she'd been dating. I remembered his name. Henry Bryant.'

'You hadn't made the connection earlier?' Lawless said. 'When you were meeting up with Bryant?'

Claire shook her head. 'At first I only knew him as Henry. His profile only gave his name and initial – Henry B. It wasn't until he emailed me that I saw his last name. At that point it rang a bell, but it was only when I was in the boot and I started thinking of Pippa that I remembered he was the guy who had broken up with her by text, right before she disappeared. Jodie had mentioned his name in passing.' Claire looked at Alfie. 'I was terrified I'd never see you again. I thought he'd do it to me, too.'

'That didn't happen,' he said. 'It's all going to be OK.' He looked at DI Wynne. 'We have to catch this guy. We *have* to.'

He meant it, but not for the reasons Wynne and Lawless and Claire would think. He didn't care about justice for Claire or keeping other women safe.

He wanted him caught because he had no idea what was going on, and he didn't like it.

Under the table, his hands were shaking. He clenched them tight. He didn't want anyone to see and think he was afraid.

Even if they did, they'd be wrong. He wasn't afraid. It was worse than that.

Alfie was close to being in the grip of a full-on panic.

iii

DI Wynne made a note on her pad of paper. 'How long were you in the boot of the car?' she said.

'I don't know,' Claire replied. 'It felt like a long time. Hours. He came a few times and gave me water.'

'Did he say anything?'

'He never spoke. I heard him once, talking on the phone—'

'How did you know he was on the phone?' DS Lawless said.

'Because there was no one replying. There were long pauses while he listened.'

'What was he saying?' Lawless asked.

'I don't know. I couldn't make out the words. He was laughing, though, and I remember feeling it was odd that he was relaxed and happy and I was only a few feet away, tied up and in pain from the cramp in my back and neck and legs.'

She took a deep breath.

'I was in and out of consciousness, and then I was woken by the engine starting up. The car started moving – I was convinced he was taking me somewhere to kill me – and we drove for a while.'

'How long, do you think?' Wynne said.

'An hour, maybe. It felt like we were going quickly at one point, but that could have been because I was in the boot. The last few minutes were very bumpy, like we were on a dirt road of some sort.' Claire glanced at Alfie. She was pale, her eyes dark. Her face was thinner, her cheekbones more prominent.

'Are you OK?' he said.

'Not exactly,' she replied. 'But there's not much more to tell. We stopped, and he opened the boot. It was early morning and we were surrounded by trees. He took me out of the boot and untied my ankles. There was a van parked a few yards away, hidden in the trees.'

'What colour?' Wynne said. 'Make? Age?'

'Quite old. White. A Ford, I think.'

'And the car?'

'It was dark blue. I don't know the make, but nondescript.'

'Thank you, Mrs Daniels,' Wynne said. 'Please, carry on.'

Claire nodded. 'He undressed me. First my jeans and underwear, and then the rest. He had to untie my hands to get my top off. I don't know why, but at the time all I could think was that he was going to rape me. Or worse. That's why he left me naked.'

'Worse?' DS Lawless said. 'What were you thinking?'

Claire looked down at her hands. 'I was thinking he was going to put me in the van and offer me to – to other men. Drive me to quiet places and let them' – she hesitated, the words almost inaudible – 'let them use me. I think that was his plan.'

'Claire,' Alfie said, 'we don't have to carry on.'

'It's fine. Because that thought was what saved me. It made me realize I had to get out of there. I shoved him as hard as I could. He banged his head on the boot, and I managed to push him in, so his legs were dangling out. Then I slammed

197

it down, three or four times. I heard a noise that sounded like something breaking, and then I ran to the trees. And eventually, I came to a road.'

'He didn't follow you?'

'I don't think so. I think he was hurt.'

DI Wynne gave DS Lawless a nod. 'Hospitals,' she said. 'Anyone with a leg injury consistent with Mrs Daniels's account.'

'On it,' Lawless said.

Wynne looked at Claire. She smiled. 'Thank you. I'm sure there will be more questions. No doubt I'll be in touch, but you've given us a lot to go on. For now, that's it.'

They got a ride home in a police car. As they pulled out of the police station she unbuckled her seat belt and leaned against him.

The PC who was driving glanced at them in the rear-view mirror. He was about to say something, but he raised a hand.

'Never mind,' he said. 'I'll drive carefully.'

Alfie smiled and gave him a thumbs up. When he looked back at Claire she was asleep.

He woke her when they got home and helped her out of the car and to the front door.

'Everything OK?' the PC said.

'Yes,' Alfie replied. 'And thank you for your help.'

'Not a problem. If you need anything, don't hesitate to call.'

Alfie closed the door. Claire walked into the living room and sat on one end of the sofa, her hands around her knees. He sat next to her and put his arms around her.

'Thank God,' he said. 'Thank God you're back.'

She nodded. 'Could you get me a glass of water?'

'Of course. Anything. Do you want tea? Or coffee? Something to eat?'

'Just water.'

In the kitchen he poured two glasses. He brought them to the living room and handed one to Claire. He set his down on the coffee table. He watched the ripples on the surface fade, and tried to understand what was going on.

What he knew was that Claire had been abducted, and managed to escape. Which confirmed that someone had taken Bryant's identity so he could meet and then abduct women, and then maybe do what Claire had suggested: farm them out as sex slaves.

It was a clever idea; those websites were unregulated, and full of people using false names. They would be nearly untraceable. They happened, in this case, to have chosen Henry Bryant, who was implicated in Pippa's disappearance.

That would send the cops down the wrong path. They would be focused on Henry Bryant, when they should be looking for other women who had gone missing after meeting men on dating websites, men who could be called anything.

Not that Alfie could tell them that.

Either way, he was starting to feel a little better about this. He thought he knew what had happened, now. It was random, and although it didn't explain the text message he'd received – the one without the name of the sender, the one which said *Miss me? Miss you too. See you soon?* – Alfie thought he had figured out what had happened there, as well. It was from Pippa – it was exactly the kind of thing she would write – but not from after he killed her. She'd sent it before, and it had got stuck somewhere in cyberspace. It was only when he went to get his phone and switched it on that it came through.

The best thing about this was that whoever had abducted Claire would steer well clear of her from now on, and also of using Henry Bryant again.

And that meant, for Alfie and Claire at least – if not for his future victims – this was over.

But it left Alfie just as trapped as before.

iv

Claire sipped her water, and then closed her eyes.

'I'm exhausted,' she said. 'I'm going to have a shower and a sleep. Will you come and lie with me?'

'Of course,' Alfie said. 'I'd like nothing more.'

He was woken by the doorbell. For a moment he had a strong sense of déjà vu – as he opened his eyes he imagined DI Wynne and DS Lawless on the front step – but then he remembered.

Claire was home.

He got out of bed quietly and walked to the front door. Mick was standing there with a large pizza box. He thrust it at Alfie and marched inside.

'Where is she?' he said.

'Sleeping.' Alfie nodded upstairs. 'She's very tired.'

'Leave her,' Mick said, as though Alfie would have done anything else. He took out his phone. 'You seen this?'

'What is it?'

'Those bastards in the press have got hold of it. They're already running it,' Mick said.

'Oh. What are they saying?'

'Read it.'

Alfie took Mick's phone and read the story.

CLAIRE DANIELS FOUND

Claire Daniels, the woman who went missing earlier in the week, has been found. Mrs Daniels was seen wandering along a quiet road in the New Forest by Barbara Linton, 61. Ms Linton informed the police.

Mrs Daniels had disappeared after arranging an extramarital liaison on a website with a man using the name of Henry Bryant. She was the second woman to vanish after arranging to meet Mr Bryant in the last two weeks. Ms Pippa Davies-Hunt has not been seen since a week ago on Thursday.

Detective Inspector Jane Wynne said the police had gained valuable information from Mrs Daniels. 'We have learned a lot about Henry Bryant and are following a number of leads. We remain concerned for Ms Davies-Hunt and hope to find her soon.'

Mrs Daniels is home with her husband, Alfie, and did not want to comment.

Alfie handed the phone back to Mick.

'It's not too bad,' he said.

'No, not yet.' Mick put the phone in his pocket. 'You know, I admire you, Alfie. For not throwing her out.'

'I thought about it. But I love her. And we'll work it out.'

'I'm grateful you feel that way. She's going to need you after what she went through.'

'I know. And I'll be here for her.'

'So what happens next?' Mick said.

'I'll take some time off work. Stay home with her. Start the healing process. I think she'd benefit from seeing someone.'

201

Mick nodded. 'Say the word. Whoever you want. I'll pay for it.'

Yes, you will, Alfie thought, *yes, you fucking will.*

'Thanks, Mick,' he said, with a smile. 'I appreciate it. I appreciate everything you do.'

Monday

i

When Alfie woke up, Claire was not there. He slid his hand to her side of the bed. The sheets were cold. He listened for the sound of movement, or the television or radio. There was only silence.

He lurched upright. There should be some sign of her – some noise, or the smell of coffee – if she was up and in the house?

He pulled on a T-shirt, then went downstairs.

'Claire!' he shouted. 'Claire!'

She was sitting on the sofa, cradling a mug of coffee, staring into nothingness.

'My God,' he said. 'I thought – I thought something had happened.'

She turned to look at him, her eyes focusing slowly.

'No. I couldn't sleep. That's all.'

'You should have woken me.'

She shook her head. 'It's OK. I wanted to be alone. To think.'

'I guess there's a lot to think about.'

'You know the thing I keep thinking?' Claire said. 'How *lucky* I am. Sounds odd, but it's the main thought in my head. I'm *lucky*.'

'Maybe you are, in a way. At least you escaped.'

'That's part of it, but not the main reason.' She beckoned him to join her on the sofa and took his hands in hers. 'The main reason is that it brought me back to you. I don't know what I was thinking when I went on that website, or when I had the other affair.'

Alfie frowned, and pulled his hands back.

'We don't have to talk about this now,' Claire said. 'I understand it must be hard for you to hear. But we'll have to, at some point.'

Alfie shook his head. 'It's OK. We can talk about it now.'

'I got lost, Alfie, in trying to have kids and not being able to. I don't know how, and I'm so, so sorry I did. It was a huge mistake. The guy at work, Bryant. But we can start again. Adoption, sperm donor. Maybe no kids at all. I don't care. As long as we have each other, I'll be fine. That's what I learned when I was being held captive, when I was sure I was going to end up dead or chained to a bed for men to use. I understood that what we have is special, and it's enough to make my life fulfilling and happy. You're all I need, Alfie. Now and forever.'

Alfie held her gaze, nodding slowly. Even now, he couldn't escape her. Maybe – thank God – he could avoid children, but he was stuck with Claire. He could hardly go through with his original plan to get rid of her, and it would be a long time before he could try another.

In the meantime, he would be trapped, and she'd be more dependent on him than ever before.

He could divorce her, of course. He had the perfect excuse. But he knew that Mick – whatever he said about admiring

Alfie – would make his life a misery. The admiration and gratitude would wear off in the time it took Claire to say *Alfie and I are breaking up, don't blame him, it's my fault* and Mick would make sure he got nothing. He'd take away the job he'd arranged, and Alfie would be left with no money and no skills. And he didn't want that. He liked his life, liked the house and car and holidays.

He just wanted to have them without Claire, and he'd thought he had a plan to get them. But that was gone now.

He squeezed her hands. 'Me too, darling,' he said. 'You're all I need, and you always have been.'

He was making some toast when his phone rang. It was DI Wynne.

'Good morning,' she said. 'How is everything?'

'As good as can be expected,' Alfie said. 'At least it's all over.'

'Yes. We have that to be grateful for. Could I speak to Mrs Daniels? I do have one request for her.'

Claire was taking a shower. Alfie didn't want to interrupt her.

'She's not available at the moment. Can I pass on a message?'

'Of course,' DI Wynne said. 'We have an identikit of Bryant and I would like to show it to her to see if it looks like him.'

'OK. Do you need to come to the house?'

'I can email it.'

'Fine.' Alfie changed the subject. 'Have you made any progress?'

'Not yet,' Wynne said. 'It's odd. We don't have any CCTV as of yet, and we can't find much evidence of Bryant. He has a passport – which he hasn't used – but we can't find much else on him. There's a possibility he doesn't exist at all. I'm starting to think that someone created him as a fake identity to hide behind. It's going to make it a lot harder, to be honest.'

Alfie was glad to hear it. 'That's not great,' he said.

'No, but I think your involvement with him is over, at least,' she said. 'I assume he'll want to keep well clear of you.'

'I hope so. But we'd still like to see him brought to justice. It would give us both peace of mind.'

'Yes,' DI Wynne said. 'It would for all of us.'

ii

Alfie had to get out of the house. Claire had moped from room to room all afternoon and he could no longer bear the sight of her. Fortunately she was asleep, again, and so he could escape.

He jotted a note – *Gone out to get milk. Back soon. Love you, A xxx* – and then walked out of the kitchen door to the gate at the end of the garden. He was wearing a baseball cap and sunglasses in case anyone recognized him. He didn't want to be disturbed. He wanted to *think*.

He was now convinced that whoever abducted Claire had been using other people's profiles as cover for what they were doing. It was simply coincidence that they had chosen Henry Bryant. At first it had seemed too big a coincidence, but the more he had thought about it the more he realized it wasn't. There were not that many people using websites to find illicit sex. Of the portion of the population who were interested in an affair, the majority would end up doing it – if they did it at all – with a colleague or with someone they met in a hotel bar on a lonely business trip. The number who were systematically seeking people out on websites was pretty small.

Then there was the fact that whoever it was would have to choose people of his own age, which reduced the possibilities yet further, as well as someone who did not show their face in their profile photo, which left hardly any possibilities. So it wasn't all that surprising he had landed on Henry Bryant.

The real surprise was that Claire had been using the websites, but even that had been cleared up. She'd been going through a tough time – by her standards – and it was simply more evidence that you never really knew someone, however much you thought you did.

But she was done with all that. She was newly committed to him. And he dreaded it. He had to get out of it, somehow.

He needed a new plan.

A new plan to kill her.

Because that was the only way to deal with this, once and for all. He'd learned that with Pippa. The problem was *how*. Push her off a cliff? Stage a burglary? Poison her? No – he'd be the obvious suspect and would be caught immediately. That was why Henry Bryant had been such a brilliant idea – it made it look like there was someone picking up women on the internet and killing them, and Claire was simply the latest. Plus, he, the luckless cuckolded husband, would get everyone's sympathy.

But his Bryant plan was gone, and he had no idea what else he could do.

Something would come to him, though. It always did, and when it came, he would be ready to exploit it. That was his great skill: he was a master opportunist. He recognized opportunities, and grabbed them, like he had done the day he first saw Claire.

He would find a way, in time. He would find a way because he wanted to, and Alfie got what he wanted.

It was good to be away from her. He was able to relax,

and think. He sat at a table outside a café and caught the eye of the waitress. She nodded – *Be there in a sec* – and turned to clear a table. He studied her. She was in her early twenties, athletic build, a plain white thong poking above the waist of her tight jeans. He'd remember her for later, and when Claire was gone he'd come back here and get chatting to her, smile his warmest smile, suggest maybe meeting for a drink.

He watched her and tried to work out her story. He decided she was single. Maybe recently broken up with her boyfriend. There was something in the way she looked at the male customers. An invitation of some sort. Obviously not well-off, or she wouldn't be doing this job, and she wouldn't be wearing clothes that were reaching the end of their useful life. But pleasant, well spoken. The kind of girl who wanted more. Who thought she *deserved* more, who would be surprised when a handsome, wealthy customer got chatting to her and asked her out, but not *so* surprised that she would be suspicious of his motives.

And then he'd fuck her a few times, each time rougher than before. Maybe he'd tie her up. Hurt her. He'd see how far he could push it. Cigarette burns on the soles of her feet? Razor cuts on her inner thighs? He thought he'd be able to push it quite a long way, especially if he told her he loved her, sprinkled some hope in with the misery. She'd let him, though, he could see that. She had the look. She was the type who liked to please, who thought that if they didn't then they'd lose their man.

Then he'd dump her. Tell her to fuck off back to her café and find some other peasant to marry. Watching her realize she'd let him do all that for nothing would be the best part of it all.

But all that was in the future. The future he could only have once he was rid of Claire.

The waitress walked over to him, order pad in her hand. As she reached the table, his phone rang.

It was Claire.

He turned it over so the screen was face down. She'd have woken up and panicked because he wasn't there, but she'd find the note. That would have to do. He didn't want to speak to her. It would destroy his peace of mind. He'd tell her he'd been paying for the milk and must have missed it.

'Coffee, please,' he said. 'Double espresso.' He smiled at her. 'Been that kind of day.'

'Me too,' she said.

'Nearly done?'

'I finish at five.'

'Then home to relax,' Alfie said. 'Put your feet up in front of the telly. You deserve it.'

This was the moment he could have said *Why not go for a drink with me?* She would have nodded, and said *Why not?* He could see in her eyes that she was almost expecting it, but he said nothing. He'd save that for later. For afterwards.

As she walked away, his phone rang, again.

He turned it over. It was Claire, of course it was. Stupid bitch. Why couldn't she leave him alone, for a few minutes? But he had to answer. He couldn't ignore her twice. She'd whine at him for the next week.

'Hi,' he said. 'What's up?'

'Where are you?' She sounded tense. More than tense. Frightened. He straightened in his seat.

'Getting milk. I left a note. Is everything OK?'

'How soon can you be back?'

'Ten minutes. What's going on?'

There was silence, at first. When she spoke, her voice was a terrified whimper.

'He's here,' she said. 'Henry Bryant. He's here.'

iii

Alfie put a ten-pound note on the table – it was the smallest denomination he had, which made this an expensive coffee not to drink – and started to run down the street. A black cab was approaching him, *For Hire* light on, and he stuck out his hand. The cab stopped and he climbed in and gave the address.

They turned into his street a few minutes later. He was perched on the edge of the seat, staring out of the window, his mouth dry. There was already a police car outside his house.

'Up there,' he said. 'By the cops.'

'Everything all right?' the taxi driver asked.

'I think so. My wife's home alone. She called and said she saw an intruder.'

'Bloody hell,' the taxi driver said. 'Country's a mess. At least the rozzers are here early.'

'Yes.' Alfie handed him another ten-pound note. 'Keep the change.'

Then he opened the door and stepped on to the pavement.

In the house, Claire was sitting at the kitchen table. There were two PCs in the room. One, a man, was standing by the kitchen door; the other, a woman, was sitting opposite her.

'Claire,' Alfie said, 'what happened?'

She looked at him, her cheeks stained with tears. 'He was here,' she said. 'He was *here*.'

'Where exactly?'

She pointed to the window. 'In the garden. I was filling the kettle and I saw him.'

'Where in the garden?' Alfie asked.

'Outside the window. Right there outside the window.' Her eyes were wide and there was a high-pitched, almost hysterical tone in her voice. 'He's coming for me. He's coming to take me away again.'

Alfie looked at the officer sitting opposite Claire. 'Did you see him?'

She shook her head. 'We arrived quite soon after your wife called. We were in the area – and this address has priority – but there was no one here by the time we showed up.'

Her colleague gestured at the garden. 'I had a walk around. It's empty. He must have left. Probably via the back gate.'

Claire was shaking. 'When I saw him, I screamed and ran out of the kitchen. I wanted to be as far from him as possible. I called you, then, when you didn't answer, I called the police. I made sure the front door was locked and then sat on the stairs.' She gave a thin smile 'I had one of your golf clubs in my hand.'

'You must have been terrified,' Alfie said. 'I'm so sorry. I should never have left you.'

'It's fine,' Claire said. 'You weren't to know.'

Alfie gestured at the back garden. 'Are there any signs of him out there?'

The male officer nodded. 'There are marks on the lawn leading to the back gate from the house – see, the grass is flattened—'

'That was me,' Alfie said. 'I went out that way this morning.'

'Oh.' The officer's face fell. 'Well, I didn't see anything else.'

'We'll talk to the neighbours,' the female officer said. 'Ask if they saw anything.' She shrugged. 'But there's not a lot more we can do.'

'OK,' Alfie said. 'Do you know Detective Inspector Wynne?'

'Yes, I do,' the female officer said.

'Good. She's been working on a case involving my wife. She can give you details. But I think she would want to hear about this. Would you mind informing her?'

'Oh, we're aware of the case. We informed DI Wynne as soon as the call came in from dispatch.'

DI Wynne and DS Lawless were at the house within an hour.

'So,' Wynne said, 'Henry Bryant was here?'

Claire nodded. 'At the kitchen window.'

'Did he say anything? Make any gesture?' DS Lawless said.

Claire shook her head. 'He just stared at me.'

'Was he there when you entered the kitchen?' DI Wynne asked.

'No. I would have seen. I was making coffee and when I went to the sink I noticed him. He must have been watching as I came in, and then moved to where I could see him. To shock me.'

DI Wynne nodded. 'And then you ran away?'

'Yes.'

'And when you came back he was gone?'

'I sat on the stairs. When the two police officers came he was gone. But I think he left right after I saw him.'

DI Wynne tapped her pen on her pad thoughtfully. 'And he didn't try to enter the house?'

'No,' Claire said. 'I heard nothing. I think he wanted to scare me. To show me he knows where I am.'

'That'll be it,' Alfie said. 'He wanted to scare Claire. He waited until I was gone. Which means he was watching us.'

'Why do you think that?' DS Lawless said, ignoring Alfie. 'Did he give any indication to that effect?'

'No,' Claire said. 'But that was the feeling I got.'

'Well,' DI Wynne said, 'it makes sense, in a way. It's still a big risk for him to take, though. I don't know what he gets out of it, other than alerting you to his presence.'

Claire looked at Alfie. 'My God,' she said. 'I don't believe this. He's back. He's coming for me!'

'I don't think we should draw any conclusions,' DI Wynne said. 'He may be thinking something else entirely.'

'Who knows what that kind of sick bastard thinks?' Alfie said. 'He's not like us. He's not *normal*.'

'No,' DI Wynne said. 'That he almost certainly isn't.'

'Did your officers talk to the neighbours?' Claire asked.

'They did,' DS Lawless replied. 'No one saw anything. A few weren't home, so maybe one of them will have something to report. DI Wynne and I will also talk to them. We'll see if there's anything more.'

'So what can we do?' Alfie said.

'I'm afraid,' DI Wynne said, 'there are not a lot of options, other than to keep looking for Henry Bryant, whoever he is.'

Alfie nodded. Who Henry Bryant was, was one question, but it wasn't what troubled Alfie the most. What he didn't understand was why Bryant was still around.

Was it Claire? Did he still have ideas of abducting her? Or was it something else, something Alfie could not even imagine?

He didn't know, but whatever it was, Bryant clearly had unfinished business.

Tuesday

i

Alfie put a slice of half-eaten toast on his plate and pushed it away. Claire was in the front room, sitting on the cushions in the bay window. It was her favourite place to read. He'd had the cushions made for their wedding anniversary.

He couldn't read; he could barely *eat*. He was too distracted. He kept turning things over in his mind, examining them from every angle, hoping something new would come up.

But nothing did.

He had been convinced someone had stolen Bryant's identity and then stumbled on Claire's profile. But why turn up at the house? It was madness. The risk of getting caught was too high.

Unless, Alfie thought, *he hadn't come to the house. Maybe Claire was imagining it.*

He picked up the toast and took a small bite. It tasted like ashes. She *could* be imagining it. He was no medical expert, but it seemed possible the trauma may have left her in shock, which could be manifesting in this way. The more he thought about it, the more likely it seemed.

Which left him with the original theory: someone had used Bryant's profile, abducted Claire, and was now out there looking for someone else to prey on.

Which, frankly, was none of Alfie's concern. He was simply glad the guy was off the scene.

He was interrupted by a loud crash.

It came from the front room.

Claire was sitting at the window, staring across the street. On the floor beside her was a teapot, brown liquid pooling around it.

'Claire?' Alfie said, breathless. 'What is it?'

'Bryant,' she replied. 'He's here.'

Alfie started. 'Where?'

'Outside.' She nodded towards the street. 'Right there.'

Alfie walked across the room and stood behind her.

And there he was.

Standing on the opposite side of the road, in dark jeans, white Adidas shoes and a maroon hoodie, his face obscured by the hood. He was wearing a backpack, and had a phone in his hand. He was Alfie's height, but thinner. It was hard to tell his age. At Alfie's appearance, he stiffened.

'The fucking bastard,' Alfie said. 'Call the cops, and wait here. I'm going after him.'

This was his chance to end this. He turned and ran out of the front room into the hall. The front door was dead-locked and it took him a few seconds to open it. When he did, Bryant was already at the end of the street, turning left towards the main road.

Alfie set off after him. As he turned left he caught a glimpse of Bryant – of something maroon, at any rate – running through the gates of the park. He was quick; the gap between him and Alfie was wider now.

Alfie slowed, then stopped. Chasing him was pointless. Bryant was faster, and once he was in the park there were any number of routes he could have taken.

He turned and headed back to the house, disappointed to have lost his quarry.

That, though, was not the worst thing.

The worst thing was that he now knew Bryant was not a figment of Claire's imagination.

Bryant was *real*.

ii

Mick sat on the sofa, a tumbler of whisky in his huge hands. DI Wynne and DS Lawless had gone, ready to circulate a description of Bryant.

'That bastard,' he muttered. 'He came here?'

Claire nodded. 'I can't believe it. I thought this was over, but he wants more. He won't leave me alone.' She blinked away her tears. 'The worst thing is how *personal* it feels. I mean, I know it was my own stupid fault for meeting him in the first place, but I thought I was just unlucky. Now I'm wondering if he was specifically targeting me all along.'

'How?' Mick said. 'How would he even know you?'

'I don't know,' Claire said. 'But the fact he came back after all this means there's something more that he wants. Something about me.'

Alfie listened. He too had a glass of whisky, but he didn't want it. He didn't want to eat or drink anything. He couldn't. He didn't know what Henry Bryant was up to, and it made him feel sick.

'He's twisted,' Mick said. 'That's all. You got away and he can't stand it. But he's making a bloody big mistake if he thinks he's going to get close to you again. Because if he keeps on sniffing about here I'll eventually get my hands on him, and after I've finished with him he's going to wish he'd been caught by the cops and locked up with all the other murderers and kiddie fiddlers. It'll be the safest place for him.'

'I hope so,' Alfie said. 'I hope that's what happens.'

'In the meantime,' Mick said, 'I've arranged for some security. They'll be here tomorrow. Two guards, twenty-four seven. You want them inside the house or parked in the street?'

Alfie didn't really want them at all, but he couldn't say that. He looked at Claire and raised his eyebrows. 'I'll leave it up to you,' he said.

'I think outside,' Claire said. 'I don't feel comfortable with the idea of having them in the house.'

'Fine,' Mick said. 'I'll pass that on. They'll have cell phones with them so all you have to do is call and they'll be inside immediately.' He looked at his watch. 'My bedtime,' he said. 'I'll head home. Call if you need anything at all, OK?' He held his arms out and hugged her. 'See you tomorrow, petal.'

Alfie and Claire went to bed not long after Mick left. Claire took a sleeping pill and was asleep soon after they pulled on the covers. Next to him, she breathed slow, shallow breaths. He watched her chest rise and fall. From time to time she started, but she slept well, considering the situation.

Not so for him. He couldn't relax, couldn't stop the whirring of his mind.

Bryant had shown up at the *house*. What the fuck was he thinking? If he wanted to meet women in secret so he could kidnap and kill them, that was one thing, but stalking one after she had escaped? It was insane. He was asking to get caught, and to what end? It would be far easier to move on to his next victim.

So, unless he was either stupid or mad, both of which Alfie doubted, he was targeting Claire. *Specifically* – to use her word – Claire.

But why? Alfie felt the panic rise again. He wasn't scared of Bryant; he wasn't scared of anything. He trusted that he would be able to deal with any situation, mainly because he would do whatever needed to be done without hesitation, like with Pippa. Most people were not able to do that, they were constrained by thoughts of morality or other bullshit, which gave him a huge advantage.

Plus, he knew what people wanted, most of the time: Pippa wanted a boyfriend, Claire wanted a husband and kids, Mick wanted to feel powerful and in charge, and if you gave them what they wanted they were happy. If you didn't, though, it could mess everything up, which was the problem with Claire; she was so obsessed with having a fucking baby she'd ruined their marriage. If only she'd accepted they were not going to be parents, he would not have been forced to try and get rid of her, and there would be no Henry Bryant. It was all, when you thought about it, her fault, like it was Pippa's fault he'd had to kill her. She'd got too needy, made herself a problem.

And Alfie knew how to solve his problems.

But not this one. The issue with this one was that he didn't know who Bryant was or what he wanted, and that left him unsettled and, in the quiet of the night, close to panic.

He needed Bryant to reveal himself. If he was after Claire, he could have her. That would help Alfie. If it was something else – well, Alfie would decide whether it was acceptable. If it was, good. If not – Bryant would have to go.

Either way, Alfie would have to put this to bed.

Early Wednesday Morning

i

Alfie became slowly aware that Claire was tapping him on the shoulder. He didn't remember falling asleep; he opened his eyes and, from the look of the window it was the middle of the night.

'Alfie,' she was saying. 'Alfie, wake up.' She was sitting up, looking at him, her face wan.

'What is it?' he said.

'He's here again,' she whispered. 'This time in the house.'

Alfie blinked. 'Are you sure?'

She nodded. 'I heard him downstairs.'

He listened. There were the creaks and clicks of a house at night, but nothing else.

'What did you hear?' Alfie said.

'A door closing. It sounded like the door of the front room. He's here,' Claire said. 'He's in the front room, hiding. Waiting for us. For me. He's in our house, Alfie.' She stared at him,

221

her eyes wide and her face flushed, almost feverish. 'We can catch him,' she whispered. 'There's two of us.'

'Don't you think we should call the police?' Alfie said.

She shook her head. 'He'll run away. Let's get him now. You have your golf clubs in the hall. We can take one each.'

'Claire, are you sure he's there? Sometimes you hear a noise in a dream and think it's real.'

'I wasn't asleep. I was lying here, wide awake, thinking about all this, and then I heard it. Soft footsteps downstairs and then a hinge squeaking as a door opened and a click as it shut. There's no doubt.'

He could hardly refuse, but then he didn't want to. If Bryant was here, this was his chance to put a stop to it. There'd be a melee of some sort. It would be dark, and distracting. If Alfie happened to hit Bryant a little too hard or a few too many times with a pitching wedge, then so be it.

Sorry, Officer. It was self-defence. I thought he had a gun. It was hard to see. I didn't mean to kill him.

Yes, Mick's lawyers would get him off, no problem.

OK,' Alfie said. 'Let's go.'

He crept across the bedroom and opened the door. He listened downstairs.

Nothing.

Taking Claire's hand, he walked slowly along the landing and halfway down the stairs. From there he could see the door to the front room.

It was closed. *Fully* closed. Wasn't it normally open, at least a crack? Hadn't it been when he passed it on his way to bed?

His heart sped up, and he stopped to listen once more.

Again, nothing.

The golf clubs were propped up inside the cupboard under the stairs. He descended the last few stairs and pulled one out, carefully and soundlessly, and handed it to Claire. He took another – a pitching wedge, as it happened – for himself, holding it halfway down so he could swing it more effectively.

He gestured to Claire to stand back from the living room door and gripped the handle.

Slowly, he began to turn it.

ii

With the curtain closed, the room was almost totally dark. As soon as the door was open, Alfie reached up to the left, the golf club poised in his right hand, and switched on the lights.

He stood in the doorway and scanned the room. It was empty.

'Bryant?' he said. 'Are you in here?'

There was no reply. Just the silence of the early hours of the morning. On the DVD player under the television the time blinked in green numbers:

02.33

Alfie turned to Claire. 'He's not here. There's nowhere in the room he could be hiding. I'll check the rest of the house, to be sure, but I think you may have heard something and thought it was Bryant. It's understandable. You're under a lot of strain.'

Which is maybe what happened with the man at the kitchen window, he thought. *But what about the guy in the street? Who knew what was happening there? That was the problem:* no one *knew.*

'I wasn't hearing things,' Claire said. Her voice was even.

'He was here, Alfie.' She stepped past him into the room and pulled back the curtains. 'Look.'

She pointed to the right side of the bay window. The sash was raised.

The window was wide open.

'That wasn't me,' Claire said. 'I didn't open it. I have no reason to.' She turned to face Alfie. 'Did you do it?'

Alfie looked at the window, then at Claire. He shook his head. 'No, I didn't.'

Claire gave a half-smile. 'Then it was him. He *was* here. Again.'

They sat in the kitchen, a pot of coffee on the table in front of them. They both knew that sleep would be impossible so there was no point going back to bed. They might as well start their day. It was going to be a long one.

Alfie sipped his drink. He caught Claire's glance. 'Tell me about him,' he said, softly. 'What's he like?' He was genuinely interested. Whoever it was had some style, and some balls.

Claire stared into her coffee. She thought for a long time, then turned to face Alfie.

'I don't really know. He was charming. Very relaxed – I was at ease with him immediately. But looking back he was kind of a blank slate. He never gave an opinion. Never talked about what football team he followed or films he liked or books he read. He laughed a lot. A warm, genuine laugh at whatever I said, which made me feel good – we all want to be funny – and which made me feel he was safe. I think I'd have been wary of someone who was very intense, or secretive. He was easy-going and open, but now I see there was nothing there. It was all an act, and I fell for it. Looking back, I think he was deliberately being the person he thought I wanted him to be.'

She looked away.

'But the truth is I was so focused on myself that I didn't really think about him,' she said, her voice barely audible. 'That's how I got into this mess in the first place.'

'What happened?' Alfie said. 'Why were you looking for another man? I thought you were happy with me?'

'I was!' Claire said. 'And I am. But all the problems we were having about getting pregnant made me think everything was falling apart. I needed an escape. And the guy at work—'

'Who was he?'

'One of the accountants, Rob. He's married. It was only a fling.'

'How many times did you – you know?'

'Twice. It wasn't very good – for either of us. We both knew we had too much to lose. Which was when I thought of the internet. I'd heard about people meeting up for no-strings-attached sex and it seemed a good idea.' She shook her head. 'I don't know why. It seems crazy now, but then? I was in a mess and I didn't know what to do.'

'I still can't believe it, Claire.'

'Me neither. It was stupid and irresponsible and I wish I'd never done it. But not because of what happened to me. Because of what I did to *you*. You deserve better, Alfie, and I'm so sorry. I don't know if you'll be able to forgive me, but I promise you – if you do, I'll never let you down again.'

She was pale, her eyes puffy and sunken in her face. She looked miserable.

Good. He hoped she never felt better, the stupid bitch.

'It's OK,' he said. 'I forgive you already. People make mistakes. Bad mistakes. You, me, everybody. And I understand why you felt so desperate. I felt the same. I want kids too.'

'But you didn't go and have sex with someone,' Claire said. 'You didn't screw the receptionist at work.'

'No. I went out and got drunk. I left you alone to deal with everything, when you needed me. And maybe I would

226

have done something else. Who knows? The point here, Claire, is that these things happen. A marriage lasts a lifetime, and there will be challenges – some big, like this one – and the main thing – the only thing – is how you deal with them.'

Claire started to speak, but Alfie raised a hand to stop her.

'Let me finish. What I want you to know is that all of this is no more than a challenge. Yes, you did something bad and hurtful. Yes, I'm upset. More than upset. But none of what happened changes the one key fact in all of this: I love you, Claire. And as long as that's true, the rest is irrelevant. So all I need to know is that you love me too.' He caught her eye. 'Do you?'

She had tears running down her cheeks.

'Yes,' she whispered, 'yes, I do. I don't deserve you, Alfie, but I love you more than I ever have.'

Alfie knew it was time to reassure her. He softened his expression and put a sweet smile on his face.

'Then we're going to be just fine,' he said.

iii

A few minutes before six a.m. Alfie poured a cup of coffee – his third – and sent DI Wynne a text message:

> Bryant was here in the night. Inside the house. He left when we interrupted him

She replied immediately. She was evidently not a late sleeper.

> OK. I'll call it in. Don't disturb anything. Will be there first thing

The doorbell rang an hour later. Alfie opened the front door, expecting to see Wynne and Lawless, but there were two men standing there. They were both in their late forties, with close-cropped hair and watchful expressions. They were dressed in dark blue uniforms, a silver tree logo on the left breast. It took Alfie a second to realize they were the security guards Mick had sent. They looked, to his untrained eye, like professionals, maybe former soldiers or cops.

'Mr Daniels?' one of them said. 'I'm Carl. This is Kevin.'

'Nice to meet you,' Alfie said. 'Thanks for coming. I'm Alfie.' He beckoned them inside. 'Come in.'

He led them to the living room. Claire stood up to greet them.

'Morning,' she said. 'Thank you for coming.'

'Pleasure,' Carl said. 'Glad to be here. I'm Carl. This is Kevin.' He kept his eyes on hers, but Alfie noticed them flickering lower as he gestured to his colleague. It reminded him that Claire was very beautiful, even when she was tired and dressed in a pair of old jeans and a hooded top. Maybe that was what was behind Bryant's perseverance. People did strange things when they thought they were in love.

'Tea?' Alfie asked.

Carl nodded. 'Thanks. Never turn down a brew. While you make it, we'll get started.'

'Of course,' Claire said. 'What do you need to do?'

'Take a look around the house,' Kevin said. He had a strong Liverpool accent. 'See where the entry and exit points are. Understand what we're dealing with.'

The doorbell rang. 'That'll be the cops,' Alfie said. 'I'll let them in.'

DI Wynne and DS Lawless were outside.

'Morning, Mr Daniels,' DI Wynne said. 'Is this too early?'

'No. We've been awake since two in the morning.'

'Was that when he was here?' Lawless said.

'Yes.' Alfie opened the door fully. 'Why don't you come in? Claire can explain what happened better than me.'

DI Wynne and DS Lawless followed him into the living room. Wynne raised an eyebrow when she saw the two men. 'Carl and Kevin,' Alfie introduced them. 'They're going to be providing some additional security.'

'Very good,' DI Wynne said. She smiled at the security guards. 'I'd like to talk to you, if I could. When we're finished here.'

'Of course,' Carl said. 'We'll have a little look around and then we'll be outside.'

'You'll need to wait to have a look around,' Lawless said. 'We've got some technicians coming to see if he left any traces. There could be fingerprints. Maybe other things.'

'No problem,' Carl replied. 'Let us know when you're ready.'

He and Kevin left the room. When they were gone, Alfie gestured at the sofa and DI Wynne sat down.

'So,' she said. 'What happened?'

'I couldn't sleep,' Claire said. 'And as I was lying in bed I heard footsteps downstairs, followed by the sound of the door to the front room closing. I woke Alfie and we came downstairs, but there was no one here.'

'The window was open, though,' Alfie said. 'It looks like he went out through it.'

'What kind of footsteps?' Wynne said. 'Loud, like hard-soled shoes, or soft, like trainers?'

'Soft,' Claire said. 'I knew it was footsteps because of the regular pattern.'

Wynne nodded. 'And the door closing? Was it the squeak of the hinges? Or the thud as it shut?'

'Neither. It was the click of the handle.'

'And when you came down, he was gone?' Lawless said. 'But the window was open?'

'Yes,' Alfie replied. 'He must have left that way.'

'Was any other window open? Or the back door?' Lawless said.

'No,' Alfie said. 'I checked.'

'Then I'm wondering how he got in,' Lawless said, glancing at DI Wynne.

Wynne pursed her lips. 'Maybe through the same window he left by,' she said. 'But that's not the mystery. The mystery is why he would do it at all. Why break in only to leave?'

'For the same reason he showed up at the window,' Alfie said. 'Because he's sick.'

'Or because he wants something,' Wynne said. 'What it is, I don't know.' She stood up. 'There'll be some SOCOs – Scene of Crime Officers – here soon. They'll look for prints. As soon as they're finished and we have their report, we'll be in touch. We'll also talk to the neighbours again to see if anyone saw him.'

She paused for a moment and then stood up. She looked at Claire, and then at Alfie. When she spoke she looked almost troubled.

'I'm glad you have those security guards,' she said. 'Be careful.'

Wednesday

i

Alfie woke up around midday. After the SOCOs had left, he and Claire had gone back to bed. It was much easier to sleep when the security guards were outside, although their presence didn't solve the rest of his problems.

He still had Bryant to worry about. Bryant, who didn't actually exist, but had become the secret identity for two people. First him, and now someone who was using it to stalk his wife.

And although there was no Henry Bryant, whoever was doing this was real. They had abducted Claire and they were still after her, despite the risks.

Which gave Alfie a problem. DI Wynne thought Claire was the second person Henry Bryant had abducted, and so she was looking for a serial criminal – probably a murderer – which was why she was so confused about why Bryant kept coming to the house. He had seen it on her face: why was he doing this? Why not move on to his next victim?

That was what he had done – so Wynne thought – after Pippa. Who was he and what motive could he have to return time and again?

There was something else going on here, and it didn't fit the pattern Wynne expected, and she was clearly bothered by it.

That was because there was no pattern. Claire was not his second victim at all, but Alfie could hardly tell Wynne that, because he would also have to tell her that he was the one who had killed Pippa Davies-Hunt. And so she would remain focused on the wrong question – who was Henry Bryant? – and not on the questions she needed to be asking. She would not be asking what was so special about *Claire*?

Which was the question Alfie kept asking himself. Unfortunately, he had no idea of the answer.

He made a sandwich for lunch and read the news on his phone. Claire and Pippa were still dominating the headlines:

Police are continuing their search for the man who abducted Claire Daniels last week. Mrs Daniels, who is married, went missing after meeting Henry Bryant on an internet site and arranging a series of illicit liaisons.

She was held captive before escaping and being found wandering in the New Forest. The police have asked anyone who witnessed anything unusual in the vicinity to come forward. They are particularly interested in any information related to a white van that may be connected to the case.

Detective Inspector Jane Wynne urged young women to exercise caution when arranging to meet people they know only from internet websites.

'There is a lot of risk attached to these kinds of situations,' she said. 'You don't know if the person is using their real name, and you don't know what their motivations are. I strongly suggest taking precautions, such as meeting in well-lit, busy places, or having a friend nearby.'

While well-meaning, this advice ignores the fact that many of these meetings are, by design, secret.

He heard Claire on the stairs and put down his phone. He doubted she wanted to be reminded of Henry Bryant.

'Hi,' she said. 'How are you? Did you sleep?'

'Yes. Woke up a while ago.'

'I slept like a log. I was exhausted.'

'I'm not surprised.'

'I feel much better with Carl and Kevin outside.' Claire kissed him on the forehead; he stroked the small of her back. 'If you want to go out for a walk, or a run, it's fine by me.'

Getting out sounded *great*, but he didn't want to seem too keen. 'I don't want to leave you,' he said.

'I'll be all right. We need to try and move on.'

'I guess,' Alfie said. 'Maybe I'll go to the office. Check in on a few things. You're sure you're OK?'

'Yes. I'm fine. You go.'

ii

Carl and Kevin were sitting in a grey van parked outside the house. Alfie tapped on the passenger side window.

'All right, mate,' Carl said. 'Everything OK?'

Alfie could sense the contempt the security guard had for him, could see in the mocking over-familiarity that he thought Alfie was a pathetic office-bound excuse of a man who couldn't protect his own home. Carl – and Kevin, no doubt – would have waited in the dark for Bryant and taken care of it themselves. He imagined them talking about him, laughing at his weakness.

Fine by him. It was what he wanted them to think. It was what he wanted *everyone* to think. He had realized years ago that being unthreatening and anonymous was the best disguise there was. It had kept him under the radar; no one thought him capable of any kind of bad behaviour, so he was never a suspect.

But they were wrong. Look at what he had done: he had created Henry Bryant, used him to get what he wanted, and, when the time came, he had killed Pippa with his bare hands.

He doubted Carl and Kevin could have done that, for all their masculine swagger. He doubted they would have driven

Pippa to the side of a wood and strangled her to death without a second's hesitation.

'Yes, all fine,' he said. 'I'm heading into the office for the afternoon. I wanted to let you know.'

Carl nodded. 'Got it, mate,' he said. 'We'll keep an eye on the place.'

He wound the window up and Alfie set off towards the Tube station. He knew what they'd be saying – he could almost hear the words – *Let's pop in there and give her one, now he's gone. Bet she's a good screw, rich birds always are.*

Like they knew anything about rich birds. This was the closest they'd get to the likes of Claire.

Perhaps he'd kill them at some point. Find out who they were and where they lived and set fire to their houses. Fire was a good way to do it; all the evidence got incinerated. The cops wouldn't suspect Alfie; he had no motive. After all, Carl and Kevin were taking care of him, so why would he wish them harm?

Because he wished *everyone* harm.

The thought surprised him, and for a second he resisted it, but then he realized it was true. He *did* wish everyone harm. If someone had an ambition he liked to see it thwarted; if they went on an expensive skiing holiday he hoped they'd break a leg on their first run; if they went to a job interview he pictured them having a brain freeze and making a fool of themselves. If he could be the instrument of their failure, all the better.

At the station he walked down to the platform and waited for a Tube to arrive. Once he'd boarded the train and it rocked into motion he smiled. Yes, killing Kevin and Carl was a nice thought. Something else to look forward to when Claire was gone.

Victoria looked up as he walked into the office. She smiled, her expression a mixture of surprise and delight at his unexpected

236

arrival. 'What are you doing here?' she said. 'Not that we're not glad to see you.'

'Thought I'd pop in,' Alfie said. 'Say hello.'

'How's Claire?'

'As good as can be expected. You all OK?'

'We're fine. Don't worry about us. It's funny you came in right this moment, though.'

'Why's that?'

'Because one minute ago I took a message for you which is quite important. I was going to email you.'

'What's it about?'

'A new instruction, in West Horsley. Nice listing. Seventeenth-century manor house on sixteen acres. Going for five million.' Victoria raised her eyebrows. 'A big one.'

Alfie did not feel like taking on a sale, however large. He needed to focus on Claire and Henry Bryant.

'Couldn't Mike or Denise handle it? Now's not a great time.'

'That's what I told the guy who called, but he said he'd heard a lot about you and he specifically wanted to work with you.'

'Oh?' Alfie was fairly sure he was not the type of estate agent who had that kind of a reputation. No one ever asked for him. He started to feel on edge. 'Who was it?'

Victoria looked at the paper in front of her. 'It was odd,' she said. 'He didn't give his surname. Only his Christian name. It's Henry.' She looked up at him. 'He said you'd know him?'

iii

Alfie blinked. He put a hand on the reception desk to steady himself.

'Are you OK, Alfie?' Victoria said. 'You look pale.'

'It's been a tough few days. Did he say anything else?'

'He asked me to tell you he'd be at the house tomorrow evening at seven, and he'd like you to meet him there, if possible.'

Alfie nodded. 'Did he leave a number?'

Victoria nodded. She passed him a piece of paper. 'He said you can try to call, but he's going to be at his place on the North Downs and might not have a signal.'

'OK,' Alfie said. 'I'll try him.'

'Are you going to be there? If he calls again?'

Alfie didn't reply for a few moments. 'I'm not sure,' he said. 'I need to check in with Claire.'

He had no intention of asking Claire; it would only make her even more worried, but he needed to buy some time before giving Victoria an answer.

'Do you know the guy?' Victoria said. She was leaning forward, intrigued. 'Is he a friend?'

'I wouldn't say a friend, exactly,' Alfie said. 'But I know him.'

* * *

He sat at his desk, staring at the phone number. After a long wait, he picked up his phone and tapped it in.

It was an automated response.

The number you have dialled is no longer in service.

Probably a no-contract phone, used once. Untraceable. Alfie's own trick. He took a deep breath, and typed in the address of the house.

It was not in any real estate database as being for sale, which wasn't surprising if it wasn't yet listed. Other than that, there was no information on it. He looked at it on Google Earth. It was a large manor house in its own grounds at the end of a long drive.

Remote. Quiet. A good place for a secret meeting, especially if you intended to do someone some harm.

He wasn't sure he was going to go, not yet. He needed to think through what this meant, why Bryant had contacted *him*. This was about Claire – Bryant had abducted her, not Alfie – so why did he want to meet Alfie at this house?

Maybe he wanted him out of the way. If he killed Alfie then he would have a clear run at Claire. Alfie shook his head. It was a risky strategy. He must have some connection to the house, and even if he didn't, how was he to know that Alfie wouldn't show up with someone? With the police, maybe?

It was the obvious thing to do, but Bryant knew he wouldn't, and there was only one way he could be confident about that.

He knew Alfie had created Henry Bryant in the first place, which meant he would also know he had killed Pippa. He knew Alfie couldn't bring anyone. Bryant would tell them what he had done.

He felt a chill run through him. Had he known about Alfie *before* he abducted Claire? Was it why he had abducted her? Or had he worked it out since?

Alfie didn't know, but then he was getting used to that. He didn't know much.

Apart from one thing.

He had to find out what Bryant wanted, and that meant going to the house.

It also meant preparing properly. Alfie walked to the front of the office. Victoria smiled at him.

'Leaving already?'

'I'm not feeling a hundred per cent,' he said. 'I probably won't be in for a few days.'

'I understand,' Victoria said. 'What do you want me to tell Henry, if he calls?'

'Tell him I'll go tomorrow evening. It's a big sale. And if he calls, please let me know.'

He left and headed in the direction of the Tube station, in case Victoria was watching. When he was out of her sight, he hailed a black cab and gave the driver the name of a pub in Harlesden.

The cab driver looked in the mirror and raised an eyebrow. 'What you going there for?' he said. 'You must be very thirsty.'

'Meeting a friend,' Alfie said. 'He lives near there.'

The pub was on the edge of a large estate. It was shabby-looking, the windows dark and uninviting. Alfie paid the driver, and walked in.

He was one of three customers. The other two were sitting alone at tables in opposite corners of the pub. One was smoking, despite the ban.

The landlord, a tall man in his fifties with tattoos on his neck and arms, was standing behind the bar, his arms folded. As Alfie approached, he did not unfold them.

Alfie sat at the bar. He looked straight at the landlord, and waited.

After a long pause the landlord spoke. 'You want a drink?'

Alfie shook his head.

The landlord narrowed his eyes. 'What do you want, then?'

'Something else. Something I understand you can help me with.'

The landlord's gaze was unblinking. 'I think you might be mistaken,' he said. 'I sell drinks here. And only drinks.'

'Then I have the wrong place,' Alfie reached into his pocket and took out a bundle of twenty-pound notes. He unfolded three hundred pounds on to the bar. 'Which is a shame. That's the first half. If you change your mind, let me know.'

The landlord glanced at the money. 'You a cop?'

Alfie shook his head.

'How do I know you're telling the truth?'

'You don't. But you know what a cop looks like. And it isn't me.'

The landlord scrutinized him in silence. 'Well, I don't know what you are, but you're not a cop.' He stared at Alfie and for a moment it seemed he would throw Alfie out, but then he gave a slight nod. 'What you going to do with it?'

'My business.'

'OK. Then what, exactly, do you want?'

Alfie told him.

He arrived home shortly after four. Claire was sitting on the sofa, under a blanket. She was watching a re-run of *Teletubbies*.

'Interesting choice,' Alfie said. 'Which one is your favourite?'

'Laa-Laa,' Claire said.

'Mine's Dipsy-Wipsy.'

'You mean Tinky Winky?' Claire said. 'Or Dipsy? There is no Dipsy-Wipsy.' She switched it off. 'It's mindless, which is what I want. I don't want to watch the news or some show about a detective solving a murder or one of those programmes where they bring people on stage to argue. You know – my mum shagged my boyfriend. That kind of thing.'

'I get it,' Alfie said. 'You watch whatever you want.'

'How was work?'

'OK. I couldn't really concentrate. I'm not going in for a few days, although there is one thing I need to do. A potential listing in West Horsley. The client wants to meet tomorrow evening at the house.'

'Are you going?'

He sat next to her on the sofa and stretched his arm around her shoulders.

'If it's OK with you. It's a big place. Could be a good commission. But if you'd prefer me to stay here then I will. No big deal.'

Claire nodded. 'You're so thoughtful,' she said. 'But I'll be OK. Go and do it.' She kissed him. 'I love you, Alfie. And we're going to be fine.'

Thursday

i

The next morning, Claire was up early. When Alfie came downstairs, she handed him a coffee.

'Do you want to go to breakfast somewhere?' she said. 'I feel like getting out of the house.'

'Sure,' Alfie said. 'I'm glad you feel up to it. I'll grab the keys.'

There were two new security guards in the van. Carl and Kevin must have been getting some rest. Alfie tapped on the window.

'We're going to Boundaries,' he said. 'For breakfast.'

The guard – a razor-faced young man with thinning hair and acne – nodded. 'You want us to come?'

'I think it's OK,' he said. 'There'll be plenty of people around.'

Alfie took Claire's hand and they walked down the street. The sun was already high in the sky and Claire turned her face towards it.

'I feel almost normal,' she said. 'Like this is over. Maybe he's given up, Alfie. Maybe he's seen the guards and realized he can't get to me, so he's moved on.'

Or maybe, Alfie thought, *he's turned his attention to me.* He nodded. 'I hope so. Then we can get on with our lives.'

They walked for a while in silence. When they reached the café, Alfie looked at her. 'Inside or outside?' he said.

'Out, I think. Enjoy the sunshine.'

They took a seat. The waitress came – the same one Alfie had spent a few minutes fantasizing about – and stood by the table.

'I'll have porridge with fruit,' Claire said. 'And a poached egg on toast. Are they free range?'

There was a flicker of contempt on the waitress's face. 'Yes,' she said. 'All our food is organic and free range.'

'Great!' Claire said. 'I'll have a cappuccino as well.'

Alfie folded the menu. 'I'll have the same. Thanks.'

When they had eaten their breakfast, Alfie ordered another round of coffees. He gestured to a newsagent a few shops up the road.

'I'll grab the paper,' he said. 'We can sit in the sun and read it.'

'OK,' Claire said. 'Sounds fun.'

Alfie got up and walked along the street. The bell on the door jangled as he pushed it open. He grabbed a copy of *The Times* and went to the counter.

'Twenty Embassy Number One as well,' he said. He thought he might need them when he was at the house in West Horsley. He handed over a twenty-pound note and waited for his change.

As he did he became aware that someone nearby was screaming. He looked at the newsagent.

'You hear that?' he said.

The newsagent nodded. He held out the change. 'Not my problem, mate. Probably just some troublemaker.'

'Yeah.' Alfie had a good idea who it was. He grabbed the change and ran to the door.

Claire was standing by the kerb, pointing up the road. The waitress was beside her, one hand on Claire's shoulder and a worried expression on her face.

'There he is!' she shouted, her voice high and ragged. 'There he is!'

Alfie followed her finger. He didn't see anyone. He ran to her, and put his hands on her shoulders.

'Claire,' he said. 'What is it? What happened?'

She was shaking, her eyes wide and unfocused. 'It was him,' she gasped. 'Again. He was here.'

'Where? Where was he?'

'In a car. He drove past.' She looked around, wildly. 'He was staring at me. And' – she choked on her words – 'he was holding up his phone, Alfie. He was *filming* me.'

'Where is he now?'

'He drove off. He's gone.'

'OK. We're going too.' He looked at the waitress. 'Did you see anything?'

She shook her head. 'No. I heard her – your wife – screaming, so I came outside.'

'And you didn't see a guy in a car, filming her?'

'No. I think he was gone by then.'

'Right.' Alfie took out his phone. 'Will you be here for a while?'

'Yes.'

'Good. The police will want to talk to you.' He dialled a number and put his phone to his ear.

DI Wynne answered immediately.

'It's Alfie Daniels. It's happened again.'

'What has?' DI Wynne said.

'Bryant. He was here. At a café where we were having breakfast.'

'I see,' DI Wynne said. 'Are you still there?'

'Yes, but we're going home. Claire's upset.'

'I understand, but I need you to stay where you are. I'll meet you at the café soon. Tell anyone who witnessed it to stay there too.'

ii

DI Wynne sat in the armchair opposite Alfie and Claire. Mick was in the other armchair. Claire's eyes were red from crying, and she was staring at her hands.

'I'll take up as little time as possible, Mrs Daniels,' she said. 'I think I got most of what I need at the café.'

Wynne had met them at the café, asked them to walk her through what had happened. When they were done they had come home while Wynne spoke to the waitress and some of the other customers. Then she'd arrived at the house with some more questions.

Claire nodded. 'It's OK,' she muttered. 'Take as much time as you like.'

'So,' DI Wynne said. 'Talk me through it again. You were sitting at the café when Henry Bryant drove past?'

'Yes. Alfie had gone to get the newspaper and I was looking in my bag for my phone. I got this strange feeling – like something was wrong – and when I looked up there was a car driving slowly past the café. He kept looking over at me, and, when he saw that I'd recognized him, he lifted up a phone and pointed it at me.'

'Horizontally or vertically?' DI Wynne asked.

'Does it matter?' Mick said.

'It helps me get a clear picture.'

'Horizontal,' Claire said. 'The phone was on its side.'

'And then what happened?'

'I jumped up and shouted at him. I wanted other people to see him. Maybe chase him down.'

'How did he react?' DI Wynne said.

'He sped up,' Claire said. 'There's a road up past the café and he turned into it. He disappeared.' She sat forward. 'What did the people at the café say? Did you talk to them?'

'I did,' DI Wynne said. 'And they recalled your jumping up and pointing at a car and shouting. Unfortunately, none of them saw the driver. And none saw him filming you. I think it all happened a little too quickly.'

Claire closed her eyes. 'He got away with it. Again.'

'Maybe,' DI Wynne said. 'But maybe there are details you can provide that will help. Did you recognize the car?'

'No. I don't think it was the one he drove me to the forest in.'

'Can you describe the one you saw today?'

'It was dark red. Maroon. Quite long.'

DI Wynne nodded. 'One of the witnesses said you pointed at a Ford Mondeo?'

'I guess,' Claire said. 'I don't really know one car from another.'

'Well, it gives us something to go on,' DI Wynne got to her feet. 'If you think of anything else, please give me a call.' She looked at Alfie. 'Could I have a word, Mr Daniels? We can do it on the way out. I'd like to get your impression of the events.'

Alfie followed her down the hall to the front door. She opened it and beckoned him outside, then closed it behind her.

'Mr Daniels,' she said. 'This could be a sensitive subject, so I'd like to keep it between us.'

'OK,' Alfie replied. 'That's fine.'

'Thank you. Mr Daniels, I think there is a possibility – only a possibility – Claire is imagining these things.'

'I don't think so. I saw him too, outside the house.'

'I know, Mr Daniels. But, apart from that one occasion, we have no evidence that any of the other things Mrs Daniels saw or heard actually happened. None of the witnesses today saw anything. And there were no fingerprints in the house after Bryant was here. Nor were there footprints or CCTV or any neighbours who recalled seeing him. There would normally be *something*, Mr Daniels. The truth of detective work is that it isn't based on brilliant flashes of intuition or complicated chains of deduction, but on CCTV and witness statements and the DNA people leave all over every place they ever go. And there's none of that in this case, which makes me wonder what is actually happening.'

There's plenty, Alfie thought. *There's a phone call and a meeting but I can't tell you that.*

'I don't think Claire is making things up,' Alfie said.

'Neither do I. I think she is totally sincere. But she has suffered a traumatic experience, and that can have profound effects. I wouldn't want to overstep any boundaries, but you may want to consider talking to her doctor later today.'

'What about the man outside in the street? I saw him too.'

'There may be some other explanation for that.'

'It seems unlikely.'

Wynne nodded. 'Unlikely, yes. But we can't rule it out.'

'So you think Claire's seeing things?'

'No. I'm saying it's a possibility.' DI Wynne clasped her hands together as though warming them. 'That's all. And I have to consider every possibility.'

'Fine. I'll mention it to her.'

'Thank you, Mr Daniels. And don't worry. We'll get to the bottom of this.'

*   *   *

Alfie sat next to Claire. He wrapped his arm around her shoulder and hugged her to him.

'Fucking bastard!' Mick said. 'Driving past like that! He must be watching.' He shook his head. 'From now on you don't go out without the security. OK?'

'Claire,' Alfie said, 'do you want to see the doctor? Maybe get something to help with the stress? I can call, if you like?'

He did not want to raise DI Wynne's question about whether she was hallucinating these events – mainly because he knew she wasn't; Bryant was real and he was meeting him later – but some medication to keep her calm might be worthwhile.

'I don't know,' she said. 'I think I'm OK.'

'Claire,' Mick said, 'you should do as he says.'

'Look,' Alfie said. 'Why don't I make the appointment and you can decide then? And I'll stay in tonight. I won't go to that house in West Horsley.'

'No!' Claire looked at him. 'I want you to go. I want things to be as normal as possible. Dad can stay with me.'

'Fine by me,' Mick said.

'OK,' Alfie said. 'I'll go. But only if you promise to see the doctor.'

He left shortly before five. He told Claire he needed to go to the office to grab something, but he headed for the pub in Harlesden.

It was much busier than the day before. The landlord was standing at the end of the bar, a half-pint of lager in his hand. He saw Alfie, and shook his head. He nodded to the back of the pub, then made a circular gesture.

Alfie understood it straight away.

Go around to the back.

He walked out and slipped down an alley that ran alongside

the pub. There was a gate at the back. It opened and the landlord stepped out.

He was holding a green Adidas sports bag. He held out his hand. 'The rest of the cash.'

Alfie took another three hundred pounds from his pocket. He gestured at the bag. 'Let me see.'

The landlord unzipped it and Alfie looked inside. What he wanted was there. He nodded and handed over the cash, then he swung the bag over his shoulder and walked back to the main street, looking like a man headed to his evening five-a-side football game.

He was anything but.

iii

The train to West Horsley was busy. He sat by the window, next to a man and his two kids. The kids, Lily and Johnny, were excited; they'd been to the Natural History Museum. They had no idea what the man opposite them had in the green Adidas bag on his lap. Alfie sat and listened to them and thought how this was exactly what Claire wanted *their* lives to be: him, coming home from some daddy time with the kids to a nice family meal.

It was not what he wanted. Not at all.

He had never been to West Horsley, but he had looked at and remembered the route from the station to the house. He got off the train and turned right on to the main road, the green Adidas bag over his shoulder.

He looked at his watch. It was six thirty-three. Good. He wanted to be early so he could have a good look at the house.

Alfie walked slowly past the house, Roseland Hall, and took it in. There was a wooden gate, covered in a thin film of mould, behind which a long gravel drive led to a large, two-storey garage. It looked like it had once been a stable and had been converted. To the left was the house itself, an L-shaped manor built of some kind of local stone. There were no cars – at least, none that were visible – and he could not see any signs of activity, although a high hedge obscured his view.

He carried on past the gate, the green Adidas bag over his shoulder. After a while, he turned on to a road. There was a bus shelter, and he sat down and waited.

He pulled his cap down low over his face, eyes fixed on the ground. At ten past seven he stood up, studied the bus timetable and shook his head, as though frustrated. If anyone was watching they'd think he was an angry passenger whose bus had not arrived. He retraced his path to the mouldy gate and put his hand on the latch.

It clicked and the gate swung open. Alfie stepped on to the gravel and walked slowly up the path. His heart was thudding and his hands were clenched with apprehension. He glanced left and right, listening for any sounds.

As he approached the house, he stopped. His scalp prickled. He was sure he was being watched. He looked at each of the windows, searching for a shadow that shouldn't be there or the flash of movement.

Nothing.

He realized he was very vulnerable. He had nowhere to hide; anyone in the house could see exactly what he was doing. Presumably that was exactly what Bryant wanted. Well, it was time to even things up. Alfie was going to start playing this on his own terms.

He pivoted to the right and walked quickly towards the garage. He headed to the far side, then walked behind it so he was hidden from view.

He put down the bag and unzipped it, then took out the sawn-off shotgun he had bought in the Harlesden pub. There was a packet of cartridges and he loaded two into the gun.

It was not the most sophisticated weapon, but it was hard to miss with a shotgun, especially at short range.

He swung the bag over his shoulder, and hefted the gun in his hand. It felt good, reassuring. He smiled. He was on equal terms with Bryant again.

He walked to the back corner of the garage and dropped to the floor. He took his phone from his pocket and slid the camera out, angling the lens slightly upwards. He took a series of photos, then brought the phone in and looked at the screen.

The house still looked deserted, but he had expected that. What he wanted was a look at the rear of the house so he could figure out how to approach it.

He studied the photo. There was a conservatory on the end of the house closest to the garage with a set of double doors opening on to a terrace.

And one of them was open.

Alfie hesitated. Was it a trap? Had Bryant – because he was sure now that Bryant was here – seen him run around the back of the garage and left this door open so he would come in that way? Was he waiting there, focused on the open door, for Alfie to appear?

It seemed likely.

Well, maybe I'll give him a surprise.

He turned around and headed back to the front of the garage. He was moving quickly – if he was right, and Bryant was at the rear of the house, then he had a short window to find another way to get in, and then he'd be in control. He'd know where Bryant was, and he could hunt him down.

He felt focused, and engaged. This was *fun*.

He sprinted across the driveway, then scanned the front of the house. At the far end, past the main door, a window jutted open. That was it. The way in. He ran harder, holding the shotgun out in front of him.

The silence was interrupted by a shout.

'Hey!' It came from above him. 'What the bloody hell do you think you're doing?'

Alfie looked up. A man in his late sixties was leaning out of an upstairs window. He had white hair and a red face, his eyes bulging behind thick glasses.

'Are you,' Alfie said. 'Are you Henry—'

'Never mind who I am. Who the hell are you?' The man fell quiet as he saw the sawn-off shotgun in Alfie's hand. 'My God. Is that a gun?'

'No!' Alfie said. 'I mean, yes, but it's not what you think.' He opened the green Adidas bag and shoved the gun inside. 'It's a long story. Forget it, OK? I'm sorry. I'm an estate agent,' he said. 'And I had an appointment here. I heard the owner wanted to sell?'

There was, he supposed, a small chance that this guy had contacted the agency asking for Alfie. Perhaps Henry was his name?

'No,' the man said. 'I'm not. And I'm not selling. I don't care what you offer – I've turned down the others and I'll turn you down too. So bugger off. I'm calling the police unless you're off my property in the next sixty seconds!'

Alfie didn't think he'd need sixty seconds. He turned, and ran.

'How was it?'

Claire was sipping a glass of wine when he walked into the living room. Her dad was deep into the whisky.

'Get the listing?' Mick said, his words slurring into each other.

Alfie shook his head. 'I don't think they're ready to sell. But I'll keep in touch with them.'

'What was the house like?' Claire asked.

Alfie had no idea; he'd only seen it from the outside. 'Fantastic. Part of it was built in the 1600s.'

'We should move to somewhere like that. It'd be safer.'

'I don't know,' Alfie said. 'It's a bit isolated.'

'But you would see anyone coming.'

'True.'

'I'm serious,' Claire said. 'Somewhere like that would be perfect for a family. If they *do* decide to sell, would you consider it?'

Alfie nodded. 'Of course.'

It was easy to agree, since he knew it wasn't coming on the market. The owner had made that clear. He'd obviously had other, unwelcome, offers, which was good for Alfie, as he'd thought his sudden appearance was more of the same. It might be enough to stop him calling the police. Alfie wasn't sure how he would explain it if it wasn't.

Which was clearly what Bryant had wanted. He had known the house was occupied and he had set Alfie up. That much he knew. But Alfie could not, for the life of him, think why.

Friday

i

In the morning, Claire brought him a mug of coffee in bed. He glanced at the alarm clock. It was almost nine.

'Hey,' she said. 'You slept well.'

He hadn't. He'd managed to finally go to sleep sometime around two, and then slept fitfully for a couple of hours. Eventually, around five, he'd finally fallen into a deep sleep.

'Yeah,' he said. Claire didn't need to know the truth. 'I guess I was tired.'

'I was thinking,' she said. 'I want to get out of the house.'

'We did that yesterday. It didn't go too well.'

'I know. But we can go with the security guards. They can drive us, drop us off, and pick us up.'

'I don't know. It seems risky.'

Claire lifted her hands, palms upright, in a gesture of exasperation. 'I know, but we can't stay in the house all day long! I feel so trapped. It's really starting to get to me.'

'It won't be forever.'

'No. But it could be days. Weeks. Months, even. I can't take it. I need my life back.'

Alfie sipped the coffee. 'OK. You have something particular in mind?'

Claire nodded. 'The theatre. Let's go and see a play.'

The *fucking* theatre. Of course. Alfie hated it. From time to time Claire decided she wanted to go and experience some high culture; every so often she dragged him to an art gallery or took him up to Stratford to watch some interminable and unintelligible Shakespeare play or paid some ridiculous amount to go and see the opera, which, as far as Alfie was concerned, was by far the worst. A bunch of people wailing in a foreign language for a couple of hours to an audience who had no idea what they were watching but were pretending to like it.

It was typical of people like her; they thought they were cultured, in some way, because they were theatre- or opera- or gallery-goers, thought they were improving themselves, when all they were doing was consuming something expensive that was wasted on them. It was like fine wine: the vast majority of people who bought it were incapable of appreciating it, especially after one or two or three bottles.

But that wasn't the point. It was a status symbol, like the latest biography of Churchill or literary novel or subscription to the *London Review of Books* that sat unread on the shelves.

And he fucking *hated* it.

'Are you sure?' he said.

'I'd like to,' Claire replied. 'If you're interested?'

'It's up to you,' Alfie said. 'You know I love the theatre – almost as much as the opera – so I'll go anytime, but it's your call.'

'Then let's do it.'

Alfie put on his best smile. 'Should I buy the tickets? Do you have a play in mind?'

'No need,' Claire laughed. 'I already got them.'

Of course she had. Of *fucking* course she had. Because Alfie was always going to give her whatever she wanted.

What *he* wanted was to scream.

ii

They were getting ready to leave when the doorbell rang. It was DI Wynne. She had a distant, strained look on her face.

'I'd like to talk through everything that happened again,' she said. 'From the very beginning.'

'I'm happy to,' Claire said. 'But I think I told you all there is to tell.'

The detective nodded. 'I'm sure you did, but I might have missed something. A small detail that could be important. Is this a bad time?'

Claire passed her a cup of tea.

'We need to leave soon,' she said. 'Twenty minutes. We're going to the theatre.'

Alfie was hoping the cop would say it was going to take much longer, but she smiled and nodded.

'That should be plenty,' Wynne replied. 'The thing is, we're at a bit of a dead end. We can't find any trace of Henry Bryant, or of Ms Davies-Hunt. She seems to have disappeared completely, and him – it's as though he doesn't exist.'

'Well he does,' Alfie said. 'He's been here.'

'We think it might be a fake identity,' Wynne said. 'We

think someone created it and got a passport and a bank account. The passport is unused and the bank account has been abandoned. There've been no transactions for a couple of weeks. He seems to have made some money selling things on eBay, but that's stopped.'

'What was he selling?' Alfie asked.

'All kinds of things. Some quite valuable. We're trying to trace where they came from. If he bought them in person, maybe we can get a description of him.'

'How is it possible?' Claire said. 'How can someone just create an identity?'

'It's surprisingly easy,' DI Wynne said. 'If you want to, you can buy a passport – which has the added advantage that there's no record of it at the Passport Office, and it comes with no photo so you can insert your own and travel freely – and all you need to open a bank account is an address. Bryant used the address of a flat in Birmingham – which is unoccupied now but which was rented for six months until quite recently. My guess is Bryant rented it purely to get the account open. The landlord never met him – they corresponded via email and Bryant sent the rent in advance, in cash.'

'I don't know why he bothered to do all that,' Claire said. 'If all he wanted was to meet people online he could have created a fake email account and stopped at that. It would have been a lot easier.'

'I think,' DI Wynne said, 'the bank account allowed him to hide that bit better. It certainly makes it harder to get to the man behind it.'

Which was exactly why he'd done it, Alfie thought. *The cops had the right idea. Unfortunately for them, they had no chance of figuring it out.*

'So,' Wynne said. 'That's why I'm here. I want every detail. Because right now we have nothing else.'

'OK,' Claire said. 'I'll do my best.' She turned to Alfie. 'You don't have to stay for this, if you don't want to.'

'I'm staying,' Alfie said, and got ready to listen to it all again.

Maybe this time there'd be a clue to what was going on.

iii

It was as bad as Alfie had feared. Some ridiculous play about a medieval queen waking up to find herself living in twenty-first-century London and discovering, to her horror, that she had no servants and no one knew who she was.

After some light comedy – her claims to be a medieval queen only made her seem deluded – she set out reluctantly to find food, accommodation and a job, but ended up on the street, revealing in the process how cruel and selfish our modern world is.

At the interval, Claire stared at the stage and shook her head in disbelief. 'This is amazing,' she said. 'It makes you think about how we treat people who we think are mad. I mean, she comes across as crazy because she claims to be a medieval queen, but she *is* a medieval queen.'

'So she thinks,' Alfie said. 'Maybe she's just mad.'

'That's the point! Even if she isn't a medieval queen, she thinks she is, and treating her like she's crazy makes her life a misery.'

'So we should treat her like she *is* a queen? I'm not sure the NHS is funded for that.'

'Alfie!' Claire said. 'You're missing the point! It's an allegory. It's not about NHS funding.'

It might have been more interesting if it was, Alfie thought.

'I know,' he said. He looked at the programme they'd bought on the way in. 'It's a twenty-minute interval. Should we get a drink?'

Claire nodded. 'Good idea.'

Alfie stood up and put the programme on the chair. The lead actor, the woman playing the queen, was on the front. She was very pretty. When this was over he'd maybe try to get in touch with her. Perhaps create an identity as a theatre-going human rights lawyer. Then he could kill her. It would create quite a storm, and it would pay her back for putting him through this drivel.

But that would have to wait.

'OK,' he said. 'Let's go.'

They managed to get a glass of white wine with about four minutes to spare before the curtain came up again. Claire glanced at her watch.

'We'll have to be quick,' she said. 'It's starting.'

Alfie didn't care if they sat there all night drinking, but he nodded.

'Don't want to miss anything,' he said.

A bell rang and a voice came over the tannoy suggesting they make their way back to the theatre for the second half.

'Here.' Alfie was wearing a linen jacket. 'Pass me your glass. I'll sneak them in.'

Claire gave him her wine, and he shrugged off his jacket. He held both glasses in one hand and draped his jacket over them.

They followed the rest of the audience. When they reached

their seats – near the front, of course – Alfie ushered Claire into the row. He bent down to pick up the programme and sat next to her.

As he did, a piece of paper fluttered to the floor.

It landed by his shoe. He looked at it. It was torn from a notebook, which meant it had not been in the programme when they bought it.

It had not been in the programme when he left it there at the intermission.

He glanced at Claire. She was looking at her phone, getting ready to switch it off. He handed his jacket and the glasses of wine to her.

'Could you hold these for a second,' he said. 'I have to tie my shoe.' He bent over, concealing the paper from her, and put his hands on his shoe as though tying the laces. He flipped over the paper.

There was a short, hand-written message, all in capitals.

ALFIE, MY GOOD FRIEND,
    ENJOYING THE PLAY? I AM. WAS HOPING TO BUMP INTO YOU, BUT THE NOTE'LL HAVE TO DO. I WANTED TO GIVE YOU A MESSAGE, JUST SO THINGS ARE CLEAR BETWEEN US: I KNOW WHAT YOU DID.
    YOURS, H

Alfie scrunched it into a ball and sat heavily on his chair. He put his hand into his pocket, both to hide the paper and to hide his shaking.

'Is everything OK?' Claire said.

'Fine,' Alfie replied. 'I stumbled. Everything's fine.'

Everything was *far* from fine.

As the play went on he grew increasingly desperate to pull the note out and read it again, parse it for any detail that might reveal something about its author. He tried to remember exactly what it had said.

ALFIE, MY FRIEND. ENJOYING THE PLAY?

Then what?

SORRY I MISSED YOU. I WANTED TO TELL YOU SOMETHING.

And then the part he remembered most clearly.

I KNOW WHAT YOU DID.

So it was indisputable now. Whatever the note said – and whatever a closer examination revealed – Alfie now knew two things at least.

One, Bryant knew about him, and that made him dangerous.

Two, Bryant was *real*. He was not a figment of Claire's damaged imagination.

And he was here.

He looked around the theatre, searching for a lone man. All he saw were faces trained on the stage, the occasional hand covering a cough or scratching an ear or picking a nose.

He had to read it again. He tapped Claire on the elbow. She turned to him, and he mouthed a word.

Loo. He shrugged. *Sorry.*

She frowned as he got up and walked along the aisle. In the bathroom he went into one of the cubicles and locked the door behind him. He pulled the note from his pocket and smoothed it out.

ALFIE, MY GOOD FRIEND,

ENJOYING THE PLAY? I AM. WAS HOPING TO BUMP INTO YOU, BUT THE NOTE'LL HAVE TO DO. I WANTED TO GIVE YOU A MESSAGE, JUST SO THINGS ARE CLEAR BETWEEN US: I KNOW WHAT YOU DID.

YOURS, H

It was written in blocky capitals. He thought there was something masculine about them, but that meant nothing. He wasn't sure there was such a thing as 'masculine' writing and, in any case, even if there was, it would have been easy for a woman to write in that way.

The note told him a few things, though: it told him someone was here, in the theatre, they knew he'd killed – or tried to kill – Pippa, and they were intent on messing with him. The playful tone – *Alfie, my good friend* – gave that away.

But beyond that, it didn't help him at all. Maybe there were fingerprints on it, or some DNA, or some clues a graphologist could unravel, but so what? He could hardly take it to DI Wynne.

What did *you do, Mr Daniels? What is the author of the note referring to? And why do you think they put it into your programme?*

And then he saw why they'd planted the note. They'd done it knowing he would want to read it in detail, and would go to the bathroom to get some privacy.

Leaving Claire alone.

Shit. He shoved the piece of paper into his pocket and unlocked the cubicle door. He ran out of the bathroom and along the carpeted corridor that led to the seats. The usher on the door motioned for him to slow down and held out his hand for the ticket. Alfie shoved it at him, then walked into the theatre.

He looked down the aisle, expecting Claire's and his seats to be empty, or – worse – for both to be occupied. The man in the hooded top, maybe, about to call DI Wynne and DS Lawless. Would the audience think his arrest was part of the play? Some meta-fictional game the author was playing on them?

But his seat was empty, and Claire was safely in hers, attention focused on the medieval queen, who was scrabbling in a dustbin on stage, feeling, he thought, about as disorientated and out of place as he did.

iv

Alfie was sitting in the kitchen, a ready-made spaghetti bolognese he'd heated up on the table in front of him. Opposite him, Claire was on the phone to Jodie.

'No,' she said. 'I'd love to, but I can't. Not yet.'

Alfie strained to hear what Jodie was saying, but her voice was too faint.

'Sorry, Jo. I really am. But thanks. I have to go. Alfie's waiting for me.'

She hung up.

'Everything OK?' Alfie said.

'Yes. Except Jodie's going out on a hen do – Heather, from school – and I can't go. I can't go *anywhere*.'

'It'll pass.'

'Will it?' Claire was pale and looked exhausted. 'The police have no idea what to do next. I'd always assumed they had all kinds of ways of finding people – I mean, you hear about the surveillance state, and how the government can listen to any phone call and read any email, but it turns out all you need to do is change your name and you disappear. It's crazy. I'm so sick of it.'

'I know,' Alfie replied. 'And in the meantime, we're trapped.

Henry Bryant is out there somewhere and we can't relax for a moment.' He shook his head. 'It has to end, but I don't see how. We can't find him.'

'I hate this,' Claire said. 'We have no control. All we're doing is waiting to see what he does.' She folded her arms. 'You know, I have fantasies of him showing up at the house during the night. We hear him and wake up and, when he comes upstairs, we're waiting for him. We grab him and pin him down and then call the cops.'

Alfie had the same thoughts, but he kept them to himself.

'But that'll never happen,' Claire said. 'Not while we're here and there are two security guards outside.'

'They're keeping us safe,' Alfie said.

'Safe in the house. But the rest of the world is a no-go area. He's winning. That's what bothers me.' She rubbed her eyes. 'And the other thing that bothers me is, even if weeks and months go by and there's no sign of him, I'll know there's always a chance of him coming back. I'll never be able to relax.'

'I know.' Alfie really meant it. He couldn't tell Claire why, but he had the exact same feeling.

'We need to get control somehow. I wish there was a way.'

'I don't see it,' Alfie said.

'If we could entice him into a trap,' Claire said. 'That would be perfect.'

'I don't know. It seems risky.' A trap sounded *perfect*, but Alfie didn't want to appear too enthusiastic, plus he had no clear idea how a trap would work. If this was going to amount to anything, it had to come from Claire.

'Imagine,' Claire said. 'We could get rid of the guards for a night, and then you go out, but you stay close. Or sneak in the back door. If Bryant *is* watching – and I think he is, I can feel it – then he'll come. But we'll be expecting him. We'll be in control.'

'No way,' Alfie said. 'What if something happened? I'd never forgive myself.'

'You'd prefer to live like this?'

Alfie let the question hang between them. He needed to appear reluctant. 'Look,' he said, finally. 'I understand. But I think it's a bit reckless. OK?'

Claire twirled the pasta on to her fork, watching it wrap around the tines as though she was deep in thought, then her shoulders slumped.

'You're right. But I feel like we're giving up.' She poured some more wine into her glass. 'I guess we have no choice.'

Maybe they didn't. Not now, at any rate.

But Alfie was starting to get the beginning of an idea.

V

After dinner, they sat on the sofa. Claire rested her head on his shoulder, the rest of the bottle of wine on the coffee table.

'You know,' Alfie said, 'it would be great if we could do something to Bryant. I know revenge is not the best motive, but I would *love* to get my hands on him.'

'I would like it if you did, too.'

'The problem is, it's too risky. We need some kind of safety net. A trap, but with no risk to us. To *you*. Imagine if it wasn't only us, but Carl and Kevin too.'

'He wouldn't come,' Claire said. 'Not with them there.'

'Unless he thought they were gone.'

'What, we get them to pretend to leave the house? I don't think he'd fall for that.'

'I know.' Alfie reached for the wine glasses. He handed Claire's to her. 'I'm only dreaming.'

She sipped her wine. 'Unless we weren't here.'

Alfie tilted his head. 'What do you mean?'

'We go away. It'll look like the most natural thing in the world for us to do after what's been going on.'

'Where?'

'Our place in the Lake District. Cartmel. It's been years since I've gone there, but I used to love it.'

She'd mentioned the summers she'd spent there as a teen-ager a few times. Alfie had assumed Mick had sold the place since they no longer went, but it seemed he hadn't bothered. He supposed that was how the other half lived.

'What happens when we're there?'

'I don't know. Maybe one day you go out hiking and leave me alone. Except I won't be alone, we'll take Carl and Kevin and hide them somewhere, and when he shows up . . . ' She clapped her hands together, a trap shutting.

'So I won't have gone hiking?'

'You'll be nearby. And Carl and Kevin will be there.' She took another sip. 'There's a bed and breakfast opposite the cottage. They can stay there. When he shows up, they'll be at the cottage in seconds.'

Alfie frowned. 'It seems very risky. What if they don't see him come in? If they're at the front, he could come in the back?'

'We'll figure it out,' Claire said. 'I'll stay in a room they can see – maybe an upstairs bedroom – and we'll agree a signal. If he comes in the house I'll open a specific window and they'll know he's there.'

'What about your dad? He'll never let you do this.'

'We won't tell him. We'll just say we're going away for a break. And we won't tell Carl and Kevin the plan either. They'll tell dad. We'll let them know when we're there.'

Alfie nodded slowly. This could work. If Bryant – whoever he was – knew they were there, and thought they were alone, he might show up.

And when he did, Alfie had his own plan. Because there was no way he could let Claire or Carl or Kevin get hold of Bryant. If they did, he would tell them about Alfie.

And that couldn't happen.

273

Bryant needed to be killed.

So Alfie had his own plan. And he was ready to agree to Claire's.

'OK,' he said. 'But on one condition. I'm *very* nearby, and as soon as he shows up, Carl lets me know. I want to be there.'

And then he'd find a way to get a moment alone with Bryant, and – in self-defence, obviously – he'd take care of this once and for all.

Saturday

i

Alfie folded a shirt into his suitcase. According to Claire, there was a restaurant with a Michelin star in the village that she wanted to get a table at. While they were there, she said, they might as well eat good food. They were planning to stay a week so they'd have plenty of opportunities to eat there, although Alfie wasn't sure they'd last that long, if everything went to plan.

It was all on Facebook, excited posts about their trip to Claire's old stomping ground. Anyone who wanted to know where they were going would have no trouble finding out.

Bryant included.

The bedroom door opened and Claire came in.

'Ready?' she said. 'We need to leave soon. The train's in forty minutes.'

They were going by train to Oxenholme and then by taxi to Cartmel. Carl and Kevin would drop them off at the station, and then drive to the cottage. They didn't want them on the train – Bryant needed to think they were going without security, but they told Carl and Kevin it was because they wanted a car when they got there. They were reluctant, but Alfie convinced them no harm could come to them on the train, and they agreed. The two guards were booked into a B & B opposite the cottage. The owners may think it was odd that they stayed in their room all day, but no matter. They weren't doing anything wrong, and hopefully they wouldn't be there long.

'I'll be down in five,' Alfie said. 'We should be OK for time.'

He closed his suitcase and zipped it up. He looked around the bedroom and smiled. The next time he saw this room everything would be back on track.

They arrived at the cottage in the early afternoon. On the few occasions she had talked about her Lakeland summers in Cartmel – the races, the sticky toffee pudding – Alfie hadn't paid much attention. He was more interested in holidays in the South of France. He had married her – and put up with her – for sunshine and glamour, not for rainy days in the north.

He had to admit, though, that in the afternoon sunshine – and today there was only endless blue sky – Cartmel was exceptionally pretty. Streams shushed their way through the village, running alongside houses and pubs and churches that were hundreds of years old, all in the shadow of the low fells of the Southern Lake District.

The taxi pulled up at a large, white-walled cottage on a quiet road not far from the village centre. Opposite was the B & B; behind was an open field, divided by stone walls that ran up the slopes of the steep hills marking the end of the farmland.

'Here you are.' The taxi driver looked at the dashboard then consulted a mileage chart. 'Forty-three quid.'

Claire handed him two twenties and a ten. He started to look for change but she shook her head. 'It's OK,' she said. 'Thanks for the ride.'

The taxi driver nodded. 'Thanks.' He took a piece of paper from the passenger seat and started writing. 'You here long? Let me give you my number. If you need a ride anywhere, give me a call. My name's Stu.'

'Will do.' Claire took the paper. 'Thanks again.'

They took their bags from the boot and walked up a path to the front door. It was made of dark wood, and opened slowly. The walls of the cottage were thick – maybe four feet – and made of a rough stone, which was probably why there were not many windows.

It was cold and dark and smelled damp. It was not an inviting place, although Claire clearly felt differently.

She grinned and flopped on to an ancient sofa. 'God,' she said, 'it's amazing to be back. I spent a lot of time here as a kid. We used to come every summer, until I was fourteen or so. Mum *loved* it. Looking back, I think she found peace here. I remember her and Dad laughing in the kitchen as they made dinner. We stopped coming after she died. There were too many memories for Dad. Still, it's funny how you can be away from somewhere for years but feel immediately at home.'

Alfie sat next to her. 'I'm glad you're happy,' he said. 'You deserve it.' He put his hand on her calf, and slid it up to her inner thigh. 'If you were that age when you used to come here, then this'll be the first time you've got up to *this* kind of thing here.'

She tensed, and her leg flinched away.

'Alfie,' she said, 'I want to, but I'm still not ready. I'm sorry. I need a bit more time.'

He sat back. 'It's fine. There's nothing to be sorry for. Take as much time as you need.' He stood up. It was, in truth, a

277

relief. They had not had sex since she'd returned, and he was glad. He'd only been trying to make things seem normal. 'I'll unpack. And then we can go and have a look around Cartmel.'

When they got back to the cottage, Carl and Kevin were parked outside. They got out and looked around.

Claire pointed to the building across the road. 'We booked you into the B & B,' she said. 'You can watch the cottage from the window. We'll have our phones on.'

'We might just have a look around. Check the back door and other access points,' Kevin said. 'That kind of thing.'

'Thanks,' Alfie said. 'We appreciate you coming up here.'

'Not a problem,' Carl said. 'Always nice to have a Lakeland break.'

'Isn't it,' Alfie said. 'Isn't it.'

Sunday

i

Alfie stared at Claire. They had decided today was the day.

'So,' he said. 'Here we go. Later this morning I pretend to leave to go hiking. Hopefully, Bryant comes. And then . . .'

Claire nodded. 'Right. And then. Exactly.'

Alfie looked at her. She seemed, suddenly, hesitant.

'You OK?' he said.

'Yes.' She paused. 'Kind of. It seemed so simple when we were in London. Now it seems – well, it seems a bit risky.'

'Do you still want to do it? We can leave anytime you want.' He held his breath as he waited for her to respond.

'I still want to. I want this over. But stay close, Alfie. Two minutes away. You can hide out at the Priory. It's not far.'

Alfie nodded. If Bryant showed up, he needed to be close, but not for the reason Claire thought.

'There'll be Carl and Kevin as well,' he said. 'Remember that.'

'I suppose we'd better tell them.'

ii

It was fair to say Carl and Kevin did not take it well.

'Are you fucking joking?' Carl said. They were sitting at a table in the B & B, a pot of tea in front of them. 'You want us to *ambush* this guy? And then what?'

'Call the police,' Alfie said. 'We need to sort this out. We can't live like prisoners.'

Carl shook his head. He turned to Claire. 'Is he putting you up to this? Is it some kind of macho bullshit plan he cooked up to impress you? If it is, say the word and we can forget it ever happened.'

'I'm sorry,' Claire said. 'But it's for real. And it was *my* idea. At least, partly.' She stared at Carl. Please. Help us do this.'

Carl closed his eyes. 'Fine,' he said. 'But if this goes wrong, it's all on you.'

Claire nodded. 'And if it goes right, you'll get a handy bonus. So. Alfie's going to leave. I'll close my bedroom window to signal that he's gone. I'll stay in the bedroom, door locked. If Bryant arrives, I open the window, and you two get here as fast as you can.'

'OK,' Carl said. 'You're on.'

*　　*　　*

Later that morning, Alfie followed the river north of the village. He was wearing a backpack with some water and a sandwich in it, just like a real hiker. The path he was on, according to the pamphlet he'd picked up at the information centre at the entrance to the car park, would loop to the right at some point, before heading back towards Cartmel Priory.

The pamphlet also informed him that the Priory had been founded in the late 1100s and had been an active part of the local community since then.

Alfie could not have cared less.

The Priory – some kind of ancient church – was close to the cottage, and it had a cell signal. As soon as Claire heard anyone in the house she would text him and he would be there in minutes. She would also open the window and alert Carl and Kevin. They, too, would text him in case her phone failed.

And then the *real* plan started. Claire wanted Bryant caught so he could be put in prison.

Alfie wanted him dead.

Of course, he'd arrive after Carl and Kevin, so he'd need to come up with an excuse to be alone with Bryant. He would, and when he was with him he'd kill Bryant. He'd get him in the kitchen, maybe. There was a set of kitchen knives there.

He attacked me! I had no option.

No option but to hack Henry-fucking-Bryant to death on the stone tiles.

And if he couldn't kill him, well, Alfie had already decided what he would do if Bryant told Claire, Carl and Kevin about him.

He'd go to Workington, and find a fishing boat that would land him, for a fee in cash, somewhere on the European mainland. He'd brought five thousand pounds with him to buy the silence of the skipper and five thousand euros, which ought to be enough to get whatever false papers he'd need to start again somewhere.

Italy, maybe. That seemed an easy place to hide for a while. Fleeing might be a drastic step, but it wasn't, not really. The marriage had been a mistake and he wanted out. If this was the only way he could escape it, then so be it. It wasn't ideal, but he'd get back on his feet. He always did.

The path forked to the right. Up ahead he saw the Priory. He walked towards it.

He spent an hour inside the building sitting in a pew and pretending to pray, then another hour wandering around the cemetery looking at the headstones. It was amazing how many people were buried with their wife or husband. Hadn't they had enough of each other in life? He couldn't fathom how anyone could want to get married in the first place, but to stay together after death? It was baffling. Not that it made any difference. When you were dead, you were dead. There was no afterlife, and there was no coming back.

'Aren't they wonderful?'

He turned to see a woman, plump and grey-haired, perhaps in her late seventies, a cheap raincoat draped over her shoulders. She was holding a guide to the Priory and peering at him.

'Yes,' he said. 'Very.'

'It's quite remarkable,' she began. 'The history of this place. This is my seventh visit, and each time I discover something new. Last time it was the tomb in the—'

Alfie's phone buzzed.

'Excuse me,' he said. 'I'm a doctor. It could be a patient.'

He glanced at the screen. There was a text message. Another withheld number.

Enjoying your romantic break? Don't want to spoil it, but remember I know what you did. Don't forget it now, Alf. PS Interesting Priory, no?

He froze. Bryant. He was here. He looked around, expecting to see a man waving mockingly at him.

There was no one.

'I'm sorry,' he said to the old woman. 'I have to go.'

As he ran towards the cottage, he looked at the bedroom window. It was shut. If Bryant was there, Claire would have opened it.

If she could.

He sped up.

Could Bryant have got in without Carl or Kevin seeing him? Could he have stopped Claire opening the window? He doubted it. She was up in the bedroom, and as soon as she heard a door open she would have signalled the guards.

Unless she thought that the person coming in was safe. Unless she knew them.

But there was no one here she knew apart from Carl and Kevin.

Fuck. How had he been so stupid? It was obvious. What better way to get close to Claire? He should have seen it earlier. He'd not asked who they were, or how long they'd been with the company. They could be brand new.

One of them was Bryant.

He could not believe he'd missed it. It was the first place he should have looked.

The front door was shut. He tried the handle and it turned immediately. Thank God it wasn't locked. He opened it and stepped inside.

Claire was standing in the hallway. She was next to a dark wood table. It was beneath a mirror, and had two heavy brass candlesticks on it. A drawer, half open, ran the length of it. She was frozen, staring at him, her eyes wide, as though she'd been caught doing something she shouldn't have been.

'It's only me,' he said. 'Don't worry. Why aren't you upstairs?'

She didn't answer. She blinked, then shook her head. She gave a slight backwards nod, as though wanting to indicate something behind her, without letting anyone else know.

'Claire? Are you OK?'

'Yes,' she said. Her voice was high and strained. 'Fine. Let me give you a hug to welcome you back.'

Alfie frowned.

She beckoned to him, stiffly. 'Come here, darling.' There was a pleading tone in her voice. 'A hug. Please.'

He took the few steps he needed to get to her, and then put his arms around her. She kissed his cheek, and then whispered quickly in his ear.

'He's here.'

Alfie squeezed her tighter.

'Don't say anything,' she murmured. 'He's here. Bryant.'

'Where?' Alfie muttered, pretending to kiss her temple.

'Here,' she said, her voice suddenly loud. 'Right fucking here.'

And then she pushed him away, something hit him in the back of the head, and the world went dark.

PART THREE

Alfie, Claire, and DI Wynne

Alfie

When he woke up, Alfie had no idea where he was. He was lying on something quite soft, which he assumed was a bed. He didn't *remember* going to bed, but then he didn't remember much. Everything was very slippery, which could have been because his head was throbbing with the worst headache he'd had in a long time. The pain came in waves, all starting at a spot at the back of his skull. He couldn't remember ever having had such a bad headache. A hangover, then? He didn't think so. There was no foul taste in his mouth.

He opened his eyes, then shut them again. The light was painful. He part-opened them, adjusting to the light. He was looking at a ceiling. Dark beams ran across it. He recognized them. He was in the bedroom at the cottage, the bedroom where Claire had been waiting for Henry Bryant.

Who had showed up after all.

He'd sent Alfie a text message, knowing it would bring him running to the cottage, and when Alfie had got there Bryant had hit him, knocked him unconscious and dragged him upstairs to the bedroom.

Well, well. Bryant was better at this than Alfie had expected. And Claire had known. She hadn't been able to warn him

– presumably because Bryant was pointing a gun at her, or something like that – but she had tried, by whispering that Bryant was there. It hadn't worked. And now Alfie was up here and she and Bryant were, he assumed, in the cottage somewhere, unless Bryant had taken Claire again.

He didn't think he had.

Alfie was almost certain Bryant was still there, waiting for Alfie to wake up so he could do whatever it was he had been planning.

He thought he had Alfie where he wanted him. He thought he was in control, that Alfie was helpless. But Alfie was never helpless. And even in this situation there was something he could work with.

He knew something Bryant didn't. He knew Carl and Kevin were watching the window. All he had to do was get it open and they'd be here and then, in the melee that ensued, he could kill Bryant.

He sat up.

At least, he tried to. Something was holding him down, and it was totally unyielding. He lifted his head and looked down the bed. He was under a duvet, on top of which three thick cargo straps encircled him, one around his knees, one around his waist and one on his chest and arms. They looped under the bed, and they were *tight*.

He struggled against them. It was pointless. They didn't give a millimetre. They were designed to secure furniture to a truck bed, so securing him to a bed was nothing.

He opened his mouth to shout – since that was all he could do – but he stopped himself. On second thoughts, he didn't want Bryant to know he was awake, not yet. He didn't want Bryant here when he had no idea what to do. He at least needed a plan of some kind before that.

But he had no idea what.

* * *

288

Ten minutes later he still had no plan. He'd tested the straps some more; he'd tried sliding down towards the foot of the bed and sliding up towards the headrest, but any movement was totally impossible. He'd wondered whether he could somehow rock the bed enough to tip it over, but even if he could, he'd more than likely end up strapped to a bed on its side, and in any case, the noise would alert Bryant to the fact he was awake.

So there was only one thing he could do. He needed to get things in motion. Right now he was trapped; there was nothing to work with. Once things were moving he could steer them. And for that he needed Bryant here. He took a deep breath.

'Bryant!' he shouted. 'Where are you? I want to see Claire!'

He tensed, waiting for a reply, but the words were met with silence.

'Bryant!' he shouted again. 'BRYANT!'

Even though he was pinned to the bed, motionless, adrenaline was flooding his body. He felt sharp, alert, focused.

He listened for a response.

It was a while coming, but eventually there it was. The creak of a stair, then soft footsteps approaching the door. The worn, brass handle turned, and the door began to open.

And an idea of how to get out of this came to him.

Wynne

DI Wynne sat opposite Jodie, DS Lawless on her left. She had called early – apologizing for disturbing a Sunday morning – and arranged to interview her again. Jodie was a link – the only one – between Pippa Davies-Hunt and Claire Daniels, and Wynne was hoping there would be some clue to who Henry Bryant was.

She didn't hold out much hope, but she had no other lines of inquiry to pursue. Bryant's trail was running cold.

Jodie had taken her through the events before Pippa Davies-Hunt had disappeared. Wynne had encouraged her to share every detail, no matter how small or irrelevant it seemed, and Jodie had obliged, walking through everything she could remember.

'She moved in. She was obsessed with Bryant. It was all she talked about,' Jodie said. 'I tried to change the topic, but it was impossible.'

'What kind of things did you talk about?' Wynne said.

'Anything. The weather. *EastEnders*. I showed her photos.'

'Of anything in particular?'

Jodie shook her head. 'Whatever was in my phone. We

went through the photos of Claire's birthday one evening. She didn't like *those* much.'

Wynne replayed the words in her mind. 'What do you mean, she didn't like them?'

'I don't know. After we looked at a few she got up and went to her room.'

'Was she upset by them?' Lawless said.

'I guess so,' Jodie replied.

'Did she say why?' Lawless added.

'No.' Jodie shrugged. 'To be honest, I was glad she'd left me alone.'

Wynne thought for a second, then looked at Jodie. 'Were there any in particular that she reacted to?'

'I don't think so,' Jodie said. 'I think she was just upset to see photos of the party. All the happy couples.'

'So she didn't focus on any specific photo?'

Jodie took out her phone and scrolled through the photos of Claire's birthday party. They were the usual kind of thing: guests pausing to look at the camera, drinks in their hands, couples posing for photos, arms around each other. She stopped on one of her, Claire and Alfie. In it, Claire and Jodie were smiling; Alfie was expressionless, as though he'd been caught out.

'She looked at this one for a while,' Jodie said. 'She'd met Claire before and she asked about her, whether she was married to the guy in the photo. I told her she was.'

'Was this the last photo she looked at?' DI Wynne asked.

'I think it was,' Jodie said.

'And would you say it was the one that upset her?'

'I guess. It was after this one that she said she didn't want to look any more.'

'Did she say anything about it? About Claire or Alfie?'

'No,' Jodie said. 'She doesn't really know them.'

'In that case, it's quite strange she would react so strongly to it, wouldn't you say?'

'I assumed she didn't like looking at photos of happy couples,' Jodie replied. 'That's all.'

Wynne nodded. 'This has been very helpful,' she said.

Jodie caught her eye. 'You think this has something to do with Pippa's disappearance?'

'I couldn't say. Not yet.' DI Wynne glanced at DS Lawless. 'Time to head back to the station. We have some work to do.'

'So,' Lawless said. 'What was all that about?'

Wynne started the engine. 'I don't know. But it's interesting, if nothing else.'

'Why?'

'I'm not sure, yet. What do you think?'

'About that?' Lawless replied. 'Not a lot. One thing did occur to me while we were interviewing Jodie, though.'

'What?'

'Bryant had dumped Pippa Davies-Hunt,' she said. 'So why would he kidnap – and maybe kill – her?'

'I don't know. But go on. I'm not sure where you're going with this, but I'd like to hear it.'

'We've been working on the theory that he's a sick bastard who preys on women he meets on the internet, but we've only been working on that theory because there are *two* of them. But say, for a minute, that Claire Daniels had never been abducted. Say Pippa was the only case. What would we be thinking then?'

Wynne pursed her lips. 'You tell me. What *would* we be thinking?'

'We'd be thinking he got rid of her,' DS Lawless said. 'We'd be thinking they had a messy break-up and maybe had an argument or she threatened him in some way, and he killed her. But because of Claire Daniels, we're thinking he's someone who gets off on meeting and abducting and killing women.' She raised an eyebrow. 'But in that case, why dump Davies-Hunt? Why dump her in such a mean way? All that does is draw attention to him.'

'Yes, it does,' Wynne said. 'It's a very good question, Lawless. So why did he do it?'

'I think something triggered him getting rid of her. I don't think he planned it from the start, but something happened and he needed her gone.'

'Right,' Wynne said. 'So after he dumped her she did something to threaten him.'

'Maybe not *did* something,' Lawless said. 'Maybe found something out.'

Wynne looked at her partner. It was becoming clear what she was driving at. 'Like his identity?' she murmured.

'Like his identity,' Lawless said. 'We know that Bryant is a fake identity. I think whoever created it did so to use the internet to find women. I think Davies-Hunt found out who he was. His real identity. And she let him know. So he killed her.'

'That sounds plausible,' Wynne said. '*More* than plausible. But it doesn't help. We still don't know why he went after Claire.'

'No,' Lawless said. 'Unless there's a link between Claire and Pippa.'

'They knew each other, didn't they?'

'In passing.'

Wynne took a deep breath. 'Maybe there's something else.'

'Do you have a theory?' Lawless asked.

'Yes,' Wynne replied. 'I do.'

'What is it?'

'Before I say it, I know there's an obvious flaw.'

'Spit it out,' Lawless replied. 'We can deal with any flaws later.'

'OK. What if the reason Pippa Davies-Hunt reacted to that photo was because she recognized Alfie Daniels? What if she knew him as someone else?' Wynne looked at Lawless. 'What if she knew him as Henry Bryant?'

'Maybe,' Lawless said. 'Ms Davies-Hunt saw the photo of him and discovered that the man she thought was Henry Bryant was in fact Alfie Daniels, husband of Claire. She got in touch and told him. So, terrified his wife would find out, he killed her.' She pursed her lips. 'But you know, he really doesn't seem the type.'

'They never do,' Wynne said. 'And remember, he came home drunk the night she disappeared. He'd been alone in bars all over the city. And then there was that period he was wandering around. Odd, don't you think?'

'Odd,' Lawless said. 'But odd isn't evidence. And then there's a problem—'

'There's at least one. I'm assuming you're about to mention the obvious flaw I referred to.'

'Let's see. The problem is that Alfie Daniels *can't* be Henry Bryant. Henry Bryant also abducted Claire, so unless Alfie did that and somehow managed to be at his home talking to us while Claire was wherever she was, then it isn't him.'

'Unless there are two Henry Bryants,' DI Wynne said. 'But that seems very unlikely, to say the least.' She turned the car into the police station. 'There's a missing part to this – to do with Claire Daniels's abduction – and when we find that it'll all be clear. But for now I'm not worried about that. I'm worried about Alfie. I think there's a chance he's Henry Bryant.'

Lawless nodded. 'If you say so, I'll go along with it. But even if you're right, there's not much we can do. We have no evidence.'

'Not yet,' DI Wynne said. 'But we need to get some.'

Claire

So Alfie was calling Bryant's name. He still hadn't worked it out.

Claire had wondered whether he would guess what had happened when he came round, but it seemed he hadn't. He'd believed her when she said Bryant was there, and had presumably come to the conclusion that it was Bryant who had hit him.

Which meant he'd believed in Bryant – her version of him – all along.

That was the problem people like Alfie always had. They thought they were the only ones who could scheme and plan and manipulate people.

But they – and he – were wrong. And it left them vulnerable.

Not that she would have ever done this under normal circumstances. She had no interest in hurting anybody. But when she had found out what he had done, and what he was planning to do – she still shuddered at the thought.

Not with fear. Or disgust.

With *rage*.

They had read parts of *The Iliad* at school and the opening line had stuck with her. In the last few days it had been on an endless loop in her head.

> Sing, O goddess, *the anger of*
> *Achilles son of Peleus, that brought*
> *countless ills upon the Achaeans.*

She had never fully understood what it meant, until now, never understood how rage – pure, unadulterated rage – could thrust all other considerations aside in its need to be satisfied. It didn't matter what else happened, what other terrible results came from it.

All that mattered was that the rage was satisfied.

Achilles didn't care who was hurt, what was destroyed: he was in the grip of his rage and it controlled *everything* he did.

And now she understood what that was like.

But rage like that didn't come from nowhere, and it wasn't sustained by nothing. It needed an equally deep emotion at its source.

And for her it came from the utter devastation she had felt when she realized how the man she loved, the man she had trusted with everything, had been lying to her. Barefaced, cynical lies from the start.

The bullshit about trust when her dad wanted the pre-nup. The bullshit about wanting children. The bullshit about loving her at *all*.

And why? For money?

And then, once the devastation had lessened enough to let in other emotions – the feeling of stupidity that she'd been so totally fooled, the humiliation, the disbelief – she had felt nothing other than rage.

She heard him shout again, and she stood up. The sofa was old and deep and she had to lever herself to her feet with her elbow. There was a cup of tea on the table next to the arm and she sipped it. It was cold, which she found odd; she was sure she'd just made it. For a moment she felt disorientated, but she shook her head and took another sip.

She put it back on the table and walked to the stairs. She entered the bathroom, ran the tap and splashed cold water on her face, then looked at her reflection in the mirror.

Her eyes seemed black. Deep, black pools. The skin around them was lined. She stared at herself, barely recognizing the person who stared back, and set off for the stairs.

The rail was worn smooth with the thousands of palms that had held it as people walked up the stairs. The smoothness was a familiar feeling from her childhood, a feeling she wanted her own children to have, so that they, too, could remember it and wish it for their children when they grew up.

It was one of the many things she wished for her children, things which she had accepted – or started to accept – might never happen. If it wasn't meant to be for her and Alfie, then she would learn to live with it. After all, she was lucky to be married to him, and maybe she'd have to come to terms with that being enough.

Or they could adopt. Alfie would do that for her. He'd do anything for her. He loved her; they were soulmates and she gave all of herself to him and he gave all of himself to her.

Or so she'd thought.

But no longer. She knew now it was all a lie.

But she still wanted her kids to come and stay here and climb these stairs and smooth the rail with their palms and sit on their grandfather's knee and lie in bed listening to their mum and dad reading to them.

And all that was going to happen, except it wouldn't be Alfie doing the reading. That, though, was for another day. For now, she had a job to do.

She crossed the landing, four, short steps to the bedroom door. It had been where her mum and dad slept. She gripped the handle and turned it. The hinges gave a low moan as she pushed the door open.

She stepped inside. Alfie was lying on the bed, eyes closed.

'Hello, Alfie,' she said.

Wynne

DI Wynne was pouring a cup of thick black coffee that someone had brewed earlier and which was on the verge of being too cold to drink when her phone rang. The more she'd thought about it, the more convinced she was that Alfie was Henry Bryant. One of the Henry Bryants, at any rate. All she needed was proof.

She picked up her phone. It was DS Lawless.

'Yes?' she said.

There was a pause. When Lawless spoke, she spoke softly.

'We got him,' she said. 'We got Alfie Daniels.'

They sat in front of a computer screen. On it was a grainy black-and-white image of a train station platform. Lawless pointed at a man stepping on to a train.

'That's him,' she said. 'Alfie Daniels, the night Pippa Davies-Hunt disappeared.'

'Where is he?'

'Tube station near his office.' She clicked to another image. 'This is him getting off at Waterloo.' Another image. 'And again . . . and then we get this.'

There was a still of Alfie walking towards an underground garage. It was followed by one of him driving out in a blue VW Golf.

Wynne peered at the image. 'You think he was going to meet Davies-Hunt?'

'I do. Somewhere south of the river. Some low-key pub out of the way. Richmond, or Barnes. The kind of place she'd go.'

'Do you have any more of Alfie? In the Golf?'

'No. We're looking, but you know how it is.'

Wynne nodded. People had the idea – from sensationalized news reports – that Britain was stuffed full of CCTV cameras and their every move was being scrutinized. It was true, to a point. There *were* CCTV cameras all over the place, but half of them didn't work and of the rest, some were low quality, or were pointed in the wrong direction.

But that didn't matter. Wynne had enough to go on.

'OK,' she said. 'We need some feet. Officers going pub to pub in Barnes, Richmond, Twickenham – any town south of the river – and showing every bartender a photo of Daniels and Davies-Hunt until they find one who saw them together. I'll make some calls.'

'Already done it, boss,' Lawless said. She handed DI Wynne a list. 'Divided up the pubs and assigned them to officers. These are yours.'

DI Wynne walked into the pub – The Feathers – and looked around. It was busy, full of late-morning drinkers taking the edge off the day before going home to more work or shouting kids or an empty flat.

She was not there for a drink, though. She was there because she was convinced that in the next few hours her theory – that Alfie Daniels had killed Pippa Davies-Hunt and that he had done so as Henry Bryant – would be proven true or false.

And she thought it would be proven true.

She was aware it left a huge question unanswered – who had abducted Claire, and why they were using the name Henry Bryant – but she was convinced this would be resolved once she knew for sure that Alfie was Bryant. That was the cornerstone; once she had that, the rest would fall into place.

The landlord was standing at the corner of the bar. He was in his late fifties and had an impressive gut straining against his black shirt. Even at a distance the rosacea mottling his face was obvious.

DI Wynne smiled and caught his eye. She walked over.

'Detective Inspector Jane Wynne,' she said, and held up her warrant card. 'I'd like a chat, if you have a minute.'

He frowned. 'What have I done?'

'Nothing,' DI Wynne said. 'Or at least, nothing of interest to me.'

He nodded. 'Then how can I help?'

'I need to know who was working on July ninth, and then I need to talk to them.'

He held her gaze. 'I'll check. Hold on.'

He disappeared behind the bar. When he came back he was holding a piece of A4 paper.

'Rock and Spike,' he said. 'Two jokers who've been working here forever.'

'Are they here now?'

The landlord nodded. 'I'll get them.'

Wynne sat opposite the two barmen. Spike – long dark hair, brown eyes – looked at the photo. He shook his head.

'I don't remember seeing them,' he said. He handed it to the other barman. 'You seen them, Rock?'

Rock – sandy-haired with a look of a young Brad Pitt – studied it. 'No,' he said. 'I don't think so.' He glanced at DI Wynne. 'Isn't that the woman who went missing?'

DI Wynne nodded. 'One of them. Thank you. You've been very helpful.'

The same scene played out at the next two pubs. She didn't doubt it was happening the same way in many others, but that was OK. That was how these things worked. You went door to door until you got a result.

She walked down the main street. There was another pub ahead. She pushed the door open, and went in.

'What can I get you?' The bartender was a woman in her mid-forties.

'I'd like to speak to the landlord.'

'Don't have one. We have a manager, though.'

'Then I'll talk to him,' Wynne said.

'Take a seat. I'll get her.'

Wynne sat at a small table in the corner. In her pocket, her phone rang.

'DI Wynne,' she said.

'This is PC Logan,' a man said.

Wynne sat up. Logan was one of the people going pub-to-pub.

'Yes?' she said. 'Do you have news?'

'I do, ma'am,' PC Logan replied. 'We have an ID. The Stones in Barnes. The barman said he saw them together.'

'Is he sure?'

'Hundred per cent. Says he has a memory for faces. Remembered her posh accent. It was them, Detective Inspector.'

Wynne fought the urge to smile. 'Thank you, PC Logan,' she said. 'Get as many details as you can.'

As she put the phone down she noticed a tall, blonde woman approaching her table.

'Hi,' she said. 'I'm Sandra, the manager. I heard you wanted to talk to me.'

DI Wynne shook her head. 'Not any more. Sorry to waste your time. I have to go.'

Sandra shrugged. 'Never sorry to see a cop leave,' she said, with a smile.

Wynne smiled back, but her mind was elsewhere. It was on what she needed to do next, which wasn't talking to Sandra.

It was talking to Claire Daniels.

And soon.

Alfie

Alfie watched the bedroom door open. This, then, was it: either his plan worked and this ended with Bryant dead, or it ended with him trying to get on to a fishing boat in Workington.

He was ready to take his chances. He was *always* ready to take his chances. He put his head back on the pillow and closed his eyes. Bryant would be expecting him to be staring at the door expectantly, frozen in terror. Well, this would be his first lesson that Alfie would not be playing his game.

There were soft footsteps as Bryant walked into the room, then the click of the door closing. Alfie lay motionless.

'Hello, Alfie.'

His eyes snapped open. It wasn't Henry Bryant. It wasn't even a man.

It was *Claire*.

She was staring at him, her face expressionless.

She must have got away from Bryant somehow. He'd obviously left the house – or been incapacitated in some way – because there was no sign of him following her up here.

He and Claire were safe.

It was not the outcome he wanted. He wanted Bryant

dead. He didn't want him out there, aware of what Alfie had done and with the constant threat that he would reveal it.

Unless he already had. Claire was unsmiling, serious.

'Where is he?' he said. 'Where's Bryant?'

'Not here,' Claire replied. There was still no hint of a smile on her face. Alfie tensed. She should have been celebrating.

'Did he leave? Did something scare him off?'

She shook her head.

'Then what happened? I need to know, Claire. I want to find him.'

'You won't. You never will. He can't be found.'

'Of course he can. He was here when I came in.'

'No he wasn't.'

Alfie frowned. There was something very badly amiss here. Something he did not understand. 'What are you talking about, Claire?' he said. 'When I got back, you told me he was at the house. He hit me on the head?'

'No,' she said. 'I was lying.'

'Then who *did* hit me?' Alfie said.

She didn't answer. She just looked at him, her eyes flat and dull. The silence was broken by her phone ringing. She ignored it. A few seconds later it rang again, then Alfie's started.

'You should answer,' he said. 'It might be important. Someone's trying us both.'

'It can wait,' Claire said.

'OK,' Alfie said. 'Fine. But would you unstrap me? Whoever hit me might still be here.'

'Oh, they're here all right,' she said, and then shook her head. 'But you're staying right there. I finally have you where I want you, and you're not moving an inch.'

Alfie shook his head as the words sank in and he finally understood. 'You?' he said. 'You hit me? Why? And what's

Henry Bryant got to do with this? Are you and him doing this together?'

'No,' Claire said. 'This is all my own doing. Bryant's got nothing to do with this. How could he? He doesn't exist.' She smiled at him. 'Don't look so surprised. You of all people should know that. After all, it was you who made him up, wasn't it?'

Alfie didn't reply for a long time. He wasn't sure what to say. The panic – the feeling he was losing control, or, more accurately, had *lost* control – was mounting. It was Claire who had knocked him out.

Not Bryant.

Who she said did not exist.

So he wasn't here. She wasn't bait in a trap for Bryant. He had not abducted her.

Then who the hell had?

'What's going on, Claire?' He could hear the tremor in his voice. 'Tell me what the hell is happening here?'

Wynne

DI Wynne leaned on a railing, her phone in her hand. She didn't like the fact that neither Claire nor Alfie had answered her calls. It wasn't late and they would have recognized her number. Maybe they were doing something else. One taking a shower, the other out running. Or watching a loud movie. Or having loud sex.

Maybe. But she didn't like it. She didn't like leaving Claire Daniels in the company of her husband for a moment longer. Not that she could prove he had killed Pippa Davies-Hunt. All she could prove was that he had met her the night she had disappeared and that, up until she saw the photo, Davies-Hunt had believed he was a doctor called Henry Bryant.

And then Davies-Hunt had confronted him with that knowledge and he had killed her for it.

Wynne imagined the conversation, over a drink in the corner of a pub, imagined Alfie Daniels asking her whether she'd told anyone else, imagined her saying no, she hadn't.

At which point he would have known that if he killed her, he'd be safe. Only she knew his secret.

She could prove none of this, yet. But it didn't matter. She didn't need to be able to prove it in a court of law to know it was true. The proof would come later – maybe in the form of a confession when Daniels learned that she knew he was lying and he had been seen with Davies-Hunt – but she wasn't worrying about that for now.

For now she was worrying about where Claire and Alfie were. She picked up her phone and made a call.

DS Lawless answered immediately. 'Yes?'

'We need to find the Daniels,' Wynne said. 'Mainly Claire. I don't want her with him any longer.'

'Have you called them?'

'No answer,' DI Wynne said. 'We need to check their house. How soon can you get there?'

'Thirty minutes?' Lawless said.

'OK,' Wynne replied. 'It'll take me nearer an hour. I'll meet you there. Take a uniform with you, but make it sound like a routine visit. I don't want Alfie getting nervous and suspecting anything. Question Claire about the day she was found. When I arrive, we can arrest him.'

'I could do it when I get there.'

'I know. But I want to see how he reacts.'

'Got it.' Lawless paused. 'Any more theories on the other Henry Bryant? The one who took Claire?'

'Not yet,' Wynne said. 'But it's all going to start to unravel. And quickly. Be careful.'

She was getting near to the house when DS Lawless called.

'No one here,' she said. 'The house is empty.'

'What about the security guards?'

'Not there either.'

'Shit.' DI Wynne banged her hand on the steering wheel. 'They must have gone somewhere.'

'That's what I thought,' DS Lawless replied. 'I checked with some of the neighbours but they don't know where.'

'All right,' Wynne said. 'I have an idea.'

She hung up the call and then dialled another number. Jodie answered. 'Hello?'

'Sorry to bother you again. This is Detective Inspector Wynne.'

'That's OK,' Jodie said, although there was a hint of irritation in her voice. 'How can I help?'

'I was wondering whether you know where Mr and Mrs Daniels are? I've been trying to contact them but haven't been able to reach them.'

'Sure,' Jodie said. 'They went away for a few days.'

'Do you happen to know where they went?'

'They're in Cartmel. Claire's family has a cottage there.'

'Cartmel in the Lake District?'

'Yes. Is that a problem?'

'It's a long way,' Wynne said. *Probably six hours in the car*, she thought. She needed to get there sooner than that. 'Did the security people go with them?'

'I think so. Claire mentioned something about them sleeping in a hotel.'

Shit. So they were alone in a cottage in some quiet Lakeland village. This wasn't good. Anything could happen.

'I'm not sure I should be telling you this. Claire swore me to secrecy.'

'Telling me what?' DI Wynne said. 'That they're in Cartmel?'

'No. She told me something else. She said they were hoping Bryant would show up so they could trap him. That's why they were taking the security people.'

It took DI Wynne a few seconds to be able to answer. When she did, the professional calm she prided herself on proved impossible to maintain.

'Are you *fucking* kidding me? What the fuck do they think they're doing?'

'Maybe this is why she didn't want me to say anything,' Jodie said.

'It's a good thing you did,' DI Wynne said. 'A very good thing. At least now I have a chance to put a stop to this stupidity, if it's not already too late.'

She hung up, and then called the station. She needed help, and fast.

Claire

'What's going on, Claire?' her husband – her loving husband, her fraudulent, pestilent husband – said. 'Tell me what the hell is happening here?'

Claire let his words fall into silence. She blinked, then opened the top drawer of a chest of drawers and took out a pair of handcuffs. She sat on an armchair and placed them on her knees. Then she spoke.

'I'll tell you, in a bit. But first let's talk about you. How are your parents, Alfie?'

His eyes narrowed. 'They're dead. You know that. Why would you ask about them? Why would you be so cruel?'

Claire was struck by how genuine he seemed. Even now he looked hurt, the little boy who missed his mum and dad.

He was a very good actor. But it was all an act. Like everything he did.

'They're dead? Are you sure? That's what I thought, too. You told me they were and I had no reason to think you were lying, but it turned out I was wrong. They're very much alive, aren't they?'

'No,' he said. 'No, they died years ago, when—'

'Oh, for God's sake, Alfie, stop lying. There's no point!

311

I've talked to them. I found them and I got in touch. Called them.'

'How?' he said. 'How did you find them?'

'Danny Bond,' she replied. 'I messaged him on Facebook. I told him I wanted to find some of your old friends and see if I could put you in touch. I thought it would be good for you, especially since you had no family. He was surprised to hear it, since he knew your mum and dad were alive and well and living in a retirement home.'

He looked away from her. She carried on.

'They seemed very nice. Old, and not enjoying the home they live in. It's crowded and dirty and the food isn't good, but that's how society treats its elders these days, isn't it? Unless they have someone – a child, maybe – to take care of them, old people are left to rot. *They* certainly have been.' She shook her head in mock disappointment. 'I was surprised you left them like that, when we have so much money, but you know what surprised me most?'

He didn't reply.

'Answer the question, Alfie. Do you know what surprised me most?'

'No,' he muttered, his tone suddenly hostile. 'I don't. What surprised you most, Claire?'

'That after I introduced myself – as your wife, who was interested in getting to know them – they didn't ask after you. And when I suggested that I bring you to see them, how do you think they reacted?' She raised her hand. 'Let me tell you. They said they never wanted to see you again. Apparently, you managed to take out a mortgage on their house, a house they'd worked all their lives to pay off – they said you forged their signatures – and when the money came you disappeared with it. They lost the house, Alfie, which was why they were in the home. They really didn't have very many kind words to say about you. In fact, they were angry. Very angry.'

312

She twirled the handcuffs around her forefinger. His eyes followed them.

'And they're not the only ones,' she said. 'I, too, am angry. Although I'm not sure that angry does it fucking justice.'

She spat out the last words. She'd promised herself she would keep control as she explained this to him, but it was hard. God, it was hard. The rage was millimetres below the surface; she felt like her skin was paper thin, that it could split open at any time and out it would surge in a livid torrent.

She took a deep breath. 'And so here we are. Here we are.'

'Why were you looking for my parents?' Alfie said. 'What have they got to do with this?'

'Why indeed? That goes to the heart of it, Alfie. I needed to find out if I was right about something. You see, I'd learned something about you and it made me wonder if you were really who I thought you were. Speaking to your parents – seeing the depth of your lies to me and the cruelty of your treatment of them – showed me all I needed to know.'

'What had you learned?' What am I supposed to have done?'

'You had a vasectomy, Alfie. And you lied to me about it. You let me think I couldn't have a child, let me suffer through the agony of test after test to see if I was fertile. And when the tests said I was, you hugged me and told me you'd taken a test and it was all OK and we'd have a baby soon. It was only when I forced you to see the doctor that you had to tell me some twisted version of the truth, although even then you lied. You said your sperm count was low. Non-existent, in fact.'

She shook her head. It was not merely the fact of the lie. It was what it meant.

'You told me you wanted to have children with me. To do the most important thing in the world together. But it was all a lie. And why, Alfie? For money? For something as banal as that?'

He didn't answer.

'And what makes me sick is that I was sympathetic to you. You let me feel bad for you, when all along you had no intention of having a child with me. You were prepared to let me believe you loved me and you wanted nothing more than for us to become parents, but it was all *lies*. All of it.' She was shouting. She forced herself to lower her voice. 'That's what I couldn't get over, Alfie. How deep the lies went. It was our whole marriage. Everything we'd ever done. It was the most important thing in the world to me, and to you it was nothing.'

He looked at her, saying nothing, and in the silence it all came back to her. The awful moment when she realized Dr Singh was telling her that her husband had had a vasectomy and he had been lying to her about it – about everything– for God knew how long. Then the long walk out of his surgery as the magnitude of Alfie's deception hit her, of what it truly meant, of how deep it went.

And, sitting there, she started to cry.

'Is that what all this is about?' Alfie said. 'The vasectomy? Kids. I'm sorry, Claire, but I couldn't tell you. I didn't want to lie to you, but I'd had it done before we met and I thought it would put you off me. I know it was wrong, but I was confused. Worried. I couldn't bear the thought of losing you. And we have other options. Adoption – whatever you want—'

'Shut up!' she screamed. 'Stop talking!'

'Claire,' Alfie said, 'we can get through this. I promise.'

'Oh no, we can't.' Her voice was low. 'There's no way we can get through this. None at all. Because I know the rest of it too, Alfie. I know *all* of it.'

Street

PC Dave Street glanced at his watch. He had five minutes of his shift left. He was planning to stop for a pint – maybe the Mason's Arms at Strawberry Bank – on his way home. He had been doing that more and more recently; he and Sheila were not getting along and he found that he was putting off the moment when he had to step across the threshold into whatever criticisms and put-downs she had ready for him.

He couldn't put his finger on why, but these days whatever they did seemed to end in an argument. There was a bubbling resentment between them that they couldn't suppress. He didn't know where it had come from, or what to do about it. At first he'd put it down to the stress of having a three-year-old boy and a new baby, but now he was wondering if it wasn't more fundamental.

If maybe they weren't suited to each other after all.

Anyway, that was what he had to look forward to. A quiet pint and then an evening of arguments or – and this could be worse – a silent cold shoulder.

He was about to walk out of the station when the phone rang.

'Cartmel and Grange Constabulary,' he said. 'PC Street speaking.'

'This is Detective Inspector Wynne,' a woman said. 'Metropolitan Police.'

He sat up. They didn't get too many calls from the Met. Especially not on a Sunday.

'How can I help?'

'Are you near Cartmel?' DI Wynne said. There was an urgent tone in her voice.

'About twenty minutes away,' he replied.

'Good. I need you to go to an address there.'

'Could I ask why?'

'There's a woman there who might be in danger. She needs to be kept safe. And there's a man who you should detain.'

PC Street saw the prospect of his pint receding quickly. This, though, was more interesting. It was certainly not the typical call the Cartmel and Grange Constabulary received.

'Is it serious?' he asked.

'Possibly,' DI Wynne replied. She hesitated. 'It could be dangerous. Is there another officer who can attend with you?'

'Yes,' he said. 'There is. What's the address?'

DI Wynne gave it to him.

'The Stewart place?'

'I don't know,' DI Wynn said. 'The woman I'm looking for is Claire Daniels.'

'That's her maiden name. Stewart. Wasn't she abducted recently?'

He knew full well that she had been. He'd followed the case closely. He knew Claire Stewart – Daniels – from years ago. They were the same age and when she'd spent summers in the cottage she'd got to know the local children. They'd had a childish fling, once, a brief dalliance that fizzled out as quickly as it had begun.

At least it had for her. Street had fallen heavily for her,

316

and had hoped all summer to repeat the one, golden evening when they'd drunk cheap cider on the shores of Windermere and kissed, lying on the grass.

It had never been repeated though, and after that summer she never came back. Over time he had forgotten about her, until, that was, she appeared in the papers.

And now she was back in Cartmel.

'She was,' the detective said. 'It's her.'

'Is this linked?' Street asked.

'Yes. But exactly how I don't yet know.'

'So who should I expect to find there with her? The abductor? Is that who I need to detain?'

'Mrs Daniels and her husband will be there. PC Street,' – he was impressed she'd remembered his name – 'it's her husband who I'm worried about. He's the man you need to take into police custody.'

'Is he dangerous?' Street asked.

DI Wynne didn't answer for a few seconds. 'Yes,' she said eventually. 'He is.'

'Are you coming here?' he asked. 'It could be a good idea.'

'I'm currently on the train from Euston to Oxenholme. I'll be arriving in two and a half hours.'

'I'll send a car to pick you up. See you later, DI Wynne.'

Alfie

Alfie pushed against the straps, in case they had somehow loosened. They hadn't. He was pinned to the bed, his head the only thing he could move. On the chair by the door, handcuffs in her lap, Claire watched him.

Why did she have handcuffs? He was already totally restrained. Did she intend to move him and wanted his hands bound when she did? If so, that was good news. He was far better off on his feet, even handcuffed, than fixed to the bed.

And what else did she know? She'd said she knew all of it, but did she? Did she know about Pippa? And Bryant? He doubted it. He didn't know how she could, but then he didn't know how she'd found out about the vasectomy.

Which was a good place to start.

'Who told you?' he said. 'About the vasectomy?'

'Dr Singh.'

Alfie shook his head. 'That's a breach of patient confidentiality.'

'It's also the least of your problems,' Claire said. 'And he didn't tell me, exactly. He just mentioned that if a man had had a vasectomy, there'd be a scar.'

'Look,' Alfie said, 'there's been some misunderstanding. I'm sure we can work it out.'

'Is that what you said to Pippa?' she asked softly. 'Before you killed her?'

Alfie stared at his wife. 'I didn't—' he began, but she waved a hand to quiet him.

'Don't bother,' she said. 'I know you did it, and that's all I need to know. I don't care how or where or why.' She caught his eye. 'And you know why I don't want to hear it? Because I know you were going to kill me, too.'

'Claire,' Alfie said, 'I would never have hurt you.'

She laughed. 'Really? You don't think there was a risk you'd hurt me by pretending to be in love with me and marrying me and telling me you wanted a family, when all along it was lies, total and utter lies?'

Alfie breathed slowly and deeply. This was worse than he had thought. She knew about the vasectomy, she knew about Pippa, she knew – or suspected – that he'd been planning to kill her. The doctor – and when Alfie got out of here he'd kill that little Paki bastard – had told her about the vasectomy, but not about the rest of it.

So how the hell did she know?

'Claire.' He was aware there was no point in denying it. 'I did kill Pippa. I admit it. But I had to.'

'I don't want to hear this. I don't want to hear any more of your lies.'

She seemed very on edge. 'Fine. I won't say any more. But can you tell me who told you?'

She smiled. 'You did, in a way. Ironic, no?'

Alfie tried to figure out what she meant. He'd not said a word.

'What do you mean, I told you? I didn't mention anything. Was I talking in my sleep?'

'No, you've always slept well, Alfie, although how I don't

know. I suppose I misspoke. You didn't tell me, as such. You *showed* me.'

'How?' he said.

'After I'd been to see Dr Singh and he told me you'd been lying about your fertility, I went to your office. I wanted to talk to you, face to face. There was no one on reception, and I went through to the back. I saw you at your desk, two phones – neither of which I recognized – in your hands. You tapped out some messages, and then put them in your drawer. You locked it, and put the key in your jacket pocket. Then you left, by the back door.'

Alfie remembered it. He'd been messaging Claire as Henry Bryant, tapping out the details of their fake affair.

'After what I'd learned, I was reeling, and then I saw you had *secret phones*. I felt like my world was falling apart, like you were not the person I'd thought. I had to know what was going on, so that evening, I went to your office and took them.'

'The phones? How did you open the drawer?'

'I took the key from your jacket pocket. I came home, then told you something had come up at work and I had to go to the office.'

Alfie nodded. He'd been happy about it, happy that she had been making some odd, unplanned evening arrangements that would make it look like she was having an affair.

'But not before I confirmed one thing. I had to know whether you'd had the vasectomy. Remember what I did, Alfie? Well, it was enough to see the scar.'

She'd given him a blowjob. He remembered it well; it was unusual. She had pushed him away.

'You stopped halfway through,' he said.

She nodded. 'I had to. I saw the scar and knew what you'd done, and I felt *sick*. And then I sat in a cab on the way to the office looking at photos of vasectomy scars – so I could

320

be sure – and starting to understand the depths of your lies.' She paused. 'At least, I *thought* I was. I had no idea quite how deep they went, not until I saw what was in the phones.'

'How?' Alfie said. 'How did you get into them?'

'I took them from your office and got one of the IT guys to hack them for me. You remember Sat? I introduced you to him once. What I didn't mention was that we went out a few times. He was keen, but it wasn't for me. I told him I had a personal problem and asked him to meet me at work. He hooked the phones up to his laptop and had them unlocked in seconds. It was frightening how easy it was.' She shrugged. 'And there it was. The whole thing laid out in front of me.'

'Claire,' Alfie said. 'Let me—'

'No, no,' she said. 'Let *me* finish. It took me a while to figure it all out. I couldn't understand what I was reading, at first. There was this series of messages from Henry Bryant to me – except it wasn't me, it was you pretending to be me.' She shook her head. 'That much was clear, but I couldn't work out *why* – I thought maybe you were trying to make it look like I was having an affair so you could divorce me, but that was crazy. I'd have denied it, and it would have been easy to prove. So it had to be something else. And then I read the messages from Pippa.'

She toyed with the handcuffs. Alfie didn't say anything. He watched her, weighing her up.

'I read the message in which you dumped her. And I remembered Jodie talking about it. Henry Bryant was Pippa's boyfriend, the one who'd dumped her by text. Which meant *you* were Henry Bryant. How am I doing so far, Alfie?'

'Not bad.' There was no point denying it now. 'You've got most of it.'

'But why? Why were you pretending to be Henry Bryant?'

Alfie shrugged. 'I was bored,' he said. 'Bored of the stupid

321

little life you led. Bored of your tedious friends and your twee, sheltered lives. You're all so obsessed with being perfect, with having the latest skinny jeans and beige walls and haircuts that you see in magazines and just have to have.'

She flinched; his words were hurting her. He allowed himself a smile. He was enjoying this. He'd wanted to say it for a long time.

'You're all fucking sheep,' he said. 'You do the same things in the same way and you call it living. But life is messy and dirty and I couldn't bear missing out. So I created Henry Bryant. He could have some fun.' He looked at her. 'Even then I couldn't bear living with you.'

'Was I really that bad?' Claire said.

Alfie laughed. 'Worse, Claire. At first it was OK. There were the holidays in the South of France, the cars. The money. It was enough to distract me. A bit boring, but I could take it. The sex was good too, at first. You lay there giving out your little gasps and moans and squeaking *Yes, Alfie, I'm coming*, but it got old pretty quick. It was bearable, I suppose. Not unpleasant. I started to think of it as glorified masturbation. But after a while I started to really *hate* you. I was so trapped in your little world. I wanted more, so I created Henry. He was *me*. He lived his life with passion and lust and struggle. And it kept me sane. It was the only way I could do it, Claire. I'd like to say I'm sorry, but I can't. It's your own fault for being so fucking mediocre.'

She sat, blinking. There were tears in her eyes, but she wiped them away. Her expression hardened.

'You're wrong,' she said. 'Very wrong. I loved you, Alfie, and that made the world amazing. I didn't need passion and lust and struggle, because I had love. That's what you lack, and it's why you're so woefully misguided. And I'll have it again, with someone else, and with the children that I'll cherish every day I'm with them. But that doesn't matter for you. What matters for you is that I figured out you were Bryant, and I figured out what you'd done to Pippa. And then I realized why you were creating this fake affair between me and Bryant. You planned to kill me, didn't you, Alfie?'

'Yes,' Alfie said simply. 'I did.'

'Why not divorce me, if you hated me so much?'

'*Because* I hated you so much,' Alfie said. 'I wanted to see the expression on your face when you understood what I was doing. And I wanted the money. Think about it. You'd be dead, murdered by the man you'd been having an affair with. I'd be Alfie, the poor cuckold who'd lost his wife. And then off I'd go, with all your cash, to enjoy the rest of my life. But then you found out about it. And all because you wanted a baby, and you wouldn't give up on it. That fucking doctor couldn't keep his mouth shut.'

'It's ironic, isn't it,' she said. 'You didn't want a child because it would ruin your life, and in the end, it was the lies you told Dr Singh that caught you out.'

'Maybe,' Alfie said. 'But I'll kill that little fucker when I get out of here. There is one other question, though. I get everything. You found out about the vasectomy, you saw the phones, you worked out what I'd done and what I was planning to do. But what happened with the other Henry Bryant? Who was he? And why did he abduct you?'

Claire smiled. 'You know, Alfie, you're not quite as smart as you think you are. And that's what led to *this*.' She gestured to the bed. 'You want to know who the other Henry Bryant was?' She leaned forward. 'I'll tell you.'

Street

PC Street sat behind the wheel. In the passenger seat was PC Angie Clifford, just arrived for her shift. He'd given her a hasty and garbled account of his conversation with DI Wynne and then hurried her to the squad car.

'Hold on a second,' she said. 'What's going on, Dave?'

'That's kind of the problem,' he said. 'I don't really know.'

'What do you know, exactly?'

'You remember that story about the women in London who were abducted? And one escaped? Well, she's here.'

'What do you mean, *here*?'

'In Cartmel. Her family have a place there. She used to spend her summers up here. I know her. She was Claire Stewart then. Now she's Claire Daniels. She's here with her husband.'

'And there's a problem?'

'So the London cop said. She wants us to go there and detain the husband.'

'The *husband*? What for?'

'So she can arrest him when she gets here.'

Angie Clifford folded her arms. She was the daughter of a sheep farmer and had forearms like Popeye.

'She's coming all this way to arrest him? Did she say what for?'

'No, but if she's coming here from London, it's not for an unpaid parking ticket.'

Twenty minutes later, they turned off the main road and on to the quiet lane that led to Cartmel.

'No sirens?' PC Clifford said.

Street shook his head. 'Don't want him to know we're coming.'

'You think he's dangerous?' Clifford asked.

'If he's got cops coming from London,' he said. 'I'd say so.'

PC Clifford nodded slowly. 'You want to call the Armed Response team?'

'Maybe. Let them know what we're doing, at least.'

Clifford grabbed her radio and spoke into it. As she did, PC Street slowed. They were approaching the cottage.

'Of course,' she said. 'If anything *does* go wrong in there they won't be here in time to do anything about it.'

'Want to wait for them? We can observe the house. Make sure no one leaves.'

Clifford thought for a second. 'The London cop asked us to go in?'

Street nodded. The car came to a halt.

'Then we go in,' Clifford said. 'You the front, me round the back. Ready?'

Claire

He had a strange look in his eyes. Up until that point he'd looked relaxed, confident even. She'd been amazed at how unemotional he was; at first she'd thought he was putting on a brave face, but now she understood it wasn't that at all.

He was unemotional because he had no emotions. He wasn't seeing this in the same way she was, he wasn't being pulled and swayed by what she was telling him. He wasn't feeling sympathy for her or regrets for his actions. He was feeling nothing.

Except now there *was* something. That strange look in his eyes was new, and she thought she recognized it.

Not quite fear, but not far off.

'Tell me,' he said in a quiet voice. 'Who was he?'

'The other Henry Bryant?' She stared into his eyes. 'The other Henry Bryant was *me*.'

He flinched as though he'd been slapped. 'You? What do you mean it was you?'

'I mean there was no other Henry Bryant. No one abducted me. I made it all up.'

'But there were emails,' he said. 'He sent you emails.'

'No, he didn't. I copied you, Alfie. I did exactly what you'd done. I established a fake account and emailed myself. You'd set it all up perfectly. When I disappeared, the police would think what you'd planned for them to think, that Henry Bryant had abducted me. But he didn't. I used your plan.'

He lay on the bed, staring at her. 'So where were you?'

'In the New Forest,' Claire said. 'Camping. It was quite fun, as it happens. Nice to be outside.'

'But he *did* things. He came to the house. Drove past the café.'

'All made up. None of it happened.'

'But I saw him. I *chased* him.'

Claire smiled. 'No you didn't. You chased someone, but not Bryant. Why do you think I spent so much time at that window? I was watching people pass by, waiting for a single young man I could smile at. He had to be in a hoodie, so his face was hidden. Then all I had to do was wave. Get his attention, get him to stop outside the house, and then call you.'

She watched the disbelief spread over his face. It was very satisfying.

'And the house appointment? You set that up?'

'I did.'

'Why?' He closed his eyes. 'Don't answer. You wanted me to think he was really after me.'

'Like the note at the theatre, and the text message to your Henry Bryant phone,' Claire said.

'How?' Alfie said. 'How did you do the note at the theatre?'

'Two programmes,' Claire said. 'When I went to the bathroom I bought another one and put the note in it. I kept it under my seat. It was easy to switch. And I needed you to believe he was real, because if you thought he was real, I'd be able to do all this.'

'All what?'

'Well, here was my plan,' Claire said. 'Originally, I was going to kill you. One night I was going to suffocate you or slit your throat, and then call the police and tell them Bryant had been there and murdered you, but I'd disturbed him and he'd fled. They would find all the weird things that had been going on – the house appointment, the theatre note – and they'd believe me. But then I was worried they'd work out it was me, so I came up with this. We come here, expecting Bryant. I kill you, and say he was here, but ran away when Carl and Kevin came in.'

Alfie laughed. 'But there's a problem. *You're* going to kill me? Come on, Claire. You're not a killer. Turn me into the police. That'll do. I'll be gone from your life. You don't need to kill me.'

'You know,' she said, 'two weeks ago, I would have agreed. I would have said that, whatever anyone did to me, I wouldn't be able to kill them. But I would have been wrong.'

She took a deep breath.

'What I learned, Alfie, is that we all have it in us. Some more than others, but we all have it. For most of us – me included – it's a last resort. But the thing I came to understand is that a last resort is still a resort. And now, the time has come.'

She reached into the chest of drawers and took out the knife she'd removed from the kitchen.

'Get ready, Alfie,' she said.

Alfie

When she said she was Bryant he knew it was bad, but he'd never thought it would get to this. He had assumed she would scare him a bit and then call her dad, or the police, and, when she did some opportunity would arise for him to get himself free and get out of there.

But then she said she was going to kill him, and pulled out a knife. It was a long, heavy kitchen knife. Alfie recognized it; he'd used it the night before to chop some vegetables for the meal he'd made.

It was *sharp*. Japanese steel, perfectly weighted. It was the kind of knife you could rest on a tomato and it would slowly sink through it, cutting it cleanly in two without the need for any pressure from the holder.

He was under no illusions about what it would do to him.

How had he missed this? It was clever; she had done it well. She had set him up and he had fallen for it. He hadn't thought she had it in her, which was why it had been possible. He had misread her. Underestimated her.

Ten minutes ago he would have laughed at the thought of her killing him in cold blood, but not now. Now he was starting to think Claire might be capable of it.

Which was a *real* problem.

'Claire, this is crazy. Think about it.'

'I have. I've thought about little else.'

'Then you'll have considered what'll happen *after* you do it,' Alfie said. 'You'll be a murderer, Claire. A twenty-year prison sentence. You might be out in ten, but that's still a decade, Claire. And it's an important decade for you. You'll be in your forties when you get out.' He raised an eyebrow. 'Too late to have kids naturally. And there's no chance you'll be able to adopt, not with a murder conviction. Is that what you want?'

'No, it isn't. But I don't have to worry about it, because it won't happen.'

'It will, Claire! Your prints will be all over the knife, you'll be covered in blood. The cops will take seconds to figure out that you did it.'

She shook her head. 'I'll tell them Henry Bryant did it. He was going to kill me, but then he fled.'

'No,' Alfie said. 'There'll be no evidence he was here, Claire. They'll know.'

'They won't. When they find me, I'll be handcuffed to the chair. I'll tell them that Bryant came in while you were out, and, when you returned, hit you on the head and brought you up here. There's a nice bruise on your skull to prove it. Then he handcuffed me and waited for you to wake up, so he could slit your throat with this knife.'

'But your fingerprints will be on the knife.' Alfie's throat was constricting and he could feel panic gathering in his stomach. 'If you're handcuffed to the chair, how will they have got on the knife?'

She shrugged. 'Because I used it this morning. It's my knife, Alfie. It won't be a surprise to anyone that my finger-prints are on it. Besides, the knife is how I save myself from Bryant.'

Alfie stared at her. This was not the Claire he knew. This cold fury, this methodical, relentless anger was something entirely new. It reminded him of him, and it was starting to scare him.

To *terrify* him.

'How do you mean, the knife is how you save yourself?' he said, in a low voice.

'Here's what I'll tell the cops. Maybe I'll cry as I tell DI Wynne,' Claire said. 'After Bryant killed you – which left me distraught, obviously – he came towards me. As he got near, something happened – you made a noise, perhaps, as some gas escaped your dead and cooling body, which I will claim was your final loving act from beyond the grave to save me – and he turned to glance at you. That gave me the opportunity to grab the knife in my handcuffed hands, which I threw at the window.' She looked at the old, brittle glass. 'That's what I'll do, after I kill you, Alfie. I'll throw the knife at the window and break it, then I'll handcuff myself to the chair. That will alert Carl and Kevin and they'll be here in seconds. In my story, I'll say I told Bryant they were coming and he disappeared.'

Alfie shook his head. He had to persuade her to stop this. 'It won't work. There'll be forensic evidence they'll expect Bryant to have left which won't be there. They'll piece it together, Claire. You have to see that.'

There was a flicker of doubt in her eyes and he thought, for a moment, he was getting through.

But then she stood up and took a step towards him. Any doubt was gone from her face, and all he saw was anger.

Pure, unadulterated *rage*.

And he knew then he couldn't talk her out of this. This wasn't about the most rational decision, about weighing the odds of getting caught against the odds of getting away with it and coming to a balanced choice.

That was how Alfie approached things. Without emotion and ready to take the path that would get him what he wanted as easily and quickly as possible.

This was something else entirely. This was someone operating in a way he didn't understand.

And, finally, he realized he was out of options.

Claire

She watched the fear spread across his face as he understood what he was facing. He would never fully get it, would never know how she felt.

Would never know how all she wanted, from the moment she'd found out what he truly was, was revenge.

She remembered sitting on the Tube on the way home after she'd seen the messages and returned the phones to his desk, remembered staring at the window, barely aware of anything outside her own thoughts.

She'd found out that her husband had been cheating on her. That he had killed one of the women he'd been sleeping with.

And he'd been lying to her since the day they'd met.

That was the worst thing. Their entire marriage was a sham. He'd fooled her into believing he loved her, that he wanted to have kids with her, that they were the perfect couple. She'd been so *proud* of their relationship, so proud of the way her friends were jealous of her. She and Alfie were the perfect couple, and she had allowed that to be the thing that defined her.

And beyond the devastation, she saw what was coming her way.

A messy divorce, Alfie on trial for murder, the whole world reading the details of what he'd done. She'd be a laughing stock. The humiliation would be total. There'd be no more smugness about her marriage; instead everyone she knew would be thinking *Poor little Claire, she's never had much luck with men, and here we go again, I feel so sorry for her.*

She couldn't bear it. Couldn't bear even the thought of it.

And that was when it started. It was just a thought at first, a little worm creeping into her mind.

It would be better if he was dead.

At that point she had no thoughts of killing him herself. At that point she was only thinking that if he fell in front of a bus or tripped into the path of a Tube train it would make it all so much easier.

And then she thought maybe she could push him. Take him hiking somewhere and give him a nudge off a cliff. Or poison him, maybe.

That was when the anger hit. Pushing him in front of a train or off a cliff wasn't good enough. It would clear up the mess, but it would leave her unsatisfied. She had given him everything and he had treated it like it was nothing and she wanted him to know she had found out. She didn't want him to die painlessly. She wanted him to die knowing it was her who was doing it, knowing she had figured out what he was and was beating him at his own game and would walk away, free to have the life she wanted.

He would know she had *won*.

And she had a way to do it.

Henry Bryant. She could use Henry Bryant.

Once she had seen that as an option, there was nothing she could do to avoid the temptation to take it.

But now, the planning was over. The preparation was done. Now the time had come to wield the knife.

She looked at the blade, turned it sideways, imagined plunging it into Alfie's neck.

Imagined the cops arriving, imagined the questions, imagined DI Wynne wondering whether there was more to this than seemed obvious on the surface.

Went through her explanation. Imagined her future without Alfie.

She'd been through this a thousand times. This was the best thing to do. The fact she was so close to it didn't change that. Her hesitation was nerves, nothing more. It was perfectly understandable, but it made no difference. She had to do it. She looked at Alfie, took heart from the hatred swelling in her chest.

Then she took the last few steps towards him.

'Goodbye, you bastard,' she said.

Street

PC Street knocked on the door. There was no bell and no door knocker, so he rapped hard with his knuckles.

He listened for the sound of footsteps, but there was nothing. He waited for thirty seconds and then knocked again.

After another wait, he spoke into his radio. 'No one home,' he said. 'Apparently.'

He reached out and grabbed the door handle. He turned it, and the door clicked open.

'I'm in,' he said. 'Poor security, leaving it unlocked if no one's here.'

He stepped inside and walked into a low-ceilinged hallway. The house was very quiet. No voices, no footsteps, no television or radio. It was the quiet of an empty house.

Or a house with occupants who did not want to be found.

To the right there was a door; to the left an opening that led to a living room and the rest of the cottage. He glanced inside; it was empty, but someone had been there recently. There was a mug of tea on the table alongside a book, open and face down.

Behind him, Clifford appeared from – presumably – the back door. 'No one,' she said.

They walked through the living room to the staircase. A few yards past it was the kitchen. Street checked it out. It was modern, and expensive-looking, with high-end cabinets and granite worktops. There was a loaf of bread on a cutting board, the serrated bread knife lying next to it. He looked at the knife block. There was a gap where the bread knife went.

And there was a second gap. Another knife was missing. He looked at the slot. It was the biggest on the knife block, the one where a large kitchen knife would have gone.

He walked over and looked in the sink. There was a half-empty bowl of cereal from the morning and a table knife, butter and breadcrumbs on the blade.

But no kitchen knife.

He opened the dishwasher. No kitchen knife there, either.

He looked back at PC Clifford. She was standing in the doorway, and he gestured at the knife block.

'Missing one,' he said, quietly. 'I think we should check out the upstairs.'

Clifford nodded, and they walked towards the stairs. They went up to the landing. At the top they faced four doors. Three were open – two bedrooms and a bathroom – and one was closed.

Street pointed at it.

'Ready?' he said, and turned the door handle.

He stepped into the room and froze.

'What on earth is going on here?' he said.

Claire

Claire heard the knock on the front door. She raised a finger to her lips. 'Don't say anything,' she whispered. 'It's probably some Jehovah's Witnesses, or something like that. They'll leave.'

They didn't. There was another knock. Claire walked to the windows and, taking care to keep out of sight, looked down at the front of the house. She couldn't see who was at the door, but she could see the car they had come in.

It was a police car.

'Who is it?' Alfie said.

She looked at Alfie. If she told him it was the cops, what would he do? Scream and shout to get their attention? Maybe, but then he'd be arrested.

Still, it was better than being killed. 'Can't see,' she replied.

And then they heard the front door open. 'Is it a burglar?' Alfie whispered. 'Knocked on the door to see if anyone's home, and now they're robbing the place?'

'Maybe,' Claire said.

'No. If it was a burglar, Carl and Kevin would have seen them and they'd be in here now, sorting it out.'

Claire realized that in a few seconds he was going to figure out the only people Carl and Kevin would let in unchallenged were the cops, and as soon as he did that he would start shouting to get their attention.

She walked quickly to the bed and grabbed one of the pillows. She put it over Alfie's head and pushed down, hard.

She heard his muffled shouts and felt him turn his face to the side so he could breathe. That was fine; she didn't want him to die, not with police here. There was no doubt she would be caught then.

She wanted him quiet so they'd leave and she could get on with it.

Except they wouldn't. If the police were here then they had come for a reason, and that reason must be to do with Alfie. And the only thing she could think of was that they had linked him to Pippa, in which case the whole sorry tale was going to come out anyway. There was no longer any chance of people believing he had been killed by Henry Bryant, no longer any chance of her revenge being private. Everyone was going to know what Alfie had done.

So she was not going to be killing Alfie, after all.

It had been taken out of her hands and, in truth, part of her was glad. As she stood there with the knife, she was not at all certain she could have done it. She wanted her revenge, of course, but she didn't want to have to kill someone to get it. Would she have killed someone to protect her children, if it was the only option? Yes, she would. But she wasn't Alfie. She couldn't take a life in cold blood, purely for her own purposes.

And she didn't need to. She'd beaten him. Alfie knew it, and that was all the revenge she needed.

She heard footsteps on the stairs. She lifted up the pillow. There was no point worrying about him shouting to the police now. They'd be here in seconds.

He looked at her, his face red and sweating. She put the

pillow down and stood up, knife in one hand, handcuffs in the other, and watched as the door opened.

Two cops came in, a man and a woman. It took a second but she recognized the man – he was called Dave, and she'd kissed him once, on a summer evening by Windermere.

He looked from her to Alfie then back to her, his eyes flicking from her face to the handcuffs and the knife.

'What on earth is going on here?' he said.

'She's trying to kill me!' Alfie shouted. 'She's crazy.'

Claire shook her head. 'No, I'm not,' she said. 'I can explain all this later. But first you need to arrest him. His name is Alfie Daniels, he's my husband, and he killed Pippa Davies-Hunt.'

Dave – she'd forgotten his last name – nodded slowly.

'I think we'll take you both to the station,' he said. 'We can sort this out there.' He unclipped a pair of handcuffs from his belt. 'It's Claire, right? I'm afraid I'm going to have to ask you to put these on,' he said. He looked at the ones she was holding. 'You'll need to put yours down. And the knife. At your feet, please, then step slowly towards me, your wrists together.'

Claire put the knife and the handcuffs on the carpet, then walked towards him, her hands extended. The cuffs clicked around them.

'PC Clifford will take you to the station,' he said. 'I'll wait here with Mr Daniels. We'll bring him in a separate car.'

'Thank you,' Claire said.

She turned for one last look at Alfie. She was disappointed to see that his eyes were closed.

Wynne

Detective Inspector Wynne looked at her phone. It was nearly midnight. On the other side of the table Claire Daniels was cradling a mug of coffee.

'Thank you for waiting,' Wynne said. 'Your father arrived. He's in the reception area and he's keen to take you back to the cottage. If you would like to leave, you can, Mrs Daniels.'

'It's fine,' Claire said. 'I'm happy to tell you everything I know.'

'He has a lawyer with him. I promised I would ask whether you would like the lawyer present when we talk.'

Claire shook her head. 'I have no need for a lawyer. I've got nothing to hide.'

DI Wynne smiled. 'Between you and me, I think that's a wise decision,' she said. 'This has been an odd day and a lawyer might complicate things. I'd prefer – and I'm sure you would too – to keep things as simple as possible.'

Claire nodded.

'I've come from talking to Mr Daniels. We have quite a lot of evidence – witnesses, CCTV – placing him with Ms Davies-Hunt on the night she disappeared. We also have footage of them leaving the pub they were in and getting into the vehicle he was using that night. I explained to him that it's only a matter of time before we learn where he took her, and that things might be easier for him if he was to cooperate with us. He agreed.'

'So he admitted it? Killing Pippa?'

Wynne nodded. 'He did. And he told us where to find her body. We'll attempt retrieval in the morning.'

'Where did he put it?'

Wynne studied her, not sure this was information she should share, but she decided that after all she had been through, Claire deserved to know.

'She's in an abandoned quarry. It's full of water, and very deep.'

Claire looked away. Wynne saw the pain cross her face. She had witnessed this before: kids finding out their dad was a thief, mothers finding out their sons were rapists. It was a toxic cocktail of betrayal and loss and grief.

'He's also claiming that you were planning to kill him.'

Claire didn't answer. There was a strange, blank expression on her face.

'I'm sorry,' Wynne said. 'I know this must be very difficult.'

'It is,' Claire said. 'But I've had a while to come to terms with it. He'll say anything to save himself.'

'Can you tell me what happened at the cottage?'

'We made a plan to trap Henry Bryant.'

'I heard. Not, Mrs Daniels, a very good idea.'

'We, or at least I, was desperate. Anyway, it didn't work. Carl and Kevin – the security guards – were supposed to come. We had a signal arranged. But then Bryant showed up and got in somehow. He texted Alfie and when Alfie arrived he knocked him out and tied him to the bed. He made me sit in the room and watch.' She shuddered. 'He said he was going to disembowel Alfie. Then the two police officers arrived and he fled.'

'Mr Daniels said that Henry Bryant was not at the house. He said you found out about his vasectomy from a doctor, and then found out about his affair, using the alias Henry Bryant, with Pippa Davies-Hunt. He said you were obsessed with having a baby and the shock of these two things drove you over the edge.'

'But I didn't know he'd had a vasectomy.' She leaned forward. '*Has* he had a vasectomy?'

'So he claims.'

'The bastard,' Claire muttered. 'We were trying for a baby. I was obsessed with it. Looking back, I almost don't recognize myself, but it was the only thing I could think about. Morning, noon, and night. The longer it went on, trying and not being able to get pregnant, the more I obsessed about it, the more desperate I was for it to happen. And all along he was lying to me.'

Wynne listened, hands in her lap. There had been a time when she had thought she might become a mother and she understood what Claire Daniels was telling her. Finding out that it wasn't going to happen was a difficult thing to take.

Wynne shifted in her chair. 'Mr Daniels also told us you were not abducted by Henry Bryant. He says you fabricated the entire episode, including sending the email messages from Bryant. There was never a Henry Bryant at all – at first it was Alfie, and then it was you. After you came back, you started to pretend to have seen him, so he was still a threat, a threat that could eventually kill Alfie.'

'That would have been poetic justice,' Claire said. 'But I'm afraid it's total rubbish.'

'I see.' Wynne drummed her fingers on the tabletop. 'His story does seem far-fetched, but there is a large question unanswered. Who is the Henry Bryant who abducted you, and who showed up in Cartmel?'

Claire shook her head. 'I don't know. I do have a theory, though.'

'Which is?'

'When he said he was going to disembowel Alfie, Alfie asked why, and he said revenge. He looked at me and said he was sorry I was caught up in it, but it was the only way.'

Wynne considered what Claire had said. 'Revenge for what?'

'He didn't say.'

'Ms Davies-Hunt?'

'That would be the obvious conclusion.'

'Yes,' Wynne said. 'It would be.'

'And if it is,' Claire said, 'I suspect Bryant is gone for good.'

What she was saying made sense: someone – maybe a friend or relative of Pippa Davies-Hunt – had found out that Henry Bryant was Alfie, and that he had killed Davies-Hunt. He had then used the same tactic to abduct Claire and set this whole thing up.

Which would only have worked if Claire Daniels was on the dating websites, waiting to be found.

That was the one thing that still didn't add up.

'Mrs Daniels,' DI Wynne said, 'isn't it a bit of a coincidence that you happened to be looking for an affair just when this person needed you to be?'

Claire nodded, and in her expression Wynne saw a resilience and toughness she had not thought was there.

'It is,' she said. 'But coincidences happen. And what's the alternative explanation?'

'The one Mr Daniels gave us.'

'What jury is going to believe him?' Claire said. 'A man who admitted to killing Pippa?'

'You have a point,' Wynne said. 'But that still leaves me looking for the man who abducted you and showed up in Cartmel.'

'I doubt you'll find him,' Claire said. 'And if you do, I won't testify against him. I won't press charges. I'm glad he did what he did. Alfie deserved it. But you can keep searching, if you like.'

Wynne got to her feet. 'I see. Goodnight, Mrs Daniels. I'll be in touch. The Crown Prosecution Service will want to talk to you about your husband. But for now, you're free to go.'

Claire Daniels stood up. She looked Wynne in the eye.

'Thank you,' she said, and then she walked out of the room.

Wynne watched her go. It was possible what she said was true. Maybe some friend of Pippa Davies-Hunt was masquerading as Henry Bryant so they could get revenge on Alfie. Maybe they had gone to the lengths of kidnapping Claire to do it, and now they were gone for good.

She found it hard to swallow.

It was more likely that Alfie – for once – was telling the truth, and Claire has set all of this up. Wynne had no proof of that, and she wasn't planning on looking for any. In fact, she rather admired Claire, and after all, what crime had been committed? Claire hadn't hurt anyone. She might have intended to, but she hadn't, in the end. There was wasting police time, possibly, but it was hardly that much of a waste if it had ended with Alfie being caught.

No, Wynne would leave it as it was. There was no point putting Claire through any more. The press would have a field day if they thought Claire was some sort of avenging Fury. Better to let it die down and fade away.

The only crime that concerned Wynne was Pippa's murder, and that case was closed. Alfie could go on telling his tale, but nobody would care.

Alfie was finding out, Wynne thought, that Karma really was quite a bitch.

Claire

The foreperson of the jury was a woman in her late fifties. After the jury had settled into their seats, she stood up.

The judge looked at her, his face red, his eyes black. 'Have you reached a verdict?'

She nodded. 'We have, your honour. On the charge of murder, we find the defendant'– she paused momentarily, and the quiet in the courtroom deepened – 'guilty.'

There were other charges – assault, intent to murder, illegal possession of a passport – but it was the murder one that counted. It was the word 'murder' that would be on Twitter in seconds.

In the gallery, Claire smiled. It had been a long time coming. At first there had been some awkward questions about Alfie's claim she hadn't been abducted at all, but eventually – under pressure from her expensive lawyers – the newspapers accepted her version of events. It was ironic, since this was the one time Alfie was being truthful, and it was her, in the end, who was telling the last lie. Then Alfie's lawyer had tried every trick in the book– insanity, provocation, statements taken under duress – to drag out the trial. It had taken over a year, but in the end the evidence was incontrovertible.

And now all that remained was the sentencing.

'Alfie Daniels,' the judge said. 'This court has heard that, having first deceived her, you murdered a vibrant young woman for no reason other than your own convenience and pleasure. More than that, you did so while treating your wife with a callousness and lack of respect that is frankly nothing short of breathtaking. You have shown no signs of remorse or regret, and, taken with your selfishness and disregard for the welfare of others, this marks you as a significant danger to society. As such I sentence you to life imprisonment, with a minimum of fifteen years.'

The gavel came down. In the dock, Alfie stared at the judge. He gave no sign of any emotion as two guards took an arm each and led him to a door at the back of the courtroom.

As they opened it, he turned and looked up at Claire.

She held his gaze, unblinking, until the guards pulled him through the door, and then he was gone.

She looked at the door – wooden, plain, functional – for a moment, and then watched as the courtroom emptied. She shifted in her seat, aware that she needed the toilet.

She'd been holding it until after the verdict, because there was something she needed to do.

She reached into her bag and took a long, thin cylinder. She'd found the pregnancy test that morning, left over from when she and Alfie had been – supposedly – trying for a baby.

She wasn't trying now – it was too early in their relationship for *that* conversation with Declan, the man she'd met two months ago – but they'd been a bit careless a few weeks back, and now she was late.

It felt different than before. She felt tired, in a way she'd never felt before.

And she'd decided this was the perfect time to find out, when Alfie was gone, and gone for a long time.

She put the test back in her bag and stood up. She walked down the stairs to the main entrance. The toilets were off to the left. She looked at the woman on the sign, the universal figure that denoted a female toilet.

It was so familiar, but when she came out, it would be different. Everything would.

She pushed the door open, and went inside, her heart racing. She wondered how Declan would take it, wondered whether he'd be happy or worried or terrified. Whether he'd run a mile.

She smiled. It didn't matter.

Everything was about to be *new* again.

Read on for a sneak preview of
Alex Lake's new novel

SEVEN DAYS

Coming soon

Seven Days To Go: Saturday

Suddenly it was so close.

Max's birthday – his third birthday, the one that counted – was right below the date she had just crossed out.

S	Su	M	Tu	W	Th	F
						~~1~~
~~2~~	~~3~~	~~4~~	~~5~~	~~6~~	~~7~~	~~8~~
~~9~~	~~10~~	~~11~~	~~12~~	~~13~~	~~14~~	~~15~~
~~16~~	17	18	19	20	21	22
23	24	25	26	27	28	29
30						

Which meant it was a week until 23 June.

Seven days away. That was all. Seven more days until it happened. She had been trying to ignore it, but seeing it there, underneath today's date, made that impossible.

It was a wonder she had the calendar at all. She had started keeping it on the fifth day after she had been locked in this basement. If she hadn't done it back then there was no doubt she would soon have lost track of time; as it was, she knew exactly how much time had passed, how many years – twelve, soon to be thirteen – since she had seen her parents and brother and older cousin Anne, who she had been on the way to meet when she made the mistake of speaking to the man in the car that slowed to a stop next to her.

When she had started the calendar she'd had no idea that more than a decade later she would still be using it – she had expected to be free well before this much time had gone by, although even after five days she was starting to understand this might be something that lasted much longer than she could have ever expected. She was glad she had, though, glad she had asked for some paper and a pencil – the pencil was a short, yellow one from Ikea, she recalled – and sketched out a calendar in tiny figures. It was her only link to the outside world. On the birthdays and anniversaries of her friends and relatives, she could imagine them having parties and opening presents, and in doing so, she felt, in a way, that she was with them.

It also meant she knew the birthday of her son, Max. Of all three of her sons, as it happened. Max – she'd named him after the boy in *Where the Wild Things Are*, because that boy was able to escape his room through a magic door and travel to the island where the Wild Things lived, and freedom was what she wanted more than anything for Max, even though she knew he never would – had been born on 23 June 2015, and ever since she'd had one dread eye on the day three years from then when he would turn three.

When Jack, her first son, turned three, the door to the basement had opened and he – the man whose name she still did not know and who she thought of only as the man – had come in. Unsmiling, as usual, but with a nervousness which was new.

He pointed at her son. At his son.

352

Give him to me, he said.

Why? she replied.

Just give him to me.

No.

I want to show him the world. I'll bring him back later.

She refused again.

It's his birthday. I'll get him ice cream. Take him to a park. Think of what you're denying him.

So she agreed.

It was the last time she saw her firstborn. The next time the man came he was alone.

She asked for Jack hundreds – thousands, maybe – of times, but he always shook his head. He refused to say where her boy was. Once, he said, *Don't worry, he's safe*, but she didn't believe it. If a three-year-old boy had suddenly appeared in his life, people would have asked where he came from, who his mother was. There was no way he wanted those questions, so she thought she knew what he had done to Jack.

He was – and she fought against the conclusion – dead. Buried in some forest grave, never to be found.

The thought made her ill. She lost weight – a lot of weight, tens of pounds – but it didn't stop the man coming to the basement and gesturing to the bed in the corner with that funny little nod of his then waiting for her to lie down and undress before he lay on top of her and did what he did while she closed her eyes and waited for it to be over and for him to be back upstairs in his house where she didn't have to look at him.

And, of course, the thing she had feared most came to pass again. Another child. She tried to stop it. Tried to starve the baby to death inside her, but all that happened was she grew thinner and thinner herself until the man noticed and figured out what was going on and forced her to eat. Why, she didn't know. Why he wanted the baby to be born was a mystery to her, but then most of what he did was a mystery to her. How could you understand a man who locked a fifteen-year-old girl in a basement for years, then stole her son? Why even try?

And then the new baby was born. A boy again. Leo. Pink and beautiful and red-haired. He was different to Jack. Smaller. More watchful. Quicker. By the time he was two he could talk, whole sentences. At two and a half he could read.

At three he was gone. On his birthday, the man came. He pointed at Leo.

Give him to me, he said.

No, she replied. *Not this time.*

Yes, he said, in his heavy, slow voice. *Yes.*

This time she fought, but it was no use. She held Leo to her chest, but the man hit her and forced her on to her back and held his forearm against her throat until he had Leo and she was unconscious. The last thing she saw before she passed out was her beautiful boy wriggling from his arms and running away.

But there was only one place to go, and he went there.

Through the open door and up the stairs. Where the man planned to take him anyway.

The next time she saw him she didn't bother asking where Leo was. There was no point.

And then, as though the universe was punishing her, the cycle repeated itself. The door opening. The nod at the bed. The disgusting act.

Then the missed period and the cramps and the feeling of being bloated and uncomfortable and then, nine months later, another baby.

Another boy.

Max, after the boy in *Where the Wild Things Are*.

Max, the curly-haired, always smiling, bright-eyed button

of joy who she loved with an intensity that surpassed anything she had ever felt before, even with Jack and Leo, if only because since the day he had arrived she had known she had only three years with him, three short years into which she had to cram a lifetime of love.

Max, who would turn three in a week.

She looked at him, sleeping on the mattress they shared, spread-eagled on his back, mouth slightly open, and she shook her head.

It couldn't happen again. It couldn't.

But it would. She was powerless. The man would come and open the door and take Max from her, whatever she did. And even if she stopped him somehow, he would put sleeping pills in her food or come another day with a club and knock her unconscious and take Max then.

She couldn't fight him every day of Max's life.

And so she had seven days left. Seven days with her son. Seven days until he was ripped from her arms.

Or seven days to figure out how to save him.

Acknowledgements

The more books I write, the more I realise how much I rely on the guidance, advice and wisdom of other people, whether as a sounding board for ideas, editorial input, or just general support and encouragement when – as they always are at some point – those are the things that are needed most.

Warmest thanks, therefore, to Becky Ritchie – unfailingly positive and supportive and an early, critical eye – Sarah Hodgson – patient, generous and insightful, which must be three of the most important qualities in an editor – and Tahnthawan Coffin, for, well, more or less everything.

A shout out to Marcus Deck for – once again – medical advice. This time he was on holiday somewhere in the Southern Hemisphere when he replied to an email asking for details of vasectomy scars. Thank you, Marcus.

And an extra-special thank you to O, F and A for their invaluable input into the cover design. It wouldn't be the same without you (although sorry the cobwebs and spiders didn't make it this time).

AFTER
ANNA

The real nightmare starts when her daughter is returned...

A girl is missing. Five years old, taken from outside her school.
She has vanished, traceless.

The police are at a loss; her parents are beyond grief.
Their daughter is lost forever, perhaps dead, perhaps enslaved.

But the biggest mystery is yet to come:
one week after she was abducted, Anna is returned.

She has no memory of where she has been.
And this, for her mother, is just the beginning of the nightmare ...

KILLING KATE

There's a serial killer on the loose.

And the victims all look like you...

A serial killer is stalking your home town. He has a type:
all his victims look the same. And they all look like you.

Kate returns from a post-break-up holiday with her girlfriends
to news of a serial killer in her home town – and his victims all look like her.

It could, of course, be a simple coincidence.

Or maybe not.

She becomes convinced she is being watched, followed even. Is she next?
And could her mild-mannered ex-boyfriend really be a deranged murderer?

Or is the truth something far more sinister?

COPYCAT

Imitation is the most terrifying form of flattery...

Which Sarah Havenant is you?

When an old friend gets in touch, Sarah Havenant discovers that there are two Facebook profiles in her name. One is hers. The other, she has never seen.

But everything in it is accurate. Photos of her friends, her husband, her kids. Photos from the day before. Photos of her new kitchen. Photos taken inside her house.

And this is just the beginning. Because whoever has set up the second profile has been waiting for Sarah to find it. And now that she has, her life will no longer be her own...

KILLER READS

DISCOVER THE BEST
IN CRIME AND THRILLER

Follow us on social media to get to know the team behind the books, enter exclusive giveaways, learn about the latest competitions, hear from our authors, and lots more:

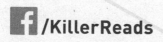/KillerReads   /KillerReads